CW00676676

ALSO BY MARY ROMASANTA

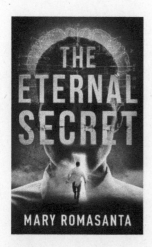

DR. PRASAD VEDURMUDI, a genius neurologist at the prestigious University of Chicago, made a mind-bending discovery during his research on Near-Death Experiences. Brace yourself for a revelation that could shatter everything we know about the afterlife. A specific region of the brain acts as a gateway, transporting the departed to the next dimension. But there's more—a tantalizing possibility nobody has ever explored... until now. Prasad believes that if he repairs that crucial part of the brain before death, he could unlock a profound secret—the key to controlling the afterlife experience itself. The implications are staggering.

He solicits the help of his colleague, renowned psychiatrist Edward Clark. With every fiber of their being, they are determined to provide a service to humanity that surpasses all that came before. Endowed with unparalleled expertise and passion, they venture into uncharted territory, driven by an insatiable thirst for irrefutable evidence. But their pursuit comes with a price. As they delve deeper into the mysteries surrounding life and death, they encounter forces eager to silence their breakthrough.

In this gripping tale of courage and scientific brinkmanship, The Eternal Secret takes you on a rollercoaster ride through a twilight realm where the line between life and the afterlife blurs. Prepare to be astounded, captivated, and haunted by the mesmerizing secrets concealed within the human mind. You stand on the precipice of a revelation that will change the world forever.

AVĪCI
SAGGA

AVĪCI SAGGA

A NOVEL

MARY ROMASANTA

Sagga Publishing House LLC

LIBRARY OF CONGRESS CONTROL NUMBER: 2023917462

Premium Mass-Market Hardback ISBN: 979-8-9886746-2-7

Premium Mass-Market Paperback ISBN: 979-8-9886746-0-3

eBook ISBN: 979-8-9886746-1-0

Audiobook ISBN: 979-8-9886746-6-5

Published in the United States by Sagga Books, a division of Sagga Publishing House LLC, Texas.

This book is a work of fiction. Names, characters, businesses, organizations, places, events, and incidents either are the product of the author's imagination or used fictitiously. Any resemblance to actual persons, living or dead, events, or locales is entirely coincidental.

Cover design and formatting by Damonza.com

Visit the author's website at www.maryromasanta.com

Printed in the United States of America

FOR ROBERT, LUCAS, SETH, AND JEREMY,
BUT ESPECIALLY ROBERT.

PREFACE

This book's title, *Avīci Sagga*, represents dualities found throughout the story. In Buddhism, Avīci is the lowest level of Buddhist hell. In Hinduism, it is one of the twenty-eight hells in the kingdom of Yama; Sagga is a place of happiness or heaven. This duality fuels this book.

It is also important to acknowledge my upbringing. I am a pastor's daughter. My father told me he felt his life lacked purpose well before I was born. That changed when he found his calling as a musical evangelist, then a preacher, then a pastor. Later, he earned a Doctor of Ministry degree. Like any good father, he raised me to understand right from wrong and, in our case, good from evil. Over his fifty-year career in ministry, he has witnessed countless demonic possessions and performed more than 40 exorcisms.

I am also the daughter of a florist, the strongest, most hard-working woman I know. Before my brother and I were born, my father grew ill and was unable to work. With a husband and four children to care for and support, my mother sold home-made candied apples to get the family by. And get by, they did. It was the makings of a business that would, over time, change our lives forever.

When I was a child, my parents purchased a small home across the street from the largest cemetery in the city. It was the perfect location for a flower shop that would become the family business. We lived there, in the business, until they saved enough money to purchase the home directly behind the shop-just twenty feet away from the cemetery gates. It's no wonder I developed a fascination with spirituality, religion, and the supernatural.

I am a lucid dreamer. I always have been. Each night I dream so vividly that I must remind myself that I am dreaming. While I was writing this book, I learned my brother is also a lucid dreamer. He says he considers his dreams a curse because of the many restless nights they have caused him. I see my dreams as a blessing because they inspired me to write this book. The process has brought me more joy than I could have ever imagined.

Finally, a heartfelt thank you to all those who witnessed and supported me through this journey. To my mother and father, you are my inspiration and role models now more than ever. Alejandra Gonzalez and Sandra Castillo, thank you for being my sounding board and for your support in completing this project. And a very special thank you to the producer and performer of Avīci Sagga's audiobook, award-winning filmmaker Lisa France. Your talent and kindness know no boundaries.

I hope you enjoy the book. Look forward to the next one!

Mary Romasanta

Oneirology: The scientific study of the connection between dreams and the human psyche in relation to brain function.

1

Day 1, The University of Chicago
10:45 a.m.

THE PUNGENT SCENT OF BURNED rubber lingered behind the piercing, high-pitched squeals of screeching tires as she rushed across the street without stopping to look out for traffic. The blaring horn was so deafening she was all but certain the driver slammed his fists on the steering wheel in a fit of rage. But she couldn't be sure. She was focused on reaching her destination and did not bother to look out for traffic, which nearly killed her.

"WHAT IS YOUR DYSFUNCTION!?" the driver shouted. His voice erupted like a volcano spewing molten lava.

She stumbled onward, her steps expeditious and unsteady. Her rapid breathing created a cloud of mist reminiscent of the smoke from a pipe. And although the vapor from her breath froze mid-air, she was sweating profusely.

A short flight of gritty cement stairs led to the building's entrance. It was only four steps, but it seemed like forty at the moment. She dug deep for the strength to keep moving.

Keep going, Emma, you're almost there.

She charged at the glass door, pushed it open with her body weight, and hurried down the hallway as if escaping from something. Her heart pounded through the heavy weight of pressure she felt on her chest. She looked back again, but there was nothing.

She stared at the stairwell ahead of her. *I'll never make it, she thought.*

The elevator.

A student passing appeared to notice her in distress. "Are you OK?" the student asked.

There was silence.

The student got closer. "Do you need any help?"

Although not one to ask for help, let alone accept it, it seemed she had no choice.

"I'm trying to get to Dr. Clark's office," she said breathlessly.

The elevator door opened.

"I know where it is. I'll help you there. We're not far," the student said.

She limped along as the student guided her into an office with an open door. Still unable to catch her breath, she released her arm from around the student's neck and collapsed to her knees.

"I'm having a heart attack," she said, barely able to get the words out.

A man seated behind a large desk stood and rushed to her side.

The student watched with a look of concern. "Should I contact emergency services?"

The man shook his head. "No, you can go now. Thank you for your help."

He kneeled. "Are you Emma Perales?"

She nodded.

"OK, Emma, I'm going to help you to the couch, and we're going to calm your breathing with a breathing exercise." His tone was calm, a stark contrast to the noise of Emma's deafening thoughts.

She bobbed her head; her chest heaved up and down as he helped her up. She spotted a blue microfiber couch just feet away.

"Good, now lay down. I need you to close your eyes and focus on your breathing. Breathe in slowly through your nose," he said.

She closed her eyes and breathed in deeply through her nose. Her focus shifted to the involuntary reactions flowing from her body as she felt it tremble.

"Emma, come back to me. Emma. Focus!" he exclaimed. "Listen to me…As you're breathing, I need you to count from one to five."

Her face flushed; her eyes widened as she nodded.

"Hold your breath for a moment, then breathe out slowly through your mouth. Count from one to five, just like you did before."

She nodded again; it was all she could do to acknowledge him.

He bent two fingers and placed them on her wrist. "Good… strong and steady. You're doing fine, Emma. I need to assure you that this is going to pass. You are in no physical danger."

She breathed in deeply through her nose as she counted, *one, two, three, four, five* and paused before exhaling through her mouth, *one, two, three, four, five.*

"Just keep doing what you're doing."

It's working. The intense pressure from her chest faded as expeditiously as it came. She exhaled slowly. "I'm OK," she said.

"Don't move just yet. I want you to relax for a few minutes before you get up."

She remained lying down, fighting every passing urge to get up. But time was of the essence. She took another deep breath before lifting herself up into a seated position.

"I thought I was going to die."

"That's to be expected. I'm glad I was here to help you through it. If it happens again, you'll know what to do," he replied.

If it happens again? She couldn't fathom the possibility. Her mind raced with questions as she thought about the countless predicaments she could find herself in. *What if it happens while I'm driving? What if it happens while I'm alone? What if it happens while I'm at work? What if it's worse next time?* she thought. "If it happens again? What do you mean? That can't happen to me again." Her tone was firm.

He exhaled audibly.

"Let's start over. Hello, I'm Dr. Edward Clark." He extended his hand. "You must be Emma," he said with a muted smile and a nod.

She shook his hand and nodded in return.

"It's nice to meet you, Emma. I was just reading up on your file."

He retreated to his desk. Although she had never visited a psychiatrist before, the desk looked like what she imagined the desk of a university professor might look like. It was long, dark brown, made of wood. It looked ancient, as if no one had moved it for years. Behind the desk was a shelf that held books from floor to ceiling. *Who reads physical copies of books anymore?* she thought.

He sat directly under a fluorescent ceiling light that revealed subtle red tones in his thick, wavy dark-brown hair. Judging by the light sprinkling of white hair that was coming in, she estimated he was in his mid to late thirties. He wore a brown cardigan over a light-blue button-up shirt and dark-blue pants, and he wore wire-framed glasses. There was a sophisticated yet approachable look to him.

"Thank you for being so thorough in answering the questionnaire," he said as he thumbed through the pages.

If you ask me, it felt more like a high school essay-writing assignment, she thought.

Her sarcasm brewed just under the surface. The list of doctors she had visited over the last three weeks had left her skeptical, distrusting, and overall unimpressed by medical professionals. She would give him the benefit of the doubt, for now.

"In the future, if the door is open, you're welcome to come right in. Hopefully, it will be under better circumstances."

She propped a pillow behind her back and allowed herself to sink into the comfort of the couch cushions. Across from the couch was a simple brown coffee table with a stack of *Psychology Today* magazines and a simple white cardboard pastry box set atop it. Her empty stomach emitted a low, rumbling growl. She looked up to find Dr. Clark watching her.

"You're welcome to take one. One of my students works at the pastry shop down the street. He brings them in daily."

"No, thank you," she replied.

She hadn't eaten yet. Come to think of it, she hadn't eaten the day before either. At least, not that she could recall. She looked through the clear window of the box that revealed powdered sugar donuts inside. She gazed at them, reminded of the shortbread cookies her grandmother made for her as a child. They were her favorite. She ate them by the dozen. Her grandmother told her they were called polvorones. Polvo is Spanish for powder or dust. Now that she thought about it, polvorones were the powdered sugar donut equivalent of a cookie. She hadn't made that connection before. Still, there was something cringe-worthy about the donuts that she couldn't place.

"Are you comfortable?" he asked as he took a seat behind his desk.

"Yes, thank you. I was expecting one of those traditional long brown leather armchairs that you normally see in the movies... This is much better."

"Oh yeah, that's a therapist cliché, and I'm not your traditional therapist," he replied with a smile.

But Emma already knew that. Dr. Clark wasn't just your ordinary therapist by a long shot. She had researched his background thoroughly and gone through a great deal of trouble to get herself a coveted appointment to see him. He was a clinical professor of psychiatry and a board-certified sleep medicine specialist with a short list of patients. Besides his work in traditional psychiatric therapy and treatment of sleep disorders, he was a globally recognized and renowned oneirologist. Given his credentials, it was no wonder why he chose the University of Chicago, home to one of the leading centers for sleep medicine research and sleep disorder treatment centers in the nation, for his practice.

"But I'm afraid there is one therapist cliché I always start with when seeing a new patient…Tell me about yourself."

"Can we fast forward through this part?" she asked. She saw clichés as a sign of unoriginal thinking and was eager to skip the pleasantries and get to the core of her visit.

"I'm afraid not," he replied.

"Dr. Clark," she said with an audible sigh, "Let's cut to the chase. Our time together would be much better spent that way."

With a tilted head, he smiled again.

Emma learned to obey strict rules from a young age. She was forever the obedient daughter, the obedient student, the obedient employee. Early on, she learned that being obedient led to rewards. So obedience became the gold standard, and she found comfort in order and process. Rules, standards, and procedures gave her a feeling of security and belonging that she could trust. But as of late, following the process had failed her, and the unspoken societal rules that once enabled her were now limiting her. She spent weeks seeing a cardiologist, hematologist, oncologist, and even an infectious disease doctor. No one could explain her declining health, let alone if her dreams were to blame. Her appetite for rules, for following the process, had expired.

She continued, "I'm here to discuss my dreams and my declining health." She spoke slowly and deliberately, emphasizing each word.

"I understand, Emma…"

She exhaled deeply. *Good, I got through to him,* she thought.

He continued, "That's why I'd like you to start by telling me about yourself."

Her blinking slowed.

She looked at the clock on her phone screen. Their session was already halfway over. Her panic attack had eaten through much of their time.

"Dr. Clark, even the most brilliant minds can benefit from listening to strong voices."

"Yes, of course," he replied. "I agree completely."

She looked him sternly in the eyes. "Then I need you to listen to mine."

2

HER WORDS COMPELLED HIM to act. He only regretted that they did not compel him to act on his own. A quick read of Emma's file had already made him aware of the countless doctors she had recently visited. And although he knew little about her, the magnitude of her panic attack told him that there was urgency behind her condition. Although not one to take shortcuts, he would have to put aside his orientation process for now.

"I'll begin by giving you a prescription for anxiety medication," Dr. Clark said.

She crossed her arms and shook her head vigorously, seemingly in vehement disapproval.

He continued, "Just until we get to the underlying cause of your anxiety."

She glared at him with a cold, withering stare. "Absolutely. Not."

His eyes glazed over as he tried to wrap his mind around her concern. She had just experienced an anxiety attack, a severe one at that. But he couldn't force her to take medication. "Well then, the only other way to ensure you don't experience another anxiety attack is to work out the underlying cause," he said.

"I understand. That's...why...I'm here," she replied with squinted eyes, seemingly unimpressed with what he had to say.

Sensing the two were off to a rocky start, he exhaled audibly. He knew she wanted fast results, and he was more than willing to help. Still, he had seen all too many patients that were looking for an easy fix. He needed to understand the problem before he could determine the solution.

"Emma, this process takes time, but we'll get there."

She rolled her eyes. "Can we please talk about my dreams?"

"By all means."

There was silence.

"My dreams, they started almost exactly four weeks ago. Every night I dream about men from my past—a former love interest, so to speak."

He watched as Emma placed her hand over her abdomen, as though signaling her stomach was in distress. "Are you OK?" he asked.

"Just the thought of my dreams is nauseating."

He walked across the office to the water cooler. He handed her a paper cup. "Here, have some water."

She took a sip. "Thank you. Anyway, the narrative of my dreams is always centered on one of seven men."

He walked behind his desk and picked up her file. *Twenty-nine years old, never married, no children*. And, although not stated in her file, *attractive*.

She looked on.

He raised a brow.

"What is it?" she asked.

"I was just checking your age."

"I've dated over seven people, if that's what you're getting at." She looked at him, gauging for a reaction.

He had none.

She continued, "Exactly how many people I've been involved with and to what extent is irrelevant."

"I agree," he replied. "It's normal for adults to be romantically involved with other people. There is no right or wrong number."

He paused.

"But why these seven men? Do they have anything in common?"

"I had a relationship with them. Some were more serious than others. But that's all in the past."

He leaned in; the leather from his seat groaned softly as he settled into the chair. "Did they abuse you?"

There was silence.

"They were each good and bad in their own way...but I only dream of the bad."

The room was quiet as he documented her response. When it came to his note-taking, he was extremely thorough, and his preference was to hand write his notes. But what she had to say, so far at least, was nothing he hadn't heard many times before. He suspected it was a common case of re-experiencing, a symptom of post-traumatic stress disorder that shows up as nightmares. Still, he was careful not to rush to conclusions.

She continued, "Every night is like a Russian roulette game show of 'Which Asshole Will I Dream of Tonight?'"

He scoffed.

Her squinted eyes narrowed in on him; she pressed her lips tightly together.

Right. Not a joke, he thought. "Sorry...How would you describe your dreams?"

"When I dream, I question if I'm awake because my dreams are as vivid as reality. When I'm awake, I question if I'm dreaming. I feel like I'm losing my mind."

He leaned in. "Emma, you're experiencing lucid dreams.

During a lucid dream, the dreamer may sense that the dream is real. A dream may feel so familiar to the dreamer that they may question whether it was reality."

Her eyes widened. "Yes, that's exactly what I'm experiencing."

"Lucid dreams are rarer than you might think. Half of people will never experience a lucid dream in their lifetime, and only one percent of people experience them regularly," he explained.

"I have maybe three lucid dreams every night, sometimes more," she replied.

His eyes widened.

"Is that bad? Is something wrong with me?" she asked.

He shook his head. "No, that's extraordinary is all," he said as he took note.

A sudden growl erupted, masked only partially by the chiming bells from the university clock tower. The clock that hung on the wall confirmed what his stomach was telling him. He looked at Emma. "That's our time for today," he said with a closed lip smile.

She remained firmly seated, her brow furrowed. "But we just got started. Don't you want to know about my dreams?"

He approached her and extended his hand. "Absolutely," he said.

She raised her hand and placed it on his.

He gripped her hand and pulled her up from her seat. "This was a great start. We'll pick up where we left off next time. You can schedule your next visit online or call the office if you'd prefer."

Because she seemed reluctant to move, he used his fingertips to apply gentle pressure on her lower back to guide her out the door. "Bye now." He closed the office door behind her. Although he was interested in learning more about her dreams, he had a competing priority.

His mouth salivated as he opened his mini fridge door and reached for his lunch—a turkey sandwich. There was an urgent knock at the door. He flinched, nearly dropping his sandwich. *What now?*

He opened the door.

There stood Emma, arms folded, tapping her toes.

"Back so soon?" he asked.

She stormed past him and marched directly back to her seat on the couch, a clear sign of her refusal to concede.

"Take a seat," he said, his tone dripping with sarcasm.

"Yes, well, we didn't get very far, did we?" she replied with glazed eyes and an emotionless expression.

To him, that look was all too familiar. "We did, by my standards," he said.

She leaned in. "Well, Dr. Clark, if I'm going to continue to see you, you're going to have to raise your standards," she whispered sensually.

He stood motionless in a trancelike state.

He cleared his throat. "What's this about, Emma?" he asked.

"Before I go, we need to level-set." Her voice was devoid of emotion. She enunciated each syllable carefully, seeming to convey the urgency of her message.

"I don't think you quite understand the severity of the issue I've come to see you for." She reached into her purse and pulled out a small spiral-bound notebook—her daily planner.

He pursed his lips. "No, I do. I understand you're having dreams you believe may be affecting your health, and you've come to the right place."

She folded her arms and glowered at him as she stood up. "Dr. Clark, you don't know anything about me." She glanced at the sandwich he was still holding. "But I can assure you that my health is of far greater importance than your lunch."

He glowered back. "First, any neuroscientist will tell you that hunger affects the brain's ability to concentrate. My lunch is a service to the both of us."

She scoffed.

He continued, "And second, I know more about you than you think."

"No, you don't." She glared at him with a squint, her arms still folded.

His steps were measured and rhythmic as he paced back and forth in front of her; the sound of footsteps echoed through the office.

He paused and looked at her with a determined stare. "May I?" he asked, as if he was about to make a grand revelation.

"Please do," she replied with a nod.

He smiled inwardly. *She does not know what she's in for,* he thought. "You're a twenty-nine-year-old Type A overachiever. You have a dominant personality, as demonstrated by your lack of patience and bluntness." *Not to mention stubbornness,* he thought, but he would keep that part to himself. "But having a dominant personality has its benefits, as shown by your relentless determination. You should tread lightly, though; when taken too far, you are borderline obsessive-compulsive, particularly when planning... Every. Detail. Of. Your. Life."

She scowled; her arms still crossed.

His attention turned towards her appearance. Although her gaunt cheeks and hollow eyes weren't quite to his taste, he couldn't deny that she was attractive. He would have to choose his words carefully. He homed in on her straight, long brown hair.

"You're hyperaware of your appearance. You give off the impression that looks aren't that important, yet your hair and makeup are perfect." He tilted his head, his eyes darted back and forth at her hair and face. "Almost, too perfect."

She gasped, as though she had taken offense to his comment. "That's enough, I get it."

He continued, "You're a perfectionist, likely because of a strict upbringing. You have excessively high personal standards and are overly critical when it comes to self-evaluations." He folded his arms, mirroring her body posture. "Which means…This. Must. Be. Killing. You," he said with an inward smile.

"I get it!" she exclaimed.

"Not bad for someone who knows nothing about you, huh?" He was joking, but her unamused expression told him she didn't find him the least bit humorous. *Did I go too far?* he thought.

Despite being a clinical psychiatry professor, he couldn't grasp women's emotional expressions.

"Did you know that the study of oneirology began with Nathaniel Kleitman and his student Eugene Aserinsky in 1955 right here in the sleep laboratories of this university?" he asked in what even he knew was a poor attempt to break the tension.

"I'm aware," she replied firmly. "Dr. Clark, you don't understand the gravity of the situation. I could lose my career. I could lose my house, my car, my family, my friends."

He nodded to express his understanding, but as he listened on, he observed her tone shift from strong and determined to despondent.

"I'm sorry I don't have all the answers yet, but I've only been seeing you for one day," he said. He let out a heavy sigh; his breath expelled his disappointment in himself.

"I know. That's why I have a plan." She stepped toward him with her daily planner in hand. "I'd like us both to commit to seeing each other every day for seven days."

He mulled over her request. It wasn't an unreasonable one. He would be in the office every weekend that month anyway to oversee a sleep study, and he couldn't in good conscience *not* do everything in his power to help what even he sensed was a dire situation.

She continued, "I know this cuts into your weekend, but—"

He interrupted, "That's fine. Seeing you over the weekend won't be an issue."

"Oh…OK," she replied, eyes wide, seemingly at a loss for words.

"Now, if you don't mind me eating my lunch in front of you, you're welcome to stay and continue."

She took a seat.

He gazed at her from behind his desk.

"What is it?" she asked.

"You're not even going to acknowledge the accuracy of my assessment?" he asked with an irrepressible smile.

"No, I'm not going to feed your already over-inflated ego."

His eyes widened; his jaw dropped ever so slightly.

She crossed her arms. "See, you're not the only one that can get a good read on people."

3

SHE PRIDED HERSELF IN who she was, who she had grown up to be. She became a strong, independent, and ambitious woman who had come a long way from her humble beginnings.

Despite having what some may consider a late start, she had developed skills that made her indispensable in her career. Her ability to develop and execute plans, coupled with her communication and decision-making skills, had taken her far. She could spot issues and vulnerabilities that others couldn't. Plan for, and effectively navigate, challenges and obstacles that no one else saw coming.

But now, she was just a shell of the person she once was. She was a prisoner to her dreams. They controlled her thoughts. They controlled when she slept, if she slept. They controlled what she ate, if she ate. She could not deny that some men she dreamed of had seared into her psyche, but she did not know others emotionally affected her. In either case, her dreams made her a prisoner to them all.

"What was I saying?" Emma asked.

Dr. Clark squinted his eyes, puzzled by her question. "You weren't. I asked you a question. Would you describe your dreams as nightmares?"

An image of Freddie Krueger flashed in her mind. Although the men in her dream bore no resemblance, the fear they evoked was far greater than any horror movie she had ever seen. "Yes," she replied.

"Why do you think you're having these dreams?"

"I don't know, but they're taking a physical toll on me. I want them gone before it's too late."

He leaned in. "Too late for what?"

Her eyes darted around the room as she struggled to come up with a logical answer, one that she hoped he could reason with or relate to. But, as hard as she tried, she couldn't.

"I just have this sick feeling that I'm running out of time." She sunk her head into her hands. "I'm not able to rest when I dream. Because I can't rest, I can't concentrate, I can't work."

Her firm had been lenient with her taking sick time off in the past, but their leniency had run out. Unable to work and with no medical diagnosis to point to, they placed her on unpaid leave. She was in jeopardy of losing everything she had worked so hard to build.

He furrowed his brows; his forehead wrinkled as he looked directly into Emma's eyes with a focused gaze. "Emma, what exactly are these dreams about?"

"Something happened when I was in college that has always bothered me." She rubbed her temples; a feeling of unease and tension spread through her body.

"Tell me about it."

There was silence.

She stared at him as she grappled with how to verbalize her clouded thoughts.

"Have you talked to anyone about it?" he asked.

"No."

"Do you think you would have done anything differently?"

"No."

It wasn't her intention to be short. Although she could make no sense of it, there was something about this experience that quieted her inner voice and shook her to her core.

He leaned closer. "I want to assure you that you're in a safe place."

She locked eyes with him. Inwardly, she acknowledged his kind words. Inwardly, she knew there was nothing to fear. Still, she remained quiet.

"What if we start with who you were with and when it happened?"

She nodded. "I was with my friend Jaden, my sorority little sis. We met when we were freshmen at the University of Texas at Austin. I told her about Sigma Lambda Gamma, the sorority I joined, and how it empowers women. I always imagined sororities as something catty and unnecessary, but the women in this sorority were strong, uplifting, and inspiring. I must have convinced her because she pledged the following semester.

"It was our senior year in college, and we were just a week away from graduation. We were meeting up with a group of close friends at a party. Someone we knew was raped after someone slipped something into her drink. The fact that it happened to someone we knew made us extra diligent and protective of one another anytime we were out.

"Since it was our last party, we wanted to get everything out of our systems. Our biggest fear was that we would look back on our college years and regret what we *didn't* do, and there was one last thing on our collegiate bucket list.

"At the party, Jaden spotted the keg. She grabbed my hand, and we pushed through the crowd toward the patio like a pair of beer-seeking missiles. Our friend Stephen was on the patio. Jaden told him we wanted to do a keg stand.

"Before he lifted her, he asked if we had a designated driver to take us home. He was like a brother to us, always looking out. We told him we had arranged to spend the night there. That's all he needed to hear before he effortlessly picked Jaden up and held her upside down over the keg.

"It was my turn. Before I knew it, my entire body was upside down and over the keg. Jaden handed me the nozzle used for pouring beer. There was no turning back. I closed my eyes and chugged while the people surrounding the keg counted down from ten.

"I returned to my feet. 'How do you feel?' Jaden asked.

"I felt fine. 'Let the celebration continue!' I exclaimed.

"We went back inside to mingle. We knew most of the people at the party that night. Like Stephen, many of the people there acted as an extended family that looked out for us. But there was one group of guys there that night that we didn't recognize. John was in that group.

"John walked up to me to introduce himself and told me he was a student visiting from some town a few hours from Austin. He was a tall, lean, and muscular guy.

He asked me to dance, but I declined. Although I enjoyed dancing, I had not yet developed the confidence to do so in public. I remember how he looked at me with puppy-dog eyes and pouted lips, but I stood firm in my answer.

"At the end of the night, I announced I was done. I put my hands in the air in surrender, and I prepared my place on the couch to sleep. Later, someone pulling my hand awakened me. Although my eyelids were heavy, I could see through my half-open eyes it was John.

"'Come with me,' he whispered.

"He pulled me up from the couch and held my hand. He tip-toed across the living room like a thief in the night. I dragged my feet and stumbled over sleeping bodies that had made beds for themselves on the floor as I followed. He led me to the bathroom.

She paused.

She shook her head. "Having a one-night stand was never on my collegiate bucket list. Especially not like that." She closed her eyes as she thought about what happened to her that night. Although she hadn't thought about it in years, she still felt powerless and ashamed.

"I'm so sorry, Emma," Dr. Clark said with a down-turned mouth. "Do you want to tell me about your dream?"

He paused.

"If it's too difficult, we can resume tomorrow."

She didn't want to say anymore. It was too hard. *But you can do hard things*, she thought. She exhaled as she opened her eyes. "I re-experienced what happened that night from the moment where he pulled me off the couch. He drags me across the living room and locks the bathroom door behind me. It's as though I am observing what is happening, but I can't move," she said as tears welled up in her eyes. *Why didn't I stop him?* she thought. "Then I hear a loud banging on the door, followed by Brianna's voice. She's yelling, 'Em, let me in!' I hear her loud and clear, but I can't move."

"Brianna? You haven't mentioned her."

"She's my best friend and the closest thing I have to a sister here. Our friendship began in kindergarten when she saw me alone on the playground."

She often pondered how they ended up together. Perhaps they gravitated toward each other because they didn't have any siblings of their own. As their friendship developed, Brianna took on the role of big sister almost immediately. She affectionately pushed Emma around the way she imagined an older sibling would rough house a younger sibling. But Emma didn't mind. "She always made me feel safe, like I was never alone... She still does."

"Did she go to college with you?"

"No, but it makes sense that she's in my dream because she's always been protective of me. And I feel so guilty. Like I let us both down."

He shook his head vigorously. "Emma, you have nothing to feel guilty about. He took advantage of you." He stood up from his chair. "I could sit here and tell you that dreams of sexual abuse reflect one's innermost fears and anxieties, but what you really need to hear right now is that guy is the scum of the universe." He spoke in a raised voice, his words deliberate and stern, his eyes piercing with intensity.

She shook her head. "I wasn't blackout drunk that night. No one put anything in my drink like the girl we knew about. I remember what happened."

Emma had full control over every aspect of her life until that point. She hadn't allowed herself to believe that what happened that night was any different. And although almost a decade had gone by since that night, it was the first time she had talked about it with anyone.

"Listen to yourself, Emma. You just told me you put yourself to bed. Let me say that again. You. Put. Yourself. To. Bed." He spoke in a low, measured voice. Each word seemed to carry the weight of his convictions. "He *lured* you out of bed, Emma. You were his prey that night, and if I were a gambling man, I would bet that you were just one of many others."

4

E THUMBED THROUGH THE PAGES of his notebook, searching for answers. He strode back and forth, his movements heavy and purposeful, his mind focused on finding an explanation. Although the trauma of Emma's experience with John explained *why* she dreamed of him, it didn't explain the sudden onset of the dreams. *Why now?*

"Let me ask you something," Dr. Clark said. "How long has it been since you've thought about John or any other men you're dreaming about?"

Emma straightened her posture. "I've given that quite a lot of thought, actually." She reached for her daily planner. "Except for one person I dated recently, I haven't thought of them for years." She flipped through the pages of her planner. "I should clarify. I ran into another one of them once, months ago, but it was a very brief encounter."

He tilted his head as he stared at the rose-gold wire-bound daily planner on Emma's lap. "What do you have there?" he asked.

She looked down at the daily planner. "They're notes I made in my planner from my journal," she replied. She handed it to him. "I researched my journal entries to pinpoint the last time I gave these men any thought. The notes from my findings are behind the red tab."

He thumbed through the pages of the planner. The planner had color-coded tabs added by Emma, showing her attention to organization and detail. "You keep years' worth of journals?"

She nodded. "I keep all my journals. I consider them time capsules."

He read through her notes. They showed that, most times, she had no thoughts of the men for five to ten years. "I assume your logic is that if you thought about any of them, you would have written about them in your journal?"

She bobbed her head. "Absolutely. I also cross-checked with Brianna to confirm I haven't talked about them to her. She confirmed that was the case for all except the last man I dated."

"I see," he replied. He trusted her process. Although he barely knew her, it was clear to him that she was the kind of person who paid close attention to minute details.

"I read an article about how memories are responsible for our dreams. Is that true?" she asked.

He scratched his head. "Yes and no," he replied in a skeptical tone. "While there's no widely accepted theory on why we dream, we believe memories to be partly responsible for what we dream about. In Emma's case, it seemed there was no other explanation, at least based on what he had heard so far."

He approached her with his notebook and pen in hand. "I want to show you something." He took a seat at the coffee table facing her. "Memories are stored in clusters of neurons in the brain called *engrams*, which are adjoined by synaptic connections." He opened his notebook to a blank page. He drew two circles connected by a single line. "It looks something like this." He handed Emma the notebook.

Emma looked at the drawing.

O—O

"The line connecting the two circles is the synaptic connection." He used a pen to point at the line in the drawing. "Every night, the brain processes memories from our experiences and decides which memories to keep and which to eliminate. The memories it decides to keep are stored in the engrams, the circles." He spoke slowly.

"OK, I'm following." She spoke so quickly that her words ran together. "Also, there's no need for you to speak slowly. I'm a fast learner."

He dropped his head. "Duly noted," he replied. "I'm sorry."

She smiled softly. "It's rare I get an apology from a man. I appreciate it."

She paused.

She cleared her throat. "You were saying."

"Oh, yes. Retrieving a memory reinforces the synaptic connection." He used his pen to trace over the line. "The more we think of said memory, the more that synaptic connection is re-enforced." He continued to trace over the line. The more he traced over the line, the darker the line appeared.

She bobbed her head. "OK, the line represents a synaptic connection and the more we think of a memory, the stronger the connection to the memory gets. The stronger the connection gets, the easier it is for us to remember." She spoke in a rapid-fire stream, barely pausing for a breath.

His eyes widened; he nodded slowly. He had taught the concept of engrams and synaptic connections in relation to memory formation and retrieval to doctoral students for years, but never had he witnessed the concept grasped so quickly or heard the explanation put so simply. "The opposite is also true—"

She interrupted, "The less we think of a memory, the weaker the synaptic connection gets. And the weaker it gets, the harder it is for us to remember."

"Exactly. Therefore, the only way to weaken the synaptic connection is to stop thinking about these men. And the only way to stop thinking about them is to stop dreaming of them. And the only way to stop dreaming of them is to…?"

He paused.

She exhaled deeply. "Process the unresolved trauma."

"Precisely."

He looked up at the clock. "Same time tomorrow?"

∽

Emma's footsteps echoed down the Psychiatry and Behavioral Neuroscience building hallway. She examined her surroundings as she questioned which direction she needed to go to reach the building's exit. In her panic, she could hardly recall how she made it to Dr. Clark's office in the first place.

She saw something from the corner of her eye; she turned her head. Her body tensed; her gaze fixed on the spot where she thought she saw the unknown object. *Was that a shadow?* Whatever it was, it seemed to materialize out of thin air.

A feeling of dread washed over her. She turned to look behind her, still on high alert. But there was nothing.

She continued to move forward.

There it is again. She turned quickly, this time in the opposite direction.

A student waved in the distance. "Are you lost?" the student shouted from afar.

"No, thank you!" she shouted back.

Without checking for the elevator, she raced down the stairs and charged toward the exit, increasing her pace to a slow jog. She stepped outside, took a deep breath, and tried to shake the feeling that she had just encountered something supernatural and dangerous. *It's all in your head, Emma. It's all in your head.*

5

DOCUMENTS FLUTTERED AND FLAPPED as he sifted through piles of papers. He scanned every inch of his desk in a frenzied search.

"Where are you?" Dr. Clark asked. Although no one was in the room, he spoke aloud, as was typical for him when he was alone. "Ah! There you are." A white spiral notebook with black plastic binding lay on his desk in plain sight. A piece of masking tape with *Emma* handwritten in black permanent marker adhered to the cover. It had become his practice to assign a designated notebook to his short list of patients. He lived by his notebooks, much like Emma seemed to live by her daily planner.

He gave Emma an explanation on memory storage to buy himself some time for the day. He recognized the vicious cycle she was caught in. Although she hadn't thought of the men in years, her dreams were triggering her to think of them all over again. And although she was clearly suffering from mental distress, she had no history of anxiety or depression. His thoughts pointed him back to the same question. "Why is she having these dreams now?"

He stared blankly at his notes. "There's nothing here!" he

exclaimed. He slammed the notebook down on his desk, further provoking the disarray of documents. He reached for Emma's medical records. "Her primary physicians' report says she's five-foot-three and weighs 132 pounds…That was three weeks ago. There's no way that's still accurate." Although he couldn't be sure, he approximated she weighed between one hundred ten and one hundred fifteen pounds.

As a board-certified sleep medicine specialist, Dr. Clark was knowledgeable about the effects of sleep on health. He knew all too well that sleep wasn't just essential for the brain; it affected almost every tissue in the body, from growth to stress hormones, the immune system, appetite, breathing, blood pressure, and even cardiovascular health. It was not out of the question that Emma's dreams could contribute to her weight loss in some form or fashion.

He picked up a brain-shaped stress ball from atop his desk and threw it in the air in a one-person game of catch as he thought through the possibilities. He couldn't deny there were theoretical reasons for her dreams. One theory suggests that the brain processes memories and emotions through dreams. Another was that dreams simulate threatening events to allow the dreamer to rehearse their actions in the face of the threats.

"But if she hasn't so much as given these men a second thought, why is she having these dreams now in the first place?" Although he had just provided Emma with an explanation of how synaptic connections work in relation to retrieving memories, it didn't explain how the connections got reactivated. "Failure to use the synaptic connections should have weakened their access to the memories stored in the engrams."

He heard footsteps; he turned to look at his door. "It's locked." He expelled a sigh of relief. Once, a student walked in on him, talking to himself through a complex case like this. Having no interest in building a reputation as a mad scientist, he had since made it a point to lock his door when alone.

He continued, "The engrams should be dormant by now."

Unable to make sense of the matter, he decided it was time to confer with a respected colleague, Dr. Prasad Vedurmudi, a clinical professor of neurosurgery at the University of Chicago. His office was in the building next to Dr. Clark's office. Normally, he would walk right over, but Prasad was not on campus today. "Hello, Prasad, this is Dr. Clark. I hope I'm not interrupting you."

"Hi, Ed. No, not at all. What can I do for you?"

He picked up Emma's file. "I want to run something by you. I have a patient that is having nightmares. This patient hasn't activated any memories related to the narrative or characters of her nightmares in years. Any thoughts on how the engrams associated with the memories could have spontaneously reactivated on their own?"

"Have you ruled out the possibility of brain disease?"

"There is no sign of brain disease. She's young and otherwise healthy," he said as he flipped through Emma's MRI and blood work results. "Everything looks normal, but I'm concerned that her nightmares are strengthening the synaptic connections to the fear-based engrams. Even with continued therapy, it would take years for connections to weaken to where they were no longer causing her nightmares."

"That's a valid concern," he replied. "Have you checked her microglia levels?"

"No, like I said, there is no sign of brain—"

He paused.

"Hello? Hello, Ed? Did I lose you?"

"No, I'm here. I appreciate the chat, Prasad. You've given me plenty to think about. I need to go. Goodbye."

His eyes widened. "Of course! Why didn't I think of this before? Microglia can eliminate synaptic connections associated with fear-based engrams!" he exclaimed as though he had just struck gold.

He was well-versed in microglia and its function to protect the brain from infection.

The research on microglia's ability to eliminate synaptic connections associated with fear-based engrams was new, but the results of using a cerebral injection to eliminate fear-based memories were promising.

He exhaled audibly. "Introducing too much microglia could introduce neurodegenerative diseases." He shook his head. "It's risky...but it may be her only hope."

6

T HE HAIR-RAISING SCREECHING of tires that reverberated against the cement walls of the parking garage brought her search for a parking spot to a startling halt. She stomped on the brake and looked around for the vehicle that created the unnecessary chaos. From her rear-view mirror, she glared at the skid-marked pavement. "What a jackass," Emma uttered.

From the parking garage, it was just a short walk across a narrow street to the main entrance of the Psychiatry and Behavioral Neuroscience building. At the street, she looked to her right, then left before striding forward, her steps long and determined.

She stopped to admire the six-story concrete building's majesty, which she had overlooked the day before. It was unlike the metropolitan-style buildings in the city. Battlements lined the top of the building's walls like a medieval castle. Above the entrance archway were three turrets, which further added to the building's feudal charm.

Inscribed on the building's façade was a quote from the famous psychiatrist Carl Jung.

❧

Thoroughly unprepared, we take the step into the afternoon of life. Worse still, we take this step with the false presupposition that our truths and our ideals will serve us as hitherto. But we cannot live the afternoon of life according to the program of life's morning; for what was great in the morning will be little at evening, and what in the morning was true will at evening have become a lie.

❧

A short flight of dingy concrete stairs led to the entrance of the building. She pushed the door open. "Oh my God." She gasped at the unexpected resonating thud of the door. Inside, she breathed into her hands to warm her numb fingers. Her chest heaved as she attempted to catch her breath. Her attention turned to a sign that hung on the wall.

❧

Welcome to the University of Chicago Department of Psychiatry and Behavioral Neuroscience! Our mission is to honor our promise to always put our patients first and to be ever mindful of each patient's dignity and individuality, we must also be at the forefront of transformative discovery and innovation in psychiatric care.

❧

She charged down the main hallway and up the stairwell with intense purpose, her steps quick and efficient as she navigated the now familiar territory. Dr. Clark's office door was open.

"Come on in, Emma!" Dr. Clark exclaimed. "Are you enjoying this beautiful Chicago weather?"

She rolled her eyes as she removed her coat. "Yeah, right," she

said, both because she downright despised the cold and because
weather chit-chat was dead last on her list of things to talk about.
She sat on the couch and rested her head on the cushion as she
stared off at the ceiling above her.

"What are you looking at?"

She lifted her head and placed her hand around her neck; her
cheeks flushed into a bright shade of red.

"There's no reason to be embarrassed. What is it?"

"It's what I do to figure out if I'm dreaming."

He leaned in; with a faint rustle, his leather chair yielded to
his weight. "You look up at the ceiling?"

She nodded.

"Do you do this frequently?"

She shrugged her shoulders. "It doesn't always work, but it's
better than nothing."

"So how does looking at the ceiling help you figure out if
you're dreaming?" he asked.

She thought back to a memory from her childhood. When
she was eleven, her aunt, her mother's sister, invited her to accompany her on a trip to Rome. At first, her father forbade her to go,
but her mother insisted that they take advantage of her sister's
generous offer to expose Emma to the religious and cultural significance of Italy and Vatican City.

Between her mother and father, her mother was the calmer
and more rational one of the two. Outwardly, her father called
the shots, but her mother always stood up for what mattered. And
when she did, she spoke with a calm but unwavering authority,
making it clear she was not to be pushed around. It wasn't until she
was nearing adulthood that Emma fully understood and appreci-
ated her mother's strength and sacrifices. But she knew it now. She
gazed off into the distance as she thought back to her trip.

"I visited the Sistine Chapel when I was a child. I remember being underwhelmed by the outside appearance of the Sistine

Chapel. It was a simple building made from red brick with white stone trim around the windows and door. The building was rectangular with a flat roof. Its only notable feature was its tall chimney. My aunt told me that the chimney released black smoke to signal the election of a new Pope and white smoke to signal that a new Pope was chosen.

"But when we stepped in, the beauty of the space struck me. I looked up to see Michelangelo's Sistine ceiling. Although I was young, I remember recognizing that there was something incredibly magnificent about it.

"I connected the scenes from the painting with Bible stories I read in Sunday school...the creation of Adam, Noah's Ark, Adam and Eve, and the serpent. I was in awe of the vivid colors and the incredible detail. Most of all, I remember how endless it all seemed.

"Even after all these years, I see it in my dreams." She covered her face with her hands, feeling the heat of embarrassment on her cheeks. "It's so stupid," she said.

Dr. Clark shook his head. "No, it's a beautiful memory." He looked at her with kind eyes. "We're getting to the bottom of this, Emma."

"I hope so..." she replied. Her eyes welled up. "Because, given what I experienced last night, I don't believe I have much time."

7

"I WOKE UP SCREAMING and covered in my vomit." She scrunched up her nose as she recalled the putrid odor that attacked her senses that very morning. Although she had experienced several terrifying episodes over the past month, vomiting in her sleep was a new first for her.

Dr. Clark dropped his head. "I'm sorry, Emma." He removed his glasses and pressed his thumb and index finger into the corner of his eyes. "Could it have been something you ate?"

"No," she replied.

"How can you be sure?"

"Because I didn't."

"Didn't what?"

"Eat."

He rolled his neck and released a weary sigh, as if the weight of the world was resting on his shoulders. "What did you dream about?" he asked.

She looked vacantly into the distance. "I dreamed of Rico," she replied with a tone tinged with sadness.

There was a click of a pen as Dr. Clark prepared to take notes. "Tell me about him."

Settling back in her seat, she crossed her arms. She didn't *want* to talk about Rico. She didn't *want* to talk about any of the men she dreamed about. A *want* implies a desire, perhaps something that can even improve the quality of life. A *need* is something that is necessary to live and function. What Emma *wanted* was irrelevant. So, she endured.

"After I graduated from college, I moved back to Chicago. I had just landed my job at the firm, I had a place of my own, and I was just happy to be out on my own in my hometown...

"I was meeting an old friend for dinner the night I met Rico. After being held back at the office, I rushed into the restaurant. I approached my friend at the hostess stand, where she was still waiting to be seated. Before I could say hello, Rico approached me. His smile was warm and inviting. I shook his hand, then glanced away, pretending to be oblivious to his stunning good looks. He said he lived in Bloomington, was studying athletic training at Indiana University, and invited me to lunch the next day. I had plans with my parents, so I declined. I'm wary of giving out my phone number, so when he asked to call me, I suggested we connect via social media instead. But he told me he didn't do social media, so I gave him my number."

Dr. Clark interrupted. "No social media?"

She nodded. "That's what he said."

"After that night, we stayed in touch daily. He initiated practically every conversation. There were many late nights when we spoke on the phone for hours. And just weeks later, he made the four-hour drive from Bloomington to visit me over a long weekend. I remember how excited we were to see each other. That weekend, it was as though we were in our own world. He was originally from Chicago, and could have visited with family or friends. But he spent the entire weekend with just me. Nothing else seemed to matter. But before I knew it, it was time for him to leave.

"We made plans for me to drive to Bloomington to be his date for a formal awards ceremony that was coming up the following month. I remember the butterflies I felt when the day finally came for me to visit. I imagined us plunging toward each other for a romantic embrace when I arrived. But there was no embrace. He seemed distant. Like a stranger.

"We walked into his apartment. The air was stale and thick with the musky scent of sweat. Floor-to-ceiling mirrors covered the walls of the shared living spaces. A weight machine took up the space intended for a dining table and free weights cluttered the floor. Posters of bodybuilders, like those of a teen idol, covered the door to Rico's room. He pointed to his room and told me to come out when I was ready.

"He wasn't the same person I spent all those hours talking with on the phone. He wasn't the same person I spent that magical weekend with at home in Chicago. This person, whoever he was, was someone I didn't want to be around. I considered gathering my bags and leaving, but I had already made the long drive there and I was going to honor my commitment to accompany him to the ceremony.

"I wore a black, sequined floor-length gown I spent weeks finding and a week getting tailored. When I announced I was ready, he didn't even look up to acknowledge me, let alone what I was wearing.

"They held the ceremony at Alumni Hall. The hall was a sea of sparkling lights and soft colors. Elegant linens draped round tables, and fresh flowers adorned each table centerpiece, perfuming the air with their scent. I remember hoping the ambiance would reignite our feelings for one another.

"As we sat at our table, I noticed a beautiful woman across the way mingling with other guests. She commanded the room's attention like a bride at a wedding reception. Although she was wearing four-inch stilettos, she floated effortlessly across the ballroom from table to table. She started walking toward us. I placed my hand over my face, hoping she hadn't noticed me staring.

"'Hey, Leah! Looking gorgeous as ever!' Rico exclaimed.

"I was so relieved. They knew each other.

"'Hey, baby! I've been waiting here all alone for you,' she replied.

"*Did she just call him 'baby'?* I thought. I cloaked my surprise with an emotionless expression. Maybe that was his nickname. Maybe she was teasing…

"He introduced me to her as his 'old friend.' *Old friend?* We'd known each other for less than three months! But I held my tongue. She explained she had planned to be out of town that weekend, but her plans got canceled.

"I should have trusted my gut. I should have gotten back in my car and driven home when I realized things didn't feel right. Instead, there I was, staring at the man of my dreams and his gorgeous girlfriend.

"I had to get out of there, so I excused myself from the table. I had my purse, phone, and keys. Although my bag was still at Rico's apartment, my decision to leave it behind was an easy one. I made the long walk back to my car and left as quickly as I could.

"On the road, I called Brianna to talk me down. She knew something was wrong before I even said a word. She has a sort of empathetic ability about her. It's like she can pick up on my emotional energy, regardless of distance. I told her how I was humiliated.

"'Of course, Rico would never go for someone like me,' I said.

"'What is that supposed to mean?' she asked in a disapproving tone.

"I explained Rico had a girlfriend and told her how beautiful she was.

"'His GIRLFRIEND!' she shouted. I could practically hear the vein from her temple throbbing on the phone. 'Em, you are *more* beautiful. I don't need to see that woman to tell you that,' she said.

"On the long drive home, I couldn't stop thinking about all the red flags I had either ignored or been oblivious to. No social media, our too-good-to-be-true weekend bubble, the way he always initiated our phone conversations. I felt so stupid, but Brianna had a different perspective. She told me I was courageous in following my heart and courageous in leaving because 'I deserve so much better.'

"We ended our call like we always have ever since we got our first cell phones, 'I'll love you forever, friend.'"

She paused.

"Actually, before we hung up, she had one more thing to say…"

There was silence.

"What did she say?" Dr. Clark asked.

She smiled. "She said, 'If I were there, I would have pulled him by the ear.' And she totally would have. That's Brie."

She stood from her seat.

"You're leaving? But you haven't told me about your dream," Dr. Clark said.

"I just need some water," she replied.

She returned to her seat. "In my dreams, I'm on a park carousel with Rico. It's just the two of us, and for a split second, I'm happy. Then the carousel picks up speed and Leah hops on. I tighten my grip and struggle to hang on as the carousel goes round and round, faster and faster. I feel dizzy and nauseous.

"'Stop, please stop!' I scream. The carousel is spinning so fast that everything I see is a blur except for Rico and Leah—I can see them perfectly clear. They're laughing and holding hands and gazing at each other like teenagers in love. I feel my heart breaking."

"Emma, are you OK? You look pale," Dr. Clark said.

She nodded. Eager to get the discussion over with, she continued. "The carousel spins even faster and faster and one by one, my fingers lose grip until I can't hold on anymore. I'm catapulted into the air and land on the ground. I lift my head to see my paralyzed, contorted body on the ground. All I can do is scream." Her eyes glazed over; beads of sweat formed around her hairline.

"Emma. Are you OK?"

She shook her head slowly. "I'm going to throw up."

Dr. Clark reached for the trash can from under his desk and rushed to her.

Still seated, she bent over. He held the trash can under her face.

She hacked and gagged until the spinning in her head slowed and came to an eventual stop. She looked in the trash bin as she returned to an upright position. "It's just water." She exhaled. "I feel better."

Dr. Clark patted her on the back. "We can resume tomorrow."

"No!" she exclaimed. She refused to concede; she flashed Dr. Clark an incredulous look. "We don't have time."

"OK," he replied. He raised his hands in surrender as he slowly stepped back toward his desk. "OK."

She placed the trash can on the floor. "Why is this happening?!" she shouted. She sunk her face into her hands.

"Because our brains don't switch off."

She lifted her head. "What?"

He took a seat. "Pent-up worries and anxieties can manifest in our unconscious brains, and when they do, they're capable of triggering the same ailments we experience while we're awake."

She released an audible sigh. "Of course they are."

8

THANKS TO HER EXPERIENCE and the connections she made as an intern during her summers in Austin, Emma had a job at a Public Relations firm waiting for her when she moved back home. The internships usually paid a measly seven dollars an hour, the minimum wage. But it was enough to pay for rent and living expenses until her scholarship kicked back in at the beginning of the next school year. And although the internships paid little, she worked hard. She approached her work ethic, much like everything else in her life, with complete dedication, and took nothing for granted. It was what her mother had instilled in her growing up. And when she started her job at the firm, it didn't take long before the execs noticed that her performance stood out.

"The firm assigned me to a special project with Zack. That's how we met. They told us they selected us for the assignment because we were the best in the firm. They called us 'rising stars.'

"Zack was tall and lean; somewhat, but not overly muscular. His hair was perfectly styled. His shoes were perfectly polished and always coordinated with his belt. His clothes were tailored and pressed. *This is someone who's got it together*, I thought.

"We enjoyed that we could rely on each other, and we made each other better…Professionally speaking, of course. And unlike so many other colleagues, there was no competition between us. Perhaps we knew there didn't need to be, or perhaps we were too naïve to care. In any case, we both excelled at our work.

"Through it all, I never considered dating him. 'Don't shit where you eat' is what Brianna always says. Although there is probably a better way to phrase it, I understood her message loud and clear, and I made it a point not to date people I worked with.

"One morning I came into work to find him emptying his desk. 'Did they finally fire you for stealing binder clips from the supply closet?' I joked.

"He told me that he had landed a junior executive role at Global PR. Initially, my heart sank at the thought of losing my closest colleague. Not because I had romantic feelings for him, but because I truly enjoyed working with him. He asked me out to celebrate at Serrano's that evening. *He's no longer a coworker*, I thought. I had no reason to decline.

"I didn't know what to expect that night. Yes, we worked together. He wasn't a stranger, but we had both been laser-focused on our work. I set the boundary early on that I don't date people at work, so any non-work conversations were limited. I didn't even know what kind of car he drove.

"He picked me up, and it surprised me to see that he was driving a new Porsche. 'Wow, this is very impressive!' I exclaimed.

"He told me he thought it was important that he drive a nice car. But that was no 'nice car.' I had never been inside anything like it. It had a new car mixed with genuine leather scent to it, and it was spotless, both inside and out. Even the back seat was completely clean and empty except for a black gym bag. I remember the bag had a logo on it that read *Elite*. And elite it was.

"I asked how he could afford his car, then immediately regretted that I asked. Maybe he came from a wealthy family. Maybe he inherited it. Maybe he won some sort of settlement. In any case, it was none of my business. I apologized for asking, but still secretly hoped he'd tell me how he could afford the car. But he didn't.

"He asked if I was OK with having Popeye's for dinner because he had a coupon. *He can't be serious*, I thought. But he was. It was getting awkward, and we hadn't even gotten to dinner. Things could only get better from there, or so I hoped.

"We entered Popeye's and walked up to the cashier to place our order. He ordered first. I assumed when he was done, he would ask me to step up to add my order. But he didn't. Not only had he just paid for his meal, but he also had his coupon fully applied to his payment. *Did he really just do that?* I thought. Don't get me wrong—it was a six-dollar meal. Paying my bill was no big deal. But he could have at least offered.

"After we ate, we headed straight to Serrano's. I was eager to see what all the fuss was about. We entered the parking lot and immediately saw the line-up of opulent luxury vehicles parked in the valet section of the parking lot. It was as if we stepped into the showroom of a luxury car dealership.

"He pulled up to the valet station. I would have taken an open self-parking spot over paying fifty dollars for valet, but who was I to judge what this guy spends his money on? After we were out of the car, Zack asked if I could pay the valet. He claimed to have no cash on him, even though the valet sign clearly read that they accepted credit. I pulled out my wallet.

"They set up a hostess at the restaurant entrance to collect a cover charge. This time, there was a sign that read 'cash only.' I pulled out my wallet once again.

"'We should consider ourselves lucky,' Zack said. 'I hear they inflate the cover charge as the night goes by.' *Lucky, yeah right*, I thought.

"Inside, I witnessed firsthand what all the hype was about. The place was a spectacle for the young and rich. Zack's eyes lit up with excitement as he gazed at the landscape of wealth in the building. We caught glimpses of local sports celebrities, from the Bulls to the Bears, White Sox, Cubs, and Blackhawks. The Bulls were the easiest to spot. You could spot them from almost anywhere in the building…You just had to look for the herd of extraordinarily tall men.

"Zack looked like he was in paradise, but except for the fleeting excitement of seeing the celebrities, I wasn't impressed. I didn't grow up with a lot of money. And although I had come a long way, I couldn't help but wonder how many of those yuppies had any real wealth at all. The celebrities, maybe. But how many of the others were wearing their wealth on their person? How many, like Zack, were driving their wealth? Were they really wealthy at all? It all felt so inauthentic, almost slimy.

"In my dreams, I'm back at Serrano's with Zack at the bar. We're people-watching like we were the night of our date. Zack is drinking Grey Goose martinis and taking inventory of his cash and credit cards as I stand nearby. Patrons are waving cash in the air as bouncers accept the highest bids to sneak people into the already packed venue.

"I gasp for air amidst a mounting sea of bodies. I reach for Zack and yell for help, but he doesn't even look up. The crush of the crowd carries me away and pushes against my chest as I struggle to breathe. Then, out of nowhere, I see Brianna in the crowd. I try reaching for her. Our fingertips touch, but we can't get close enough.

"'Em, I'm not going to leave you!' she shouts.

"I fade in and out as I'm depleted of oxygen. Then I awaken, gasping for air."

Emma breathed in deeply. Her chest puffed up as her lungs filled with air, then fell as it quickly expelled the air. Though seated, she felt unsteady. Her complexion grew pale. She planted her palms on the couch cushions for balance and blinked slowly to clear her blurry vision.

Dr. Clark pushed his seat out in a rush; the sharp scraping from his chair scuffing the floor echoed through the room as he stood up. "Emma!"

9

EMMA GAZED VACANTLY at the buzzing fluorescent lighting above her. Her body lay stretched out on the couch; her head rested on a soft pillow. She breathed slowly and steadily. *I'm not dreaming,* she thought. She turned her head toward Dr. Clark. "What happened?"

"You fainted," he replied.

Her eyes widened. "I've never fainted in my life," she said.

"If I had to guess, your dreams of Zack are causing sleep fainting episodes, just like your dreams of Rico caused you to vomit."

Sleep fainting? Her dreams had caused her to question her sanity on more than one occasion, but now she was questioning whether it was Dr. Clark who was insane. "That makes absolutely no sense. How is it possible for someone to faint in their sleep?" she asked.

"Sleep fainting occurs when a person is in an unarousable state while already asleep or faints upon waking. In either case, unless a person is being actively monitored, it's difficult to detect if sleep fainting has occurred.

She crossed her arms and glanced around the room, reluctant to hear more. "If it's alright with you, I'd like to continue."

He nodded. "If you insist."

"I met Noah when I was a freshman at UT Austin."

"That's a long way from home. Was moving to Texas difficult for you and your parents?" he asked.

"Yes, but I went on a full scholarship, so it didn't really matter," she replied.

"That's very impressive."

She scoffed. "More like a miracle, I'd say. My father wouldn't let me go, but I went anyway."

"Why wouldn't he allow you to go?"

"It's complicated. He's a pastor with a small bilingual Pentecostal church on the west side. I grew up with a strict upbringing, and he said it was too dangerous for me to go away to college."

To say that Emma had a strict upbringing would, by many people's standards, be an understatement. When she was a child, she wasn't allowed to do many things children experience growing up. She didn't take part in after-school activities or attend birthday parties. Sleepovers, for Emma, were a thing that only happened in movies. She hoped her father would be more lenient as she got older, but that wasn't the case.

When it came time for Brianna's sweet sixteen, she thought surely her father would make an exception and allow her to attend her party. Her parents knew Brianna well, after all. There would be boys at the party. There would be music and dancing. It was not an environment her father would allow her to be in, not for a single moment. Not on his watch. Not while she was living under his roof. She begged and pleaded with him, but her father told her it was for her own good. He claimed he was protecting her. And for that reason, she never so much as considered going away for college. Until one day, she was called into her high school guidance counselor's office.

It seemed Emma's upbringing came with a bright side. While

others her age enjoyed active social lives, she studied. And studied. And studied. Aside from attending church, her time with her books had become her sole pastime. And her perfect grades reflected it. Emma's guidance counselor thought she would be the perfect candidate to apply for a prestigious presidential scholarship to the University of Texas at Austin.

Although Emma felt honored that her guidance counselor suggested her for the opportunity to apply, she explained her parents wouldn't allow her to leave the city, let alone the state, to attend college. But her guidance counselor insisted. So, believing it was a long shot anyway, she completed the college admission form and scholarship application in the guidance counselor's office. She would soon learn that being awarded the scholarship was the easy part of her journey to college.

"How did you convince your father to let you go?"

"I didn't," she replied. "I remember overhearing my mother try to convince him one evening after church service...

"'No! It's too dangerous!' my father shouted. 'No way, no how,' he said.

"'We need to let her go,' my mother said. 'We can't protect her forever.'

"Later that night, after my father went to bed, my mother woke me from my sleep. 'You're going to go to Austin,' she whispered.

"'But how?' I asked.

"'I'm going to help you,' she replied. 'Don't worry about your father. I'll take care of him.'

"I couldn't believe my ears. My seemingly submissive mother was going to help me sneak away to college. My sleepy eyes widened with excitement, but my excitement faded when I thought about the roadblocks still ahead. Although I had earned a full scholarship, the university required that I submit two hundred dollars with my acceptance letter to secure my spot. I also needed a one-way plane ticket to get to Austin. Two hundred dollars and a one-way plane ticket stood in my way, but it was my Mount Everest.

"'I'll give you the money,' my mother told me.

"'Where will you get it?' I asked.

"'You let me take care of that…all we need right now is two hundred dollars to secure your spot; we can worry about the plane ticket later,' she said.

"I knew my mother would come through for me. They pulled her out of school at a young age to work on a farm with her family, and she married my father when she was just sixteen. But somehow, she saw value in education. She always told me, 'When you go to college, you get to choose what you want to do with your life. When you don't, life chooses for you.'

"The night before I left for Austin, I said goodbye to my father, although he didn't know it. I hugged him tightly and fought back my tears.

"'Where is all of this coming from? Am I dying?' he asked.

"He had no clue that I was preparing to leave. It wasn't until I was on the plane that my mother told him I had left.

She paused.

"Four years passed before I spoke to him again."

"Do you resent him?" Dr. Clark asked.

She sat quietly as she reflected on his question. Not because she didn't know how to answer it, but because she didn't know where to start. So, she responded the only way she knew how. "Do you mean, aside from the fact that I was robbed of a normal childhood, or that I was socially crippled as an adolescent?"

"That would certainly be reason enough."

"My father kept me in line. Perhaps he went too far, but that's all in the past."

"How did he 'keep you in line?'"

"There was no talking back to him." She bit her lip and furrowed her brow.

"What would be the consequence if you talked back?"

"He never touched me, if that's what you're trying to get at," she replied, shaking her head. "He'd tell me to go to my room and have me read the Bible."

"Hold on. Did you say he locked you in your room and forced you to read the Bible as punishment?"

Her face paled as she realized the weight of her words. "I didn't use those exact words. It's no big deal."

"Do you resent him for how he punished you?

Not as much as I resent this conversation, she thought. "Yes, but like I said, that's long in the past."

She realized that some things she had accepted as normal in her household could be considered abusive behavior and she resented her father for some time. A few months after she went away to college, her father tried to make amends. He called and wrote, but she was unwilling to put herself in a position where she might fall back into his control.

Still, her father never gave up hope; he never stopped trying. Every birthday and holiday while she was away, she received a card from her mother and father with a modest cash gift. And before every mid-term and final, she received a hand-written letter from her father with a special prayer and words of encouragement. It helped, but the risk of reconciling with her father and getting pulled back into his control while she was in college was not one she would take.

After she returned home from college, her father continued to ask for her forgiveness. And after agreeing to meet him for coffee one day, he explained that although his intentions stemmed from his concern for her safety, he recognized now that his actions were wrong. He told her he should have left her choices in God's hands rather than attempt to force control over a matter that was out of his hands. And she believed him.

"You've forgiven him?" Dr. Clark asked.

"Yes, I forgave him long ago. Now, we have a healthy relationship with healthy boundaries. I can assure you of that. But Dr. Clark, you're focusing on the wrong thing."

She paused.

"I know my father isn't perfect—no one is. But that's not what I'm here to discuss."

There was silence.

Dr. Clark gazed at her with a muted smile.

"OK, Emma. What would you like to discuss?"

She inhaled deeply. "Noah," she uttered as she expelled her breath.

She paused again.

"I feel like he's haunting me."

"*Haunting* you? That's an interesting choice of words. Is he alive?"

"Of course!" she exclaimed.

Ten years had passed since she last saw him. After college, they no longer shared the same friends. She didn't know what had become of him. Given that he always talked about wanting to start a family, she imagined he was married and with children by now. "At least, I think he is," she said.

He leaned back in his chair and propped his feet up on his desk. "Tell me about him."

"When I moved to Austin, I didn't know a soul. I met Noah at a Greek life event held for incoming freshmen. It turned out that he was there on the same scholarship that I was on, so it was important to both of us to keep our grades up or risk losing our scholarships. We spent many late nights studying together at the campus library. The air was cool and crisp on those late fall nights in Austin, and the UT tower shined brightly. Something about our walks together back then made our time feel even more special.

"We had a lot of fun together. We went to the movies, bowling at the student union, ice skating, and all the fun activities friends do, none of which I had ever experienced before. I had never been in love before, but the feelings I was growing for him were like nothing I imagined possible. By spring semester of that year, we couldn't put aside our feelings for each other and became a couple. Everything was wonderful, but we soon started growing apart."

"What happened?" Dr. Clark asked.

"I was eighteen when I had my first drink in college. Unlike me, Noah started drinking at a much younger age. He was a self-proclaimed 'pro.' Drinking with him was fun at first. On some weekends, we'd experiment with a bottle of liquor he got a hold of even though he was under the legal drinking age.

"By sophomore year, we were both well into the college social scene. Noah was in a fraternity. I was in a sorority. We were making friends and having the time of our lives, but Noah started drinking more heavily as time passed. While I enjoyed having fun as much as the next person, I never lost sight of what I was there for. But he did. Many nights I pleaded with him to go home so that I could work on a paper that was due, or because he had an exam he needed to be up early for, or whatever the case was.

"'Stop being a prude!' he'd say.

"By the end of our sophomore year, he was drinking heavily every day. And once he started, he wouldn't stop. His grades suffered, and they placed him on academic probation. He even lost his scholarship.

"I didn't notice it right away, but many of the traits that drew me to him faded away by then. As much as I loved him, he wasn't the same person I fell in love with, and we were on completely different paths. He was heartbroken when I broke off our relationship. I was, too. A part of me thought he was 'the one.'"

"Well, that's normal, and it sounds like you did the right thing," Dr. Clark said.

"How old were you when you fell in love?"

"I was seventeen, almost eighteen," Emma replied. "Why?"

"Well, those are formative years in brain development. First loves have lifelong effects because of hormonal imprints on the brain from memories formed during adolescence. As a result, it's normal for people to dream of their first loves long after they've moved on, even after decades," he explained.

Although interesting, something about Dr. Clark's explanation didn't add up. She never doubted her decision to break up with Noah. And as difficult as it was, she stuck to her decision and never looked back. She never wondered what he was up to, never attempted to reconnect, never searched for him, let alone followed him on social media. Yes, she'd dreamed of him before, but her dreams of him were few; not even close to the frequency of her dreams of him now. And the narrative of her recent dreams was disturbing, unlike anything she'd dreamed of in the past. "That was such a long time ago. Why is he haunting me now?"

He brought his feet to the floor and placed his palms on his desk; he leaned in. "You said it again—what do you mean he's *haunting* you?"

"He's haunting me in my dreams. I can't explain it. It just feels different from my other dreams, like he's all around me." Her mouth trembled as she spoke. "I dream that I'm back in college with Noah. He's drinking, and he's completely wasted. He forces me to get in his car.

"He shouts at me as he's driving. His speech is slurred and stumbled, disjointed and lacking coherence. I listen closely, but I can't understand a word he's saying. Suddenly, his words are more clear. 'Why don't you love me anymore?!' he shouts over and over. His breath reeks of alcohol and vomit; I look away because I can't take the smell. I feel like I'm about to throw up. I need some fresh air; I turn to the door and desperately try to open the car window...But it's locked.

"I turn to look at him. He's pounding on his chest like an

angry gorilla. 'Is it because I'm not good enough for you?!' he shouts. The sound of his voice is deafening. Then it occurs to me. His mouth isn't moving. The sound of his voice is blasting from his car's sound system.

"I don't know what to make of it; fear consumes me. I try to escape. Suddenly, I hear a horn blaring and I'm blinded by headlights. Noah has crossed the median, and we're about to hit a semi-truck head-on. My body lunges forward as we collide with the truck. That's when I wake up. That's when I always wake up, gasping, my body spasming and dripping in sweat." Beads of sweat formed around her lips as she spoke.

"Lots of people who have experienced abuse dream about their abusers. These dreams can be extremely upsetting and can feel very real."

She fixated on his word choice. *Abusers?* "How does this apply to me?"

He scratched his head. "At any point in your relationship, did you feel threatened or unsafe when you were with Noah?"

Memories flooded her mind. Although Noah never hit her, she could recall countless incidents where she felt threatened by him, like the times he refused to let her drive despite his drunken stupor. She remembered sitting in the passenger's seat of his car, terrified for her life. It never occurred to her it was abuse. Until now.

"Yes," she replied. She watched as Dr. Clark placed his palm under his chin and stared blankly at his desk, as if lost in thought. "What is it?" she asked.

He removed his palm from his chin. "I can't help but wonder..."

He paused.

"What?" she asked; she gnawed nervously on her fingernail.

He crossed his arms. "What if Noah *is* dead?"

10

HAUNTING. HAUNTING. HAUNTING. Dr. Clark considered the number of times Emma had used the word while discussing Noah. She had not used that word at any point while discussing the other men in her dreams.

"You can't be sure he's alive, can you?" he asked.

She shook her head. "I guess not. I remember seeing him around my junior and senior years, mostly at parties. I don't even know if he graduated, let alone what became of him after I moved back home."

"He certainly sounds like someone that would engage in risky behavior."

Dr. Clark was familiar with many published articles on *dreams of the departed.* Many psychologists and psychotherapists use dream interpretation to understand their patients' mental and emotional states. Although it was likely a long shot, he decided it was worth checking. He turned to his computer. "Do you remember his last name?"

"Evans," she replied.

He hammered away at his keyboard as Emma looked on from her seat. *Noah Evans, Austin, Texas.*

He adjusted his glasses as he leaned in toward his computer screen. "You've got to be kidding me," he said.

Emma stood up and rushed to his desk. "Did you find him?" she asked.

He leaned closer to his screen and gestured for her to come around. "You're going to want to see this for yourself."

᪗

Austin Police: Driver fatally shoots himself while being arrested for drunk driving

AUSTIN (KXAN) – Authorities are investigating an incident where a driver shot himself after a multi-vehicle accident in Austin, Texas.

According to a press release from the Austin Police Department, at about 2:50 a.m. on Saturday, Feb. 18, officers responded to a three-vehicle accident on southbound I-35 frontage road near Stassney Lane.

Police say they were placing one of the drivers under arrest for DWI when he began resisting arrest. Officers report the driver then pulled a gun he had on his person and shot himself.

Authorities attempted life-saving measures, but the driver was later pronounced dead at a hospital. The driver has been identified as Noah Evans, age 29, of Houston, Texas.

KXAN has also learned that Evans was driving with a suspended driver's license and that an ignition interlock device was installed in his vehicle. Evans would have faced felony charges of DWI 3rd or more. It would have been his ninth offense in just as many years.

"The driver was more than likely trying to avoid extensive jail time. This was just a very sad and unfortunate outcome," Abel Tayler, a spokesperson for the Austin Police Department, said.

This comes after a jury in Texas sentenced a 44-year-old woman to life in prison following her sixth driving while intoxicated (DWI) conviction.

※

He turned to her. "The article is dated a month ago."

Her eyes widened; she placed her hand over her mouth. "I can't believe he's dead."

Her reaction confirmed what he suspected. She truly didn't know what became of him.

"So, what, his ghost is actually haunting me?" Her eyes were wide, the white showing around her entire iris.

"Calm down, Emma. That's not what I'm saying."

She placed her hands on her head and paced nervously around the room. "What are you saying, then?"

Dr. Clark didn't believe in the spirit world, per se. Unlike some he knew, he had never experienced a ghost encounter. And even if he did, he certainly didn't believe Noah's ghost had somehow flown across the country to haunt Emma. But he couldn't ignore that dreams of the departed are among the most remarkable and most important categories of dreams. He crossed his arms as he leaned back in his chair. "There have been several studies on what's known as visitation dreams, where the dreamer dreams of someone that recently departed."

"And?"

"And studies show that this type of dream feels very real, and the dreamer often awakens with intense emotions. Perhaps that's what you're experiencing here."

She shook her head. "I don't care what they're called...How do I stop them?"

Struggling to respond, he stood up. He still didn't have all the answers, but given her symptoms, he saw a trend of her body physically reacting to both her dreams and the re-telling of her dreams; he was both unwilling and unable to mask his concern. It was becoming increasingly clear to him that whatever was telling Emma she was running out of time was something he couldn't ignore. "Your subconscious may be trying to warn you that you are in imminent danger," he said

"What kind of danger?" she asked, rubbing her throat.

"It could have something to do with your work or your health. I don't know exactly. But given the vividness of your dreams, I'm concerned that the warning may overextend itself into your sleep. People have died in their sleep because of dreams that triggered a medical emergency." He knew of countless testimonies on record where, for example, a character in a dream shoots a dreamer in the heart, and the dreamer wakes up having a heart attack.

"Are you saying I could be in danger while I'm dreaming?" she asked with a look of disbelief.

"That's exactly what I'm saying," he replied. "Just last year, a man living just outside of town dreamed his home was being burglarized. While asleep, he grabbed his handgun and opened fire. He awoke to find he had shot himself in the leg."

"You're kidding," she replied.

"Absolutely not kidding." Papers rustled as he searched his desk. *I know it's here somewhere*, he thought. His eyes widened. "Here!" he exclaimed.

He handed her a newspaper. "See for yourself," he said.

She looked at him as if he had just handed her a foreign object. "What's this?" she asked.

"It's the Chicago Tribune." He pointed to the front-page headline. "There. Read it."

"Lake Barrington man facing firearm charges after shooting himself while dreaming burglars were breaking into home, authorities say." She cocked her head to the side. "Why was he facing firearm charges?"

"Allegedly, the firearm was unregistered. Anyway, that's not the point."

She heaved an audible sigh. "OK, I'll take you up on the prescription for anxiety medication."

He shook his head. "It's not that simple."

"Why not?" she asked.

"Because medication won't change the narrative of your dreams."

She lowered her head. "So, how do we change the narrative of my dreams?"

He paused.

His eyes grew wide. "That's it—we need to change the narrative."

She lifted her head. "But how?"

"Through dream training," he said with a tingle of excitement. "Have you ever considered taking the wheel, so to speak, to change the outcome of your dreams?"

She shook her head. "I didn't think I could affect what was happening in my dreams. Is that even possible?"

"Not only is it possible, but using the mnemonic induction lucid dream technique, known as MILD, and given the high frequency of your lucid dreams, the outcome will likely far exceed my expectations."

"What is it?"

"It's a technique where a dreamer rehearses a dream and its outcome using sleep hypnosis," he replied. His excitement intensified at the thought of the results the technique could yield. "Lucid dreaming is critical to the success of the technique, particularly during the rapid eye movement, REM, stage where dreams are the

most prolific and intense," he explained. As an expert in oneirology, he conducted dream training countless times. The process
involved using sleep hypnosis to change how the mind thinks, a
sort of re-wiring of the brain. In doing so, the dreamer can change
the narrative of their dreams, thereby altering the course, the narrative, of their dreams. Although he had conducted dream training
many times before, he had only done so with above-average lucid
dreamers, those who reported having lucid dreams several times a
month. Never had he conducted dream training on someone who
had the ability to lucid dream several times every night.

"Are you willing to try it?" he asked.

"Yes, of course. I'll try anything," she replied. From the look
on her face, his excitement had rubbed off on her.

"Come back this evening, at five-thirty. I'll be ready for you."
He stood up, signaling the end of their time.

She remained seated as she stared off into the distance. She
appeared deep in thought.

"What is it?" he asked.

She turned to him. "Do you think any of the others are dead,
too?"

11

THE SKY WAS A BLEND of pink, orange, and purple hues as the sun began its slow descent below the horizon. Emma sprinted across the street, desperate to make her appointment on time. It was unlike her to be late, but the social media rabbit hole she had jumped into before she left caused her to lose track of time. Losing track of time was the very reason she limited her time on social media to begin with, except for work where she depended on it. But the revelation that Noah had passed left her wondering if the same could be true for the others. However, their active social media footprints revealed that wasn't the case.

She rushed up the steps that led to the entrance of the building.

She gasped at the sudden appearance of a man seated on a bench just outside the building. He wore a black jacket over a hoodie that covered his head. It was as if he had always been there, and it seemed as if he appeared out of nowhere. He sat silent and unmoving as he stared down at his phone.

An uneasy feeling washed over her. Her knees trembled, causing her to lose her footing. She rolled her ankle as she fell to the ground.

The man stood up.

Perhaps the man only wanted to help, but something she couldn't rationalize was telling her she was in danger. Maybe it was instinct. Maybe it was anxiety. Whatever it was, she couldn't ignore it. She stood up and powered through the throbbing pain that accompanied every hurried step.

She pushed the door open but found no solace from making it inside. Clenching her teeth, she hurried forward. The halls were empty and quiet except for the sound of her rapid footsteps.

She stepped into the elevator. Fear gripped her as she heard footsteps from a distance growing louder. She lunged forward to press the close button. "Come on!" she exclaimed in a whisper as she pressed the close door button in rapid fire fashion.

Alas, the elevator door closed. She crouched down to examine her injury. *It's just a scrape.*

She gasped, startled by the ding of the elevator door as it opened. Unwilling to step out blindly, she peaked out of the elevator from the inside; her index finger hovered over the emergency call button. *The coast is clear.*

Dr. Clark's office was just a few steps away.

That's strange, she thought. The door was open, and the lights inside the office were off. She reached for her daily planner tucked securely in her purse.

5:30 PM @ Dr. Clark's office.

She looked at her watch. *5:37. Maybe he left.* She knocked on the door. "Hello? Is anyone here?"

"Come in," Dr. Clark whispered.

The door let out a high-pitched groan as she pushed it all the way open. The office was dim.

"Close the door behind you."

She looked around the office nervously, uncertain of what she was walking into.

He guided her to the couch. "Lay down." He placed a blanket over her. "Are you comfortable?" he asked.

"Yes," she replied, but if he could see her eyes, they would tell a different story. She was a careful planner, accustomed to knowing exactly what she was getting into. Placing her trust in Dr. Clark, practically a stranger that she'd known for just a couple of days, did not come easy for her.

"I want to let you know that I'll be recording our dream training session today, and I'll be providing you with a copy of the recording so that you can repeat the exercise as much as possible on your own."

The sound of a click signaled to her that the recording was starting.

"Emma, I need you to close your eyes... I need you to imagine a situation where someone is being inappropriate towards you or putting you in a situation you don't want to be in." His voice was like a gentle breeze, his speech slow and calm. Her body sank into the couch cushions.

She imagined John guiding her to the bathroom like he did that night in college. It conflicted her mind and body, her mind filled with anxious thoughts, her body relaxed. With each passing moment, her body relaxed further, succumbing to the weight of her exhaustion.

"Or maybe the person you are imagining is abusing a friend. This person is a bully, Emma...Imagine that you stand up to this person. You won't allow this person to bully you, hurt you, or force you to do anything you don't want to do, Emma."

Sound asleep, she shook her head, as though her subconscious was exposing her inability to accept the truth of Dr. Clark's words. Her breaths were quick and shallow, coming in rapid succession like a drumbeat.

He continued, "You may not believe it yet, but you will. Now, again, I need you to imagine that you stand up to this person. You won't allow this person to intimidate you, hurt you, or force you to do anything you don't want to do, Emma."

She dreamed she was a scared young girl, the childhood version of herself, being led away by a faceless man. The man was slender and dressed in black from head to toe. Panic set in. She grew more fearful and uncertain of what to do. She looked up at the man. Just beyond him, she saw the ceiling of the Sistine chapel. Although she now knew she was dreaming, it brought her no peace. Her heart raced and her thoughts became clouded. The man was much bigger than her, and she was all alone. *There's no way out of this,* she thought as she followed him.

Dr. Clark continued, "No matter what this person looks like or how they made you feel in the past, this person does not scare you, Emma...You are not afraid because there is nothing to be afraid of. This person is incapable of inducing fear in you. This person cannot intimidate you, Emma."

Her breathing slowed; her heart rate normalized as her psyche internalized his words.

She looked around, suddenly aware of her surroundings. Her thoughts were no longer clouded. She could think clearly. The sound of children giggling surrounded her as she walked through a park. In the distance, she saw families playing games of Frisbee and tag.

"This person cannot control you, Emma. You are in control. You are always in control," Dr. Clark said. His words echoed through her psyche and into her dream like a voice from the heavens.

He continued, "This person cannot control you, Emma. You are in control."

She looked down at her feet and dug her heels firmly into the earth beneath. The man pulled at her arm, nudging her to continue.

"No!" she shouted.

The faceless man pulled harder.

She fought to free herself from his tight grip. "Let me go!"

He picked her up and threw her over his shoulder as he laughed deviously at her efforts to escape.

She kicked and screamed. Powerful punches exploded from her small, clenched fists. "Get away from me!" she shouted with all her might.

From a distance, a woman in the park heard her cries. She spotted Emma fighting off the faceless man and alerted others around her.

"Hey! Let her go!" a man shouted from a distance.

"Put her down. Now!" another man shouted from closer proximity.

One by one, men and women surrounded her, and they pried her from the arms of the faceless man.

She opened her eyes.

"How do you feel?" Dr. Clark asked.

A tender smile graced her lips. "I feel…free."

12

Day 3, The University of Chicago
10:55 a.m.

BEADS OF SWEAT FROM his forehead and upper lip glistened in the light. It was unlike Dr. Clark to deviate from his standard office uniform which comprised of a long-sleeve button-up shirt and cardigan, but today he had peeled away his attire down to his white undershirt. His cheeks were flushed, and his skin glazed. He despised the heat. In fact, Chicago's cool weather was a major consideration when he decided to work at the University of Chicago.

He spoke on the phone. "What do you mean it won't be fixed today?" He shook his head. "Fine. Goodbye!" he exclaimed. With an incredulous scoff he slammed down the phone.

"Good morning," Emma said.

"Good morning," he replied with his back to her.

"It's warm in here."

"The heater won't shut off. I'm afraid we'll have to have our session today in less-than-optimal conditions," he groaned.

"That won't be a problem. I don't mind the heat as much as the cold."

The sound of papers being shuffled filled the room. He took a seat behind his desk.

"People can't sleep when they're hot," he said in an agitated tone.

"Excuse me?"

"Nothing, sorry."

She cleared her throat. "I'm ready whenever you are."

He raised his head. "Sorry, I'll just be a moment." His eyes widened. *Oh my,* he thought as he laid eyes on her for the first time that day. She typically donned a turtleneck blouse and pants, but on this unseasonably warm day, she wore a cargo skirt that fell just above her knees and a simple white tank top. There were parts of her body he had never seen exposed before—her arms, neck, collarbone, even her wrists, were all in plain sight and glistened with a dewy moisture in the light.

"What are you looking at?" she asked. She pulled a compact mirror from her purse and held it up to her face. "Do I have something in my teeth?"

He dropped his head. *Oh boy,* he thought; he used the back of his hand to wipe the sweat from his forehead. "You're not wearing what you usually wear."

"What? Is my outfit too revealing?" she asked. She glowered at him, her disappointment clear on her face.

As the heat of the tension intensified, his armpits became slick with sweat, leaving moist patches on his shirt. He searched for something, anything, to say to get past the awkwardness of the situation.

He cleared his throat again. "I'm sorry, I'm just a little distracted...because of the heat issue."

She stared at him with squinted eyes. "What's the matter with you? You don't seem like your usual self today."

It was clear from her expression that she didn't buy his explanation. And who could blame her? He wouldn't buy it either, but he was a horrible liar, and it was the best he could come up with. Still, he couldn't reveal the real reason for his distraction. Not yet. He was a professional. He would allow the situation to play out on its own and bite his lip for now.

"Can we get started? I've got a lot I'd like to get through today," she said.

He cleared his throat. "Yes, of course. Let me just grab my notebook." He fumbled nervously through the paperwork on his desk. "Found it!" he exclaimed. "Oh wait, I need a pen." He fumbled some more. *You can get through this,* he thought. *Just. Don't. Stare.*

13

THE FIRST THING SHE NOTICED was the way he looked at her. It was a look that stretched out way too long. It was a look she had seen many times before, but never from him. He looked at her like she was a specimen. Who knows what he was thinking, but it was a look she had an issue with, and it had to be addressed. She glowered at him from across the room. A storm brewed just beneath her burning gaze. "I know what you must be thinking," she said.

He squinted his eyes as he connected with her gaze; he leaned in. "Tell me, what must I be thinking, Emma?"

"You're thinking that I brought this on myself."

He furrowed his brow and placed his palms on his desk as he leaned in closer. "Emma, I do not think that for a single second." He spoke softly and slowly, his tone warm and empathetic. "I'm trying to help."

She sensed he was speaking authentically. Her posture loosened; her shoulders dropped. She believed him. "Thank you, Dr. Clark."

Perhaps it was the way he looked at her before. Perhaps it

was her own pent-up, unwarranted guilt. Maybe it was a blend of both. But she had seen women, including herself, being judged and condemned for actions or appearance that were not considered "decent." Therefore, she refused to be labeled as promiscuous or sexually provocative. She remained unconvinced that the uncomfortable look he gave her was just her imagination, but she believed he respected her enough to move forward.

She inhaled deeply. "Well, let's get on with it," she said.

"Ready when you are," he replied.

"I didn't dream of Jonah last night, but I've dreamed of him many times in the past month. My colleagues and I were at a downtown pub for happy hour when we met. Jonah came right up to our table as if he knew us. He was friendly and eager to converse with perfect strangers. When his attention turned to me, I put my back to him and pretended he wasn't there. I needed a break from the whole dating scene.

"When I arrived home that evening, I received a text message from one of my colleagues letting me know he came around looking for me after I left. She said she had given him my contact info. I groaned at the top of my lungs. I had just spent the entire evening trying to avoid this guy and now he had my name and phone number. *Maybe he won't call*, I thought.

"The next day, I received a call from a number I didn't recognize. I let it go to voicemail. It was Jonah. He followed up with a text message soon after. I didn't respond, but something told me I hadn't heard the last of him.

"Another day, another phone call. He was persistent. After several days of voicemails, I decided I needed to act. He clearly wasn't getting the picture. The next time he called, I planned to pick up the phone and make it crystal clear to him he needed to lose my number.

"As I predicted, he called again. Before I could get a word out, he asked if I would join him and some friends at some trendy new spot that evening. I declined and told him I only picked up to ask that he respect my wish to stop calling.

"'I'm a nice person. I'm not asking you to marry me. I'm only asking you to hang out—just once,' he said.

"For reasons I don't myself understand, I agreed to see him. And it turned out he was a fun guy. His bigger-than-life personality drew me in. He brought this giant energy into any room he set foot in. So, we started seeing each other.

"He told me he had just lost his job in marketing. So, when we went out, I covered the bills. I didn't even think twice about it. But before I knew it, several months had passed, and I was becoming financially drained. I decided it was time for me to hold him more accountable, but he insisted he was actively searching for a new job and blamed his unemployment on the job market. So, I let it go.

"Jonah loved to sleep as much as he loved to have fun, maybe even more. No matter how much I tried, I just couldn't sleep as much as he did. I regularly cleaned while he slept to pass the time. Even the blaring sound of a vacuum cleaner against his ear wasn't enough to wake him from his slumber.

"One day, while I was folding his laundry, his roommate told me how nice he thought it was that I did that for Jonah. I said it was no big deal; I was just keeping busy while I waited for Jonah to wake up.

"'Having a girlfriend who cleans my room and does my laundry while I live somewhere rent-free would be a dream,' his roommate said.

"*Jonah is living rent-free?* I thought. I hadn't even considered how he paid for living expenses, but it made me think I was being taken advantage of.

"I marched back to his room, surprised to find him awake. He was sitting on his bed, playing video games. 'Are you staying here rent-free?' I asked.

"He shrugged his shoulders.

"I was practically supporting this guy, and he had nothing to say about it. I turned to leave the room with no intention of coming back.

"'Emma, wait,' he shouted.

"*Thank goodness,* I thought. There must be more to this.

"'You haven't been supporting me, not completely anyway,' he said. 'I sell marijuana.'

"I couldn't believe my ears. Not only was my boyfriend a full-time marijuana dealer, but he hid it from me the whole time, too. It was over."

She looked at Dr. Clark. He was staring intently at his note-pad, his pen moving rapidly without stopping. "Go on," he said, without stopping to look up.

"In my dream, I'm back at Jonah's place. I gag from the smell of marijuana mixed with the stench of decaying meat from week-old takeout—garbage and dirty laundry cloak the floor. Flies are everywhere. I'm in the center of the room lying on a mattress on the floor, and Jonah is lying next to me. Suddenly, the walls close in on us like a trash compactor. I scream for help. Jonah opens one eye, then rolls over to go back to sleep.

"The walls continue to close in, pushing every bit of garbage and dirty laundry closer and closer to me. I fight to climb out of the garbage pile, gasping for air. The ceiling is visible to me. Then I realize...I can't feel my legs. I direct my gaze downwards at my mangled legs."

Dr. Clark leaned in. "Does this feeling of paralysis extend beyond your dream?"

"Yes, how did you know?" A feeling of dread washed over her as she recalled the paralysis she experienced regularly since her dreams started. It was as though something outside of her control, perhaps even something supernatural, was interfering with her ability to physically move upon awakening, as if she was being

physically restrained to her bed. Inevitably, under these circumstances, panic and fear gripped her. She tried to scream, but she
couldn't. She was, yet again, a prisoner.

"You're experiencing something known as sleep paralysis—a
temporary inability to move or speak while falling asleep or upon
waking," he explained. "It happens when a person's mind and body
are out of sync. Their senses and awareness are active and awake,
but their body cannot move because, well, the body is asleep."

"That sounds exactly like what I'm experiencing."

He continued, "It happens during the REM sleep stage, where
you're likely to have dreams. When you're asleep, the brain pre-
vents the muscles in your limbs from moving to protect you from
acting out your dreams and hurting yourself."

"So, it isn't just me?" she asked.

He shook his head. "No, as a matter of fact, in Germanic and
Slavic folklore, the paralysis is attributed to a *mare*, a malicious
entity, said to bring on nightmares. It's believed that the mare rides
on people's chests while they sleep."

Her eyes widened. *A mare?* She imagined a horned demon
with a sinister smirk crouching on top of her chest as it looked
down at her in pure delight. "How can I stop it from happening
again?"

He stepped toward her as his gaze focused on the floor; he sat
at the coffee table in front of her.

There was silence.

Why isn't he saying anything? she thought.

"Dr. Clark?"

She stood up and stepped toward him. He was still, his eyes
wide open. His pupils appeared larger than usual, overshadowing
his irises. She waved her hand in front of his face. "Dr. Clark? Are
you OK?"

14

DEEP IN HIS THOUGHTS, Dr. Clark still had more questions than answers. Anxiety attacks, re-experiencing, sleep fainting, vomiting, visitation dreams, sleep paralysis. In his years of research and practice, he had seen it all. But never had he seen everything all at once from just a single patient over such a brief span of time. Emma's case was proving to be extraordinary. As he sat engrossed in his thoughts, his body tensed at a sudden, unexpected caress of his arm.

"Yes!" he exclaimed. He jumped to his feet from his seated position on the coffee table, jolted back to reality.

"For Christ's sake, you scared the living daylights out of me! Why weren't you answering me?" Emma asked.

He strode across the office toward the water cooler. "I must have drowned you out," he replied. "I was thinking about your question."

Her brow furrowed; her eyes darted back and forth, as if trying to make sense of the situation. "Why did you look like that?"

"Like what?"

"Your eyes—your pupils were dilated."

"Oh, were they?" He laughed. "Fun fact...Pupils change in size in response to increased cognitive activity."

She glowered at him with her arms crossed and a look of disdain on her face, making it clear to him they did not share the same sense of humor.

He approached her with a cup of water. "Here you go," Dr. Clark said.

She took the cup with an unforgiving glare.

"Do you think about Jonah a lot? When you're awake?" he asked.

She shook her head. "No, never. Like I told you before, I haven't thought about any of these people in years, except recently, because of my dreams."

He knew they had discussed this before, and he intentionally asked again. Like an investigator questioning a witness, he needed to be sure her answer remained consistent. Although he could not deny that there was a part of him that wanted her to give him an inconsistent answer, at least that might help explain her dreams.

She raised the cup to her mouth and tilted her head back to drink.

As she drank, he saw something he had not noticed before. Perhaps it was because of the way the light hit her face. He wanted a better look. But given the issue she had just addressed with him, the awkward lingering look he gave her before, he was sensitive not to stare. "Did something happen to your eye?" he asked.

"No, why do you ask?"

He pulled his handkerchief from his pant pocket. "Do you mind?"

"What are you doing?" she asked.

He dipped the tip of the handkerchief in the water that remained in her cup. "I'd like you to wipe the makeup away from under your eye. If it's alright with you."

She nodded. "That's fine."

He handed her the moistened handkerchief and looked on as she wiped. "That's enough, thank you," he said.

"You have discoloration under your eyes," he said.

"Yes, I know," she replied. "It's like I told you, I'm not getting enough rest." She reached for her purse and pulled out a tube of beige concealer. "I don't even recognize myself anymore." She applied the concealer under each eye and used the tip of her ring finger to blend it into her skin.

He tilted his head. "That's very impressive. You don't require a mirror to apply your make-up?"

"I try to avoid mirrors when I can. Lately they make me feel self-conscious."

His eyes narrowed; a glint of skepticism shined within his gaze. He certainly did not take her as the type to avoid mirrors.

"The medical record from your primary physician indicates you are five-foot-three and weigh 132 pounds, but that was documented weeks ago. Do you know what you weigh now?" he asked.

She shrugged her shoulders. "Not a clue," she replied, shaking her head.

He crossed the room to the corner of his office, where a dusty scale sat on the bottom of a shelf. He didn't ordinarily weigh his patients. Ordinarily, there was no need. He blew on the display window of the scale and placed it on the floor in front of her. He gestured at the scale. "If you don't mind?"

She stood up. "I don't mind." She looked away as she stepped on the scale.

He noted her weight. *110 pounds.*

And that's with her coat on. At this rate, she'll be dead in a week, he thought.

He looked at her. "Emma, given what I have observed over the past three days, it's time that we discuss a more invasive option."

15

WHEN EMMA WAS A YOUNG GIRL, her father read Bible stories of miracles each night before bed. He read of vision being restored to the blind, the healing of a man with a withered hand, and the healing of paralytics. Her father told her that anything was possible if only she believed. And she did. But as she grew older, like a child who no longer believes in Santa Claus, her beliefs faded. Still, she always hoped miracles were possible. And now, hope is all she had.

"I'm willing to try anything," she said. Her face lit up with a wide smile.

"Have a seat." Dr. Clark gestured toward the couch. He sat on the coffee table across from her. "You may be a candidate for a procedure known as *memory extinction*, but it's not an option you should take lightly. Consider it your last resort. Are you familiar with the procedure?"

She shook her head. "No."

He opened his notebook. "Remember, I explained how synaptic connections retrieve memories?"

"Yes, of course."

He gripped his pen and moved it across a page. "What do you think would happen if we snipped the synaptic connection, this line in between the two circles?" He turned the page to her and pointed to a space between the lines in his drawing.

O—O

She examined the drawing and imagined electricity running through an extension cord, and the extension cord being cut at its center. "I assume the connection to the memory would be eliminated," she said.

"That's exactly right," he replied.

She stared at him with a mixture of delight and disbelief in her eyes. "How is that even possible?" she asked.

"It's very possible, thanks to microglia, the brain's resident immune cells. And now we are at the cusp of manufacturing it."

Her eyes narrowed, squinting with confusion at his conflicting explanation. "Does the brain produce microglia naturally, or is it synthetic?" she asked.

"Yes, and yes!" he exclaimed.

Her eyes widened; she sensed his excitement growing.

"The brain produces it naturally, but the procedure uses synthetic microglia to target specific regions."

Her expression turned to one of awe, but she could not deny that there was a part of her that was weary. She wanted to be optimistic, but she was a realist at heart. And it sounded too good to be true. "Why haven't you brought this up before?" she asked.

"The only way to administer synthetic microglia is through targeted intra-cerebral injection," he replied.

Her muscles locked in place.

He continued, "You would be sedated, and you could go home the same day." He spoke in a soothing tone, as if each word was carefully chosen to reassure her. "The effects are almost immediate."

It was now clear to her why Dr. Clark referred to this option as a last resort. But questions remained. She thought about the times she danced with her mother as a child to her mother's favorite song, *The Mashed Potato*, the tickle fights with her father, the endless laughs with Brianna. *Would those memories go away, too?* "Will all of my memories be eliminated?" she asked.

He slapped his palm on his forehead; he shook his head. "I forgot to address that. That's what makes microglia so fascinating—it only prunes the connections associated with the *fear-based* memories." He clapped his hands together and displayed a wide grin that revealed his teeth. "That's the magic of the microglia."

She was not yet nearly as delighted as Dr. Clark appeared. "How much will it cost?"

"It won't cost you a thing. If you agree to have the procedure performed at a university hospital."

She cringed at the idea of having surgery performed by students, but her desperation overrode any objection she would otherwise have in the matter.

"One of the best neurosurgeons in the country, Dr. Prasad Vedurmudi would perform the procedure."

She breathed a sigh of relief.

He continued, "And medical students would observe through a window overlooking the operation suite."

Although the idea of students observing wasn't ideal, it seemed there was no other choice. She had no other options. "I'll do it," she said.

"You'll need to consult with Dr. Vedurmudi first. He'll make the ultimate decision on whether you are a suitable candidate for the procedure." He pecked at his computer. "I just sent him a message. He'll be ready to see you right after you visit with me tomorrow."

The idea of seeing yet another doctor daunted her. She had already undergone many blood tests, cat scans, MRIs, and ultrasounds. All of which took time. She feared seeing yet another doctor would take up the little time she felt she had left. "If he thinks I'm a suitable candidate, how long before I can have the procedure done?" she asked.

"He's penciled you in for Friday."

Her eyes widened. "That's incredible. Thank you." She looked at the time; it was the top of the hour.

"If he agrees you are a suitable candidate for the procedure and you show signs of improvement on your own, we can call it off."

She stood up. "I understand." She reached for her things and stepped toward the door.

"You should also continue your dream training. It will be an ongoing part of your therapy and it will prevent the development of new fear-based memories."

She nodded. "OK, I'll see you tomorrow."

She stepped out of the office; his words re-played in her mind. *Microglia will only snip the connections associated with fear-based memories.* She trusted Dr. Clark over the past three days but couldn't repress her thoughts that his explanation sounded too good to be true. And like Brianna always said, *Trust but verify…*

᛫

A mile away from the Department of Psychiatry & Behavioral Neuroscience building, Emma gazed at the Crerar Library located on the University of Chicago campus. The building's sharp edges, straight lines, and flat roof reminded her of the undergraduate library she spent countless hours at the University of Texas. It was a much simpler time back then. *I miss those days,* she thought.

She strode through the glass door of the library's entrance. In the building stood a twelve-foot wooden sign that pointed to various areas in the library. She stopped in front of the sign. *The John*

Crerar Library LL Circulation & Bookstacks. That's where I need to be, she thought. She proceeded to the lower level of the library.

The library's lower level housed numerous resources, including collections in science, medicine, and technology. But there was no need for her to search through the library's physical collection. She took a seat at a public computer. The university's online catalog appeared on the home screen; she entered *Microglia* on the search bar. Almost instantly, the search results yielded countless books, articles, and studies on the topic.

She scrolled through the pages of information.

Microglia contribute to the formation, pruning and plasticity of synapses.

Microglia play a pivotal role in transferring traumatic memories from short to long-term memory and the memories subsequent extinction.

Microglial deletion and inhibition alleviate the behavior of post-traumatic stress disorder in mice.

Preclinical studies using fear conditioning suggest microglia are involved in fear memory dysregulation.

Each source supported Dr. Clark's claims. Her face lit up with an irrepressible smile. *Maybe miracles happen after all,* she thought.

16

SHE GLARED AT THE WHITE cardboard pastry box containing Dr. Clark's daily delivery of powdered sugar donuts and wondered what it was about them that she loathed. She wasn't averse to powdered sugar, donuts, or pastries in general. In fact, she had enjoyed countless powdered sugar donuts over the years. They had even become a staple at her firm's break-room. And although she didn't always indulge, she didn't avoid them all together. She scrunched up her nose. "Can you please put those away?" Emma asked.

"Put what away?" Dr. Clark asked in return.

She picked up the stack of magazines that lay on the coffee table and placed it on top of the pastry box. "Forget it." Although she would prefer not to be in the room with them at all, having them out of sight would have to do for now.

She folded her arms as she sunk into her seat. "I had a panic attack last night. I woke up feeling like my soul was trying to escape through my chest…probably to avoid the inevitable horror of my dreams."

"Ah, that's known as a nocturnal panic attack," he replied.

She exhaled deeply. "You've got to be kidding."

"I'm sorry, Emma. Stress, poor sleep, and nightmares can all trigger nocturnal panic attacks. Did you dream of someone we haven't discussed yet?"

"Yes, I dreamed of Herod." She spoke in a subdued, somber tone. Her voice carried a tinge of sorrow that hung over her like a cloud.

"Herod? That's not a name you hear very often."

He paused.

"Why does it sound so familiar?"

She shrugged her shoulders. "He's the only Herod I've ever met. Anyway, I broke my rule when I started dating him. He worked in the technology division of my firm, but I met him outside of work at a hotel bar downtown. A group of us were there celebrating the win of a major account.

"He wasn't with our group; he just happened to be there. I'd seen him around before; we had passed each other in the halls at work. He always flashed me a warm smile as if he'd known me for years.

"He walked up to me to introduce himself. Apparently, he already knew who I was. He said I was a 'big deal,' which I thought was nice of him to say. But then he went on.

"'I hear you are brilliant and extremely talented. I hear you are the youngest person to make vice president at the firm by a long shot,' he said.

"And on…

"'I know you went to UT on a full scholarship and that you own two homes, one of which is a rental property.'

"*OK, now this is getting creepy*, I thought. But it turned out he was friends with my good friend Jim. Jim took me under his wing when I joined the firm. I often came to him for professional and personal advice. He's a mentor, big brother, and grandfather figure wrapped in one.

"'Jim is so proud of you. He talks about you all the time,' he said.

"Now, all the facts Herod spit out about me made sense. Jim didn't have any grandchildren, so he saw me as a granddaughter that he could brag to his friends about. It also made sense why I felt like he knew me when we passed each other in the halls.

"Days later, I found myself thinking of him and hitting replay on the memory of the night. I asked Jim to pass along my phone number. Within minutes, I received a message from him on my phone.

"The evening of our first date, I was surprised to hear my doorbell ring. Having been on many first dates before, I grew accustomed to getting a phone call from my date to let me know they were outside. But Herod was very chivalrous. He took me to an amazing Italian restaurant called Scuzzi's. When we walked in, I was transported to a different time and place. Dim lighting set the mood for the perfectly dressed tables with crisp white linen tablecloths, glassware, and fresh flowers. The romantic sounds of Italian music serenaded the restaurant patrons.

"The host approached us and asked if we had a reservation.

"'Reservation for Romo,' he said.

"'Right this way, Mister and Missus Romo,' the host said.

"Herod and I exchanged looks.

"'Oh, we aren't married,' I said.

"The host paused. He looked at Herod, then at me, then back at Herod. 'Well, perhaps not yet,' the host replied with a smile.

"At our table, my thoughts remained on the host's comment. I told Herod that I had never had someone confused for my husband."

"'Who knows, maybe it's fate?' Herod replied.

"*Maybe it's fate?* With any other guy, those words would have triggered me to call for a ride and change my phone number. I wasn't looking for a husband. I never saw myself as someone who cared all that much about getting married, settling down, and having a family. And perhaps my recent heartbreaks had left me with a fear of commitment. But coming from Herod, those words didn't scare me the least bit.

"Our conversation over dinner was effortless. We talked about our backgrounds. His family immigrated to the United States when he was a toddler. He told me about his struggles with identifying as an American, yet being held to the standards of his parents' culture and a country he knows little about. It was such a deep and meaningful conversation. Although I couldn't exactly relate, the depth of the conversation made me fall for him even more.

"He continued to impress me all evening will his intellect, chivalry, and sense of humor. He even took me to a dance studio for a Salsa lesson, where we worked off our meal and laughed with each other as we fumbled through the steps."

"It sounds like a fairytale," Dr. Clark said. "How did it end?"

Her eyes teared up. "I'll get there." She inhaled deeply. "After that night, we were inseparable. Not a single day went by when we didn't spend time together. I journaled every single encounter in my daily planner, like a schoolgirl in love. We were so happy.

"A couple of months later, Herod walked me to my door after a night out like he always did. But instead of his usual farewell, he said something I wasn't prepared to hear.

"'You know I love you, right?'

"I gasped. 'Why would you say that?' I asked.

"He stared down at his feet. 'I said it because I love you,' he replied.

"I didn't give him the reaction he expected. And I didn't understand why I reacted like that but I didn't want to fall in love just to get hurt again. I didn't want to find out that he had a girl-friend, or was living a double life, or whatever bullshit you hear about that is actually much more common than it seems. Things were going so well. Why couldn't we leave it at that?"

"Perhaps he thought you loved him, too," Dr. Clark said.

"Of course, I loved him!" she exclaimed. "The feeling in my heart was visceral, like nothing I had felt before. Still, I didn't speak to him for days after that.

"He sent me text messages daily to check in on me, but I didn't reply. I was trying to come to grips with my feelings, but every day that passed that I didn't see him made me feel that much worse. I missed him. I loved him, too.

"After several nights, I decided it was time to call him. I wasn't prepared for how quickly he would pick up. It was as if he was standing by, waiting for my call. I asked him to come over so that we could speak in person.

"Just minutes later, my doorbell rang. It had been less than a week since I saw him last, but he looked noticeably thinner. He stared at the floor as he stepped inside and took a seat. It was as if he was preparing himself for the worst.

"'I'm sorry,' I said.

"Although his eyes were staring at the floor, I could tell he was tearing up. There was no doubt he sensed I was ending it. Ending us.

"I continued, 'I'm sorry for how I reacted.'

"He picked his head up.

"'The truth is, I love you, too,' I said.

"Before I could continue, he sprung up from his seat and lifted me off the floor. We kissed and cried, and kissed and cried some more. A warm tingling sensation overwhelmed me from head to toe. A sense of peace and contentment filled me within. *This is what it must feel like to be madly in love,* I thought.

"Then one day it all changed." Emma spoke in a quiet voice,

her words shaky and hesitant. She dropped her head, her shoulders slumped.

"Brianna had joined us for dinner at Scuzzi's. She was buzzing with excitement about the fact that Herod and I decided to meet each other's parents. Herod and I had never been in a relationship where we met the parents, so it was a big deal, and Brianna was harping about being my maid of honor.

"He was running late, which was unlike him. When he finally arrived, he sat down and looked at the menu without saying a word. I had never seen him act like that before. Something was clearly bothering him. 'What's the matter?' I asked.

"He put his menu down on the table and glowered at me as if daggers were preparing to shoot from his eyes from across the table. 'Do you really want to know?' he asked.

"'Yes, I really want to know.' *That look, that tone...what could he possibly have to say to me?* I thought.

"'Do you really want me to say this in front of Brianna?' he asked.

"Brianna stood up. I placed my hand on her lap and told her to stay. *Anything he can say to me, he can say in front of her*, I thought.

"He told me he had run into his friend John. 'Does that name ring a bell?' he asked.

"*John*—it's such a common name, but I couldn't place it with anyone I knew. 'No,' I replied.

"He crossed his arms and looked deep into my eyes. 'You're lying,' he said.

"I straightened my posture and my eyes widened at the accusation.

"'Don't you recall that night with John in the bathroom back in Austin?' he asked; his voice shook with rage.

"Instantly, I knew what he was referring to. My eyes bulged with disbelief. I was too stunned to say anything.

"'I figured that would get a reaction out of you,' he said.

"He was seething with anger. He told me he thought I was different and was glad he found out before introducing me to his parents. He pushed his chair out with so much force that it fell over and stormed out of the restaurant... That's how it ended."

Dr. Clark stood up. "What John did is a classic predator move!" he exclaimed in an agitated voice. He paced the length of the room, his clenched fist and furrowed brow revealing the anger within.

"What do you mean?" she asked.

He turned to her. "Predators spin the narrative of true events and, as an act of self-preservation, tell their version of the story to anyone who could potentially learn of their transgressions."

His gaze, his posture, and his tone carried a shadow of disturbance that made her believe this was something he had seen many times before. And his explanation made so much sense. It was so clear now. *John lied about what happened that night to shame me and protect himself,* she thought.

"Didn't you say you met John at a party in Austin?" Dr. Clark asked as he thumbed through the pages of his notebook.

"Yes," she replied.

"And Herod worked at your firm. You met him here in Chicago. Correct?" The intensity of his gaze revealed a hunger for answers.

She nodded. "That's correct."

"How did the two of them know each other?" he asked.

She shook her head. "I don't know. I used to ask myself that all the time."

He paced across the office with his arms folded. "What are the odds that Herod and John know each other, let alone run into each other on opposite sides of the country?"

She shrugged her shoulders. "Just my luck, I suppose."

"And your dream? What's it about?"

"When I dream of Herod, I re-experience the devastation of that evening at the restaurant just as it happened, word for word. I re-experience the fear I felt from hearing John's name. I re-experience the guilt I carried with me from that night with John. My heart breaks from losing the man I thought I was going to marry." She exhaled deeply. "If it wasn't for Brianna, I don't know what I would have done."

"Is Brianna in your dream?"

"No, but that night in the restaurant after Herod left, she tried to console me, but I was mortified. I locked myself in a bathroom stall. 'Em, you need me right now…Let me in! I'm not going to leave you!' she shouted as she pounded on the stall door. But I just wanted to be alone."

"Wait, what did you just say?"

"I said I just wanted to be alone."

"Before that," he said, thumbing through his notes. "'Em, I'm not going to leave you.' That's what Brianna said in your dream about John."

Her eyes widened. "You're right. And in my dream, Brianna was pounding on the bathroom door."

"And here's something else. You just told me Brianna said, 'I'm not going to leave you.' She said the same thing in your dream about Zack."

Her jaw dropped and her eyes widened in wonder as she fixated on the revelation. "They're my memories."

17

HER FACE CONTORTED TO a barely recognizable version of herself; her shoulders shook as she struggled to catch her breath in between sobs. It was as though the pain she buried away from her breakup with Herod had insidiously made its way to the surface. Yet through her pain, her thoughts remained fixed on Brianna. Something about Brianna being in her dreams made her wonder if there could be more to it. Dr. Clark said her dreams could be trying to tell her she's in danger. Could their bond and Brianna's empathetic energy be so strong that she made her way into her dreams? Could Brianna be trying to warn her about something? If so, why wouldn't Brianna just tell her to her face?

"How long has it been since you last spoke with him?" Dr. Clark asked.

"Who?"

"Herod."

"Oh, right." She took a deep breath. "It's been two years," she whimpered.

"And you never got over him?"

She jumped to her feet. "I did!" she exclaimed.

She paused.

"I thought I did." She thought back to her experience after the breakup. To avoid her crying spells, she recalled sleeping as much as possible. She remembered ignoring the rumbles from her stomach begging for sustenance, and how the more time passed, the less hungry she became.

During that time, she withdrew from her family to shield them from her pain. She didn't want them to worry. Hiding from her parents was easy, but there was no hiding from Brianna. She witnessed the breakup in all its glory, after all. Although her calls and text messages were mostly silenced, Brianna checked in on her daily. And after a couple of days of being completely ignored, she made an unannounced visit to pitch an idea. It was an idea that Brianna assured her would get her out of her slump and make her forget all about Herod—a cruise vacation. She thought the idea was insane until Brianna booked the cruise in front of her. They would fly nonstop to Houston (paid for with frequent-flyer miles), then make the hour drive to Galveston, where a five-day Royal Caribbean cruise to Mexico and the Bahamas awaited. But Emma didn't have the desire nor the energy. She insisted she wasn't going. That is until realizing Brianna would drag her along kicking and screaming if that's what it took. So, lacking the energy to argue, she conceded.

"Thanks to Brianna, I actually got over him rather quickly."

"How so?"

"She thought it would be good for me to leave the house, so we went on a cruise together a week after the breakup." She stared off into the distance. A smile briefly flashed across her face. "Have you ever been on a cruise?" she asked.

"I can't say that I have."

"You should. It was amazing, despite—"

She paused.

"Despite what?" he asked.

"Despite the fact it's how I met Davis."

"I take it Davis is the seventh man in your dreams?"

She nodded. "I met him on the first day of our cruise.

"I remember rushing to keep up with Brianna to get on the ship and being absolutely taken aback by the sight of the imposing vessel towering above us. 'Holy cow, the ship must be larger than the *Titanic!*' I exclaimed. When we got inside, I took in the sights like a small child visiting Disney World for the first time. Elegant glass staircases spiraled around each end of the Centrum, the ship's main lobby. From there, I could see each of the floors above us lit up with the most magnificent glow. Glass elevators zipped up and down, transferring passengers to different floors at what seemed like the speed of light. Everyone seemed so…happy.

"We went straight to the pool deck where servers walked around with cold drinks on trays as passengers lounged by the pool soaking up the sun. The smell of sunscreen filled the air like aromatherapy for the soul. The sounds of laughter and music drowned out any thoughts I had about Herod, and life rekindled within me.

"Brianna and I had taken Salsa lessons, so it thrilled us that a live salsa band was performing on the pool deck. Then the music transitioned to an unfamiliar sound—the rhythm was slow and sensual, romantic yet tropical. Couples swarmed the dance floor. It was like nothing I had seen before—they embraced each other closely, their bodies almost intertwined. As they moved across the dance floor, I could tell each step, every hip movement, was deliberate yet fluid, passionate, sensual. It was as if they were using their bodies to tell their unique stories of love, heartbreak, longing.

"I became fixated on the dance. I didn't intend to capture Davis's attention, but he caught me watching. He asked me to dance, but I was unwilling to make a fool of myself by dancing a type of dance I had never danced before with the best dancer on the ship, so I declined. Despite everything, he was convincing. From there, our connection was magnetic."

"What was the music called?" Dr. Clark asked.

"Excuse me?"

"It's just that you spoke so highly of it. What was it?"

"Oh, I learned it was called Bachata and that it originated in the Dominican Republic. Anyway, he asked me where I was from. Worried about where the question may lead, I considered how much to reveal about myself. Reluctantly, I told him.

"His eyes bulged. He was from Chicago, too. He told me he flew into Houston to visit family and they surprised him with a family cruise. *OK, no big deal. It's a coincidence, that's all. Don't make a bigger thing out of this than it is,* I thought. We got to know more about each other throughout the night, and I learned he was a police officer. After what happened with Jonah, hearing about his line of work was refreshing.

"When the evening was over, I wondered if I would see him again. Brianna assured me I would.

"'Just be careful,' Brianna said. 'You know what I always say.'

"I searched through my mental catalog of Brianna sayings that might fit the situation. 'Oh right,' I replied. 'Never trust a man who can dance.'

"Davis and I leisurely bumped into each other throughout the cruise, mainly at the ship's coffee bar. Each time, he ordered the same thing…a tall cappuccino with almond milk and three powdered sugar donuts. Before I knew it, the cruise was ending. On our final evening, Davis and I planned to meet at the Centrum for the farewell dance. I took mental snapshots of every detail about him that night, especially his mesmerizing hazel eyes. That may have very well been the end had it not been for the string duet that magnificently played 'Quando, Quando, Quando.' Like a fool, I took the song as a sign that I should see him again."

"What's 'Quando, Quando, Quando?'"

She scoffed. "You're kidding me, right?"

"Not kidding," he replied.

She shot him an incredulous look. "It's a classic!" she exclaimed.

"I don't know what to tell you; I've never heard of it. What are the words?"

She opened her mouth, then promptly closed it. "I know what you're doing," she said.

"What am I doing?" he asked.

She crossed her arms. "You're trying to get me to sing."

His face blushed ever so slightly. "Oh, come on. What are the words?"

"Look it up."

He scoffed. "If I must," he said as he turned to face his computer.

She approached his desk. "There, that's it," she said, pointing to the top of the search results.

> *Tell me when will you be mine*
> *Tell me quando, quando, quando*
> *We can share a love divine*
> *Please, don't make me wait again*
> *When will you say yes to me?*
> *Tell me quando, quando, quando*
> *You mean happiness to me*
> *Oh, my love please tell me when*
> *Every moment's a day*
> *Every day seems a lifetime*
> *Let me show you the way*
> *To a joy beyond compare*
> *I can't wait a moment more*

Tell me quando, quando, quando
Say it's me that you adore
And then, darling tell me when...

"I don't believe in signs, but I see your point," Dr. Clark said.

"When he asked if he could see me again, my gut told me to say no. By now, I should have learned to listen, especially after what I experienced with Rico." She shook her head. "If only I had said no."

18

URING HER TIME AWAY at college, without her parents there to guide her every step or tell her what to do, Emma developed her sense of self. It took some time, but eventually, she learned that there was a difference between who she was and who her parents, particularly her father, wanted her to be. She learned that, given the freedom to make her own choices, once she established a goal, there was no stopping her from taking the right steps to achieve it. Some called her a visionary. And in some ways, she was. She attributed her success to her ability to anticipate next steps while welcoming failure. Should things not go entirely as planned, she didn't sulk; she pivoted. And somehow, her pivots always propelled her to something better.

Still, she couldn't help but wonder how different her life would have been had she not reconnected with Davis after the cruise. Not because she had lost time. She was in no rush to settle down. She wasn't even sure if she wanted to have children. It was just that every part of her life became more complicated after Davis entered the picture. That's when she started to doubt herself and her abilities. She questioned things she never thought twice about.

Even the simplest decision became a daily challenge, like what to have for dinner. She often felt drained and didn't see Brianna or her parents as much as she used to. It was as if she lost who she was and, for the first time, she felt like a failure. It would be the single most failure in her life she wished she could go back and erase.

She looked at Dr. Clark; a veil of unease settled over her face as she recalled her time with Davis at the Rumba Room, a salsa club known for its live music and energetic atmosphere, that now left her emotionally drained just thinking of it. "I sometimes worked late, so meeting up with Davis at the Rumba Room wasn't unusual. On that night, my car was being serviced, so a colleague gave me a ride there. When I arrived, he was well into his dance rotation of women who had lined up to dance with him. That's how the salsa scene went. You dance with different people. You learn different styles."

She paused.

"But I only danced with Davis. So when I arrived, I took my usual seat on one of the velvet couches around the dance floor, where I would wait until he was ready for me.

"There was a tap on my shoulder. 'Would you like to dance?' a male voice asked.

"I turned to him; my eyes widened with surprise. It was Rico.

"'It's nice to see you,' he said.

"*If only the feeling was mutual,* I thought.

"The music was blaring, so he crouched down to speak into my ear. He told me he had moved back into town after he graduated and that he managed the Elite Gym. 'You should come by,' he said. I struggled with how to respond. Then I spotted Davis approaching. *Thank goodness,* I thought.

"He walked right up to us. 'Davis, this is Rico,' I said.

"Rico extended his hand for a handshake; Davis accepted. But then I observed something strange… Rico's forehead wrinkled; his eyes squinted as if he were in pain. When I looked down, I saw Davis was tightly gripping his hand.

"Rico shook off his hand. 'What's your problem?' he asked.

"Davis glared at him with fire in his eyes and puffed out his chest. He pushed Rico to the ground. 'This is my girlfriend; stay the fuck away from her,' he shouted.

"I was stunned. We hadn't been dating long, but it was a side of him I had never seen before. I was speechless, and I wasn't the only one. The band stopped playing, and the room fell into an uncomfortable silence.

"'What the fuck are you staring at? Mind your own business!' he shouted to the club patrons, many his regular dance partners.

"*How could he get so angry?* I thought. My eyes welled up with tears; he grabbed my hand and pulled me out of the club. It all happened so fast.

"He stopped outside. *Surely, he was going to apologize*, I thought. Whatever just happened must have been a fluke. He was a police officer; he must have had the worst day of his life. There had to be an explanation.

"'You are a fucking embarrassment!' he shouted. His eyes narrowed; he placed his index finger on my collarbone and pushed me away with such force that I nearly fell to the ground. 'You'd better never pull that kind of shit on me again,' he said.

"I refused to hold my tongue. I refused to accept that what had just happened was my fault. I told him it was him who overreacted and made a fool of us both.

"There was silence. I thought I got through to him. He coughed slightly and took a deep breath through his nostrils. He held his breath. *He must be calming down,* I thought. Suddenly, he made a hocking sound; he turned to me with pursed lips and pushed the air from his lungs through his mouth.

"There was spit all over my face.

"'You're disgusting,' he said as he walked away.

"He left me there, stranded."

Dr. Clark leaned in. "Do you think it's a coincidence that he left you stranded on the particular night when you didn't have your car?" he asked.

She sensed his question was rhetorical by the stark look in his eyes. She answered anyway. "No, of course not."

"How did you get home?"

A muted smile broke the look of devastation on her face. "I called the only person who I could call in a moment like that. Brianna answered my call right away. And like before, she could sense I needed her. It wasn't long before her car came screeching down the parking lot. When I got in her car, I didn't say a word, but I didn't need to. My face said it all…She hugged me and told me I didn't deserve what happened to me that night."

"Did he exhibit any kind of abusive behavior prior to that?" Dr. Clark asked.

There was silence.

"In retrospect, there may have been signs."

"Like what?"

"I remember him acting like he was jealous when someone would ask me to dance on the cruise ship. He'd insert himself and yell, 'Mine!'"

She paused.

"I thought he was just being cute."

Dr. Clark shook his head. She could sense his disappointment. "I assume that's how it ended?" he asked.

She swallowed hard and stared at him blankly. "That's how it should have ended."

Why would anyone stay in a relationship after being treated like that? Does she have no self-respect? Does she not think she deserves better? These were all the questions she asked herself after what happened. So, the decision to end their relationship was an easy one. He practically decided for her. But when he came over unannounced the next day, he attributed what he had done to his feelings for her. He didn't apologize for his behavior; he said something about *her made him* do what he did. It was something he needed to protect. Somehow, he convinced her it was something he did for them. And in the end, in a bizarre turn of events, it was Emma that apologized to him.

"The incident at the Rumba Room was just the beginning. One evening, we dove into a fast-food restaurant for a quick bite. There was nothing special about the restaurant. I just remember thinking that it was nice to spend time with Davis outside of the Rumba Room. It just sort of felt like a safer environment to be in."

"Safer environment? Tell me what you mean," Dr. Clark said.

She shrugged her shoulders. "I don't know. Safer than the Rumba Room, or anywhere where I risked upsetting Davis for casually speaking to another man."

"You had to tip-toe around him?"

She sat quietly; her gaze grew distant, her mind consumed by the weight of her thoughts. "I suppose."

She paused.

"Anyway, while we were in line, I noticed a stranger ahead of us looking back at us. *Does he know me?* I thought. I certainly didn't recognize him. My suspicions were confirmed when he stepped out of line and started walking toward me. I worried that any potential interaction with this person might not go over well with Davis, so I tried to avoid eye contact.

"'Emma is that you?' he asked.

"'Hello,' I replied sheepishly.

"'You don't recognize me, do you? It's me, Joey!' he exclaimed. 'We went to high school together.'

"I stared at him blankly. He must have sensed by my lack of expression that he would need to say more if he expected me to recognize him. He told me we were in the National Honor Society together; he said we were in all of the same honors classes. *He must have me confused with someone else,* I thought. I turned to Davis; fortunately, he appeared uninterested.

"'Ah, I know why you don't recognize me,' he said. He raised his arms and turned around as if revealing a new body.

"'Joey, of course!' I exclaimed. His appearance had changed drastically from what I remembered. He had lost a lot of weight and his skin cleared up. He was barely recognizable from the clumsy, awkward nerdy kid I remembered from high school. Our reunion didn't last long…

"'Oh, just stop already!' Davis shouted.

"I attempted to defuse the situation, but he was a ticking time bomb. That's when I figured out once Davis was triggered, there was no stopping the damage that was to come.

"I watched his breathing become heavy and erratic; the veins on his forehead throbbed, his nostrils flared. He puffed out his chest like he did that time with Rico at the Rumba Room.

He shouted, 'You clearly want to fuck him!!!' His voice boomed with rage.

"My eyes homed in on Davis's hands; they were clenched into fists, his knuckles white. I feared for what he might do next."

Dr. Clark interrupted. "Did you think he was going to hit you?"

There was silence.

Her blinking slowed.

"Or were you concerned for Joey?" he asked.

She remembered how afraid she was when the incident unfolded. If she was honest, she didn't know what he was going to do or what he was capable of, especially after what unfolded next. Regardless, it wasn't something she cared to discuss. "Yes, I was concerned for Joey," she replied, crossing her arms. "Anyway, after Davis's outburst, an eerily familiar silence blanketed the restaurant. Then he stormed out and slammed the door behind him. I was so embarrassed. I turned to Joey to apologize before running out after Davis.

"I rushed outside to find Davis standing by my car. Although

I didn't want to be near him, I didn't have the heart to abandon him in the parking lot… If only I could say he would have done the same for me.

"We got in the car and sat silently as I pulled out of the parking lot. He lit a joint; smoking was his modus operandi after a blow-up. I tried to say something, but he suddenly had a competing priority. He got on the phone with his marijuana supplier; he called him his 'White Whale.' That was the thing about him—he made me feel like he should be my number one priority, but I was never his.

"I couldn't hold my tongue any longer. 'Why did you do that back there?' I asked.

"'Why do you give a fuck about him?!' he erupted.

He reached over to my seat while I was driving and my eyes were focused on the road. *What is he doing?* I thought. In one swift motion, he pulled the emergency parking brake. The car spun out of control in what felt like the longest five seconds of my life. *This is it,* I thought. *I'm going to die.*

"When the car came to a stop, I couldn't believe I wasn't hurt. And luckily, I didn't hit any vehicles. A police officer nearby saw what happened and approached us. Davis saw the police car coming and jumped out of my car. He threw his joint on the ground and ran away without even closing the door behind him. *Coward,* I thought.

"The officer knocked on my window and asked if I was OK. I told him I was fine. He asked what happened. My heart raced as I searched for what to say. I settled on saying, 'I must have hit a patch of ice.'

"He examined the road conditions. 'I don't see any ice around here,' he said.

"I was out of excuses; I shrugged my shoulders.

He asked me if I knew where the person who ran out of the car was headed. I shrugged my shoulders again, but I could sense he wasn't buying my story.

"'Would you like to press charges?' he asked.

"I said, 'Of course not, it was an accident.' I couldn't bear the thought of Davis being charged. His career would be ruined. Still, I know I should have told the officer the truth. I should have told him that Davis had lost his temper and pulled the parking brake while I was driving. He could have killed us both." She shook her head with a look of despair. "But I didn't."

19

LIKE BEFORE, SHE KNEW what she had to do. And just like before, Davis justified his actions, as if she had given him no choice but to pull the emergency brake while her car traveled at fifty miles per hour. He told her that *she* was the issue, not him. *She* was making a big deal out of nothing. *She* was being dramatic. *She* was overreacting. The deflecting and accusations went on and on. And under 'ordinary' circumstances, she might have believed him. But this incident was far more dangerous than the previous ones. His actions were intentional and reckless. He could have killed her. He could have killed them both. She couldn't just let that go, so she ignored his attempts to get back in touch with her. This time, it was over.

But things are never as easy as they seem. If they were, she would have ended it with him long ago. Breaking up with Davis would require her to go to great lengths. She spent nights at her parents' house, told them her house was being fumigated, to avoid his announced visits. She would have changed her phone number if she wasn't sure he would use his connections to get a hold of it again. Instead, she turned her phone off and sent all work calls to voicemail. Then he had flowers delivered to her work.

Every.

Single.

Day.

"I tried to break it off with him, but it became clear he wasn't going away, and his attempts to get me back interfered with my job. So, one early morning, before I was to go to work, I drove to his place, intending to make it clear to him we were over.

"I knocked on his door. His roommate answered. I'll never forget the look on his face. It was as though he'd seen a ghost. He told me it probably wasn't a good time, but I made my way in anyway. Davis was interfering with my work, and I couldn't let another day go by without settling this. I charged straight to his bedroom.

"His roommate stared at me intensely as I approached Davis's bedroom door. In retrospect, it was as if he was preparing for a show to begin. Nothing could have prepared me for what I was about to walk into. I opened the door and stepped in. There he was in bed, as I expected, but he wasn't alone. Another woman slept next to him. Her hand was on his chest. She wore a white T-shirt that I recognized instantly. It was the same V-neck white T-shirt Davis swore by.

"I didn't recognize the woman, but her hair stood out. It was red-orange, with long tight curls. She was not someone I would forget on the off chance we ever met while Davis and I were dating.

"I stood by the door and covered my mouth with my hands as I attempted to contain myself. Even though I went there intend-ing to break up with him, I began hyperventilating and sobbing uncontrollably. I still loved him…You don't just stop having feel-ings for someone overnight.

"The sound of my wailing and heavy breathing caused him to wake up. He slowly opened his eyes. 'What's wrong?' he asked. His eyes bulged. It was as if, for a moment, it slipped his mind that his curly-haired mistress lay next to him.

"He jumped out of bed. 'Calm down, you're being crazy,' he said.

"The curly-haired woman awoke. She took one look at me, and her eyes grew large. She looked down at her bare thighs and searched for cover, then scurried off to the bathroom.

"I fell to my knees. 'What did I do to deserve this?' I sobbed. He couldn't have known it, but my question was not directed at Davis. I thought back to my past and searched for what I could have possibly done to deserve the pain, the gut-wrenching agony that I was experiencing at that moment.

"'You're overreacting!' he shouted. 'This is my friend.'

"'Your friend?' I fired back. 'What is your *friend's* last name?' I asked.

"He didn't have an answer. He just looked at the floor…The coward couldn't even look me in the eye.

"'I don't feel sorry for you,' he said. 'You're doing this to yourself! You're delusional!' he shouted.

"The intensity of my emotions raged inside me…I felt as if I were on the brink of exploding. My attention turned to a bright-orange wax mold on a shelf in his room. It was a souvenir from a museum visit that Davis and I made by dipping our clasped hands in wax. The memento was both cheap and gaudy and had lost all its significance to me. It was less than meaningless. Its very sight enraged me.

"I lunged to grab it.

"'What are you doing?' he asked.

"I held up the souvenir and slammed it down on the floor with all my might, but because of the cushioning of the carpet, it barely cracked. That wouldn't do, so I stomped on it until it was unrecognizable.

"He looked down at the pile of orange wax pieces at my feet. 'Clean it up,' he ordered. 'Now.' He spoke in a deep, commanding tone as if on duty.

"Although I was terrified by the fire in his eyes, I didn't move. I couldn't move.

"He jumped out of bed and grabbed me; he twisted my arm behind my back and forced me to the floor. Surely it was a move he practiced on the job. I fell to my knees and followed his orders.

"As I picked up the pieces, the curly-haired woman stepped out of the bathroom. She wore a short black tube-top dress and four-inch stiletto heels. She stood there for a moment and glowered at Davis...Her eyes narrowed to slits; brows furrowed deep as she shook her head. But then she looked at me, and her demeanor changed. Her eyes softened; the corners of her mouth curved ever so slightly. Although she said nothing, her gaze had an unspoken look of understanding and compassion. For the first time in a long time, I didn't feel alone. Still, I imagined she felt sorry for me, but perhaps that's only because I felt sorry for myself."

Dr. Clark exhaled deeply. "I'm sorry you went through that, Emma."

"I'm an intelligent, educated woman. How could I find myself in that kind of situation?" She looked deep into his eyes, as if searching for answers.

"Many people find themselves in similar situations. Educated or not. Male, female, non-binary...It doesn't matter."

"What do you mean?" she asked. "Are you implying this is a case of domestic violence?"

"Not exactly. Maybe. I would have to learn more about him to be certain, but from your description, Davis showed signs of Narcissistic Personality Disorder."

"Can you elaborate?"

He flipped through the pages in his notebook. "You said he's a police officer, correct?"

"Yes."

"I don't want to cast too wide a net, but many narcissists are drawn to law enforcement because they thrive on the admiration, power, control, and drama that comes with the job."

"What gives you the impression that he thrived on admiration?" she asked.

He leaned back in his chair. "It sounds like Davis has a need for attention and thinks highly of himself based on what you said about the Rumba Room incident. You said women lined up to dance with him. I would bet that he thrived on being the center of attention. And when he wasn't, as was the case when your attention was on the high school friend you ran into, it was too much for his ego to handle, and he exploded."

He continued, "Which brings me to my next point—narcissists want their victims to be afraid of what will happen if they don't comply with their demands. The narcissist's use of fear, obligation, and guilt manipulates their victims and keeps them from seeing the abuse."

Blinds them? "Do you mean victims are in denial about the narcissist's abusive behavior?"

"Most likely, yes. They cannot see what's happening right in front of them, what's happening *to* them. For instance, consider what you told me earlier about Davis's behavior on the cruise ship."

She gazed into the distance, deep in concentration, as she tried to recall what she said before. She shook her head. "I have no idea what you're referring to."

"You said, on the cruise ship, when someone asked you to dance, Davis would insert himself and yell, 'Mine!' You said you thought he was being cute. But he was exhibiting jealous behavior. You just couldn't see it."

She inhaled deeply. Hearing her own words come out of Dr. Clark's mouth made it so clear. She had believed that *she* had caused Davis to behave the way he did. But that's what Davis wanted her to believe. *How did I not see this before?*

He continued, "Narcissists are very cunning and convincing people. They appear charming at first, just like Davis did. But once they've entangled their victim in their web, so to speak, they use manipulative tactics to get what they want—regardless of the impact on their victim."

"What in the morning was true will at evening have become a lie…"

"Yes, exactly."

"Can a narcissist be rehabilitated, or cured, or whatever the term is?" she asked.

He shook his head. "No, treatment might help manage some symptoms for people who rank lower on the narcissism scale, but that's not likely the case for him."

"Oh," she replied with a look of defeat.

"Don't be so hard on yourself. Some people never come out of the FOG. Some people *marry* narcissists. Some people have parents, in-laws, or siblings who are narcissists that they must deal with their entire lives. Fortunately, you're not tied down to Davis."

"What do you mean by, 'some people never come out of the FOG?'" she asked.

"FOG—it's an acronym for fear, obligation, and guilt. The FOG disappears when the victim of a narcissist stops allowing themselves to be manipulated by the fear, obligation, and guilt tactics."

She nodded slowly. She didn't know exactly what to make of Dr. Clark's explanation, but it made so much sense.

He looked at his watch. "That's our time for today. Dr. Vedurmudi should be ready to see you."

20

THE CENTER FOR Advanced Medicine building houses the Neurosurgery Department, next to Psychiatry and Neuroscience at the University of Chicago. Holding the handwritten directions from Dr. Clark, Emma walked on the elevated walkway that joins the two buildings. She couldn't help but gaze out the walkway windows and observe the buzzing activity outside. Her eyes caught people walking, talking, and laughing. She observed a driver stopped in traffic that was dancing, arms raised, so freely that she could see her from afar. She smiled. For her, the walkway was more than just a way to get to the Neuroscience building. The walkway represented a path to freedom from the terrorists that had hijacked her dreams. Freedom to regain control of her life, get back to work, rest, eat, live a normal life. But it all hinged on one man's professional opinion.

She continued into the building.

This must be it. She knocked on the office door.

"Come in," a male voice with a British accent shouted.

She entered the office with caution. A man sat behind a desk, focused on his computer screen. "Hello, are you Dr. Vedurmudi?" she asked.

His attention turned to her. "You must be Emma," he said. He extended his hand toward her as he stood up.

She nodded and stepped further into his office.

They exchanged a firm handshake.

"I was just reviewing your file," he said.

Her eyebrows drew together. "Is this your first time reviewing it?" she asked.

He shook his head. "No, of course not. I've engaged in daily conversations with Dr. Clark about your condition. We have been working closely together."

She exhaled a sigh of relief.

"Take a seat, please," he said. He turned his attention back to his computer screen. "You've seen a neurologist before, yes?" he asked.

She nodded. "Yes, but nothing came of it."

He looked at her and flashed her a smile that showed his teeth. "That's because your neurologist was working alone. Here you have the benefit of an inter-professional team." His attention turned back to his computer screen. "I am going to read Dr. Clark's observations. Please listen carefully and let me know if there is anything you disagree with or anything you feel he may have missed."

"OK," she replied.

"Patient is sleep deprived and suffers from headaches and fainting spells. Patient suffers from anxiety and panic attacks. Patient has reported diminished quality of life and concern for potential loss of employment."

He paused.

"Do you agree so far?"

"Yes," she replied.

He continued, "Patient is experiencing sleep paralysis and night terrors on a regular and ongoing basis. Patient has experienced significant weight loss over a three to four-week period. Further weight loss could result in life-threatening medical emergencies. Patient has skin discoloration consistent with contusions."

He paused.

"That's everything. Do you agree with Dr. Clark's observations?"

She furrowed her brow. "Contusions? Is he referring to the discoloration he observed under my eyes?"

"That's possible. I realize the word may be alarming, but a contusion is simply used to describe a region where blood capillaries have been ruptured."

Her eyebrows drew together in a knot of confusion.

"If you are concerned or have questions about the observation, I can investigate."

She shook her head. "No, that's OK. I think I understand. That covers everything."

"Are you aware of what the procedure entails and related risks?" he asked.

She nodded. But despite Dr. Clark's thorough explanations, she filtered out anything that would deter them from undergoing the procedure.

"And are you aware that there is at least some chance the procedure may not work?"

She blinked rapidly. "Why wouldn't it work?" she asked.

He stood up from behind his desk. "There are at least three areas of the brain involved with explicit memory. They are the hippocampus, the cerebellum, and the amygdala." He pointed to a poster of the anatomy of the brain that hung on the wall. "Most evidence suggests that the hippocampus carries the functions of memory; that's the area we will be targeting."

She nodded. "That's what Dr. Clark told me."

"But we also know that many brain regions are activated during the recall of memories." He stepped closer to the poster and moved his hand in a broad circle.

Her shoulders drooped. Her hope dwindled.

"I don't intend to discourage you," Dr. Vedurmudi said. "There is a good chance it will work, at least to some extent; therefore, I recommend you proceed with the scheduled procedure. That is, if you choose to do so."

But she was discouraged. "Just tell me where I need to be and when I need to be there."

He picked up a manila folder from his desk. "This folder contains everything you need to know. Including what time you should arrive, the address, and what you can expect after."

She took the folder.

"You can drive yourself to the facility, but you should plan on having someone pick you up—your parents, perhaps?"

Her parents were unaware that she was considering the procedure. They would be worried sick if they found out. "I'll have my best friend drop me off there and pick me up when I'm released."

"You'll need to go somewhere where you can rest after, ideally not alone."

She nodded. "That won't be a problem. I can rest at my best friend's house."

"Alright then, try to get some rest. I'll see you tomorrow."

She gathered her things and stepped out of his office.

"How did it go in there?"

Her body jolted; she released her daily planner and manila folder from her grip. "Jesus!" she exclaimed. "You scared the living daylights out of me!"

"I'm sorry," Dr. Clark replied. He crouched down and picked up her things. "Are you moving ahead with the procedure?"

"Yes…Is that why you stalked me?"

He handed Emma her things. "I need to give you some instructions for after the procedure. Don't forget to pack the dream training recording from our session. You should continue with your dream training, even during your recovery."

She nodded.

He handed her a yellow sticky note. "This is my personal mobile number. Call me if you need anything. I mean it."

She took the sticky note and placed it in her daily planner. "Is there anything else I need to know?"

He shook his head. "That's it. Just hang in there.

21

Day 5, Northwestern Memorial Hospital
4:30 a.m.

THE DOOR OPENED to a dark room overlooking the neurosurgery suite where nurses prepared for surgery. Dr. Clark was the first to arrive. A herd of medical students came in after him. He didn't typically observe patient procedures, but Emma's unique case compelled him to be there. He sat in the front of the room. To his right was a podium equipped with a microphone intended for use by medical students to answer questions during the procedure. The floor-to-ceiling glass wall in front of him allowed for direct visibility into the neurosurgery suite below.

In the neurosurgery suite, Dr. Vedurmudi wore a barely visible microphone attached to the collar of his surgical scrubs. Emma lay awake on the surgical table next to him. Her eyes darted around the room aimlessly. *She looks nervous;* he thought as he gnawed on his fingernails.

Dr. Vedurmudi looked up at the glass wall; the sound of his voice blasted through an intercom in the operation theater. "I'm excited to be here as part of a collaborative effort between the University of Chicago's Psychiatry and Behavioral Neuroscience Department, the University of Chicago's Department of Neurosurgery, and Northwestern University's Department of Neurological Surgery," he said.

Although highly unusual for a neurosurgeon affiliated with one university to perform surgery at the facility of another, it happened under very specific or unusual circumstances. Emma's condition and willingness to undergo a procedure that had been extensively studied but rarely performed more than qualified as unusual.

"As you know, microglia are the resident immune cells of the brain. In addition to regulating brain development, microglia function to maintain and repair injuries to the nervous system," Dr. Vedurmudi said. "Our patient today is having debilitating nightmares. Can anyone tell me how injecting microglia into the hippocampus may improve her condition?"

In the operation theater, an eager student rushed to the podium. "The hippocampus is where memories are stored," the student said. "Introducing the microglia in the hippocampus should eliminate the synaptic connections associated with the fear-based engrams that are mostly responsible for the patient's nightmares."

Dr. Clark watched as the student held his breath; he appeared hungry for validation.

"Very good," Dr. Vedurmudi replied.

The student exhaled audibly.

Dr. Clark smiled inwardly. *I remember those days*, he thought.

Dr. Vedurmudi approached the sink and dispensed a generous amount of liquid soap into his hands. He worked the soap into a rich, foamy lather and rubbed his hands together vigorously.

"Until recently, it was believed that microglia solely functioned to maintain and repair synaptic connections. We now know that it's much smarter than that. Can anyone tell me how?" he asked.

Dr. Clark side-bent toward the podium. He reached for the microphone; his feet still planted where he stood. "Microglia can distinguish between fear-based and non-fear-based engrams and prune away at connections it no longer deems necessary or valuable," he said.

Dr. Vedurmudi and Emma looked up at the operation theater. He flashed a smile and a wave.

Dr. Vedurmudi nodded. "That is correct, Dr. Clark. Thank you for joining us today." He held his hands out to the surgical scrub nurse. One at a time, the nurse placed latex gloves on his hands and methodically slipped each finger into place, tugging at the wrists to ensure they were securely in place.

"I would be remiss not to mention that we previously believed that memory engrams were isolated to just one part of the brain," he said. "Thanks to the application of cutting-edge technologies, we now know that memory engrams are widely distributed throughout the brain, spanning many regions. Would anyone care to give me an example?"

A student strode up to the podium, his chest puffed out. He turned to Dr. Clark. "I got this," he said with a smirk.

There's always an arrogant one in the class, he thought. He shook his head and rolled his eyes.

"After forming in the hippocampus, memory engrams may be rooted through the anterior thalamus, particularly with long-term memory storage," the arrogant student said. He stepped back and smirked at Dr. Clark again.

"That's a wonderful example," Dr. Vedurmudi replied. "Until recently, we associated the thalamus with only sensory relay; that it is associated with cognitive activity is an unexpected finding, to say the least."

Dr. Clark felt a warm breath in his ear. "Did you hear about the study that came up with that finding?" a male voice whispered.

He turned toward the voice. It was the arrogant student.

"Do you want to know how they did it?" the arrogant student asked.

"Let me guess, they used lab rats," Dr. Clark replied.

"Actually, they used mice. But do you know what they did to them?"

Uninterested in engaging with him, Dr. Clark stared straight ahead into the neurosurgery suite.

The arrogant student continued, "The researchers developed a virtual reality maze for the mice."

A virtual reality maze? Dr. Clark thought. As annoyed as he was by the student, he couldn't suppress his curiosity. He turned to the student.

"The virtual reality maze took the mice into different rooms that offered sugar water or a puff of air to the face. They repeated the process for days to give the mice time to create long-term memories."

Although he did not want to reward the arrogant student, Dr. Clark thought acknowledging him would be the only way to get him to go away. "Very interesting. I wasn't aware," he said. He turned his gaze back to the neurosurgery suite.

"But wait until you hear the best part," the arrogant student continued.

Oh, dear God, there's more? Dr. Clark thought.

"They strapped the mice's heads into these tiny little headpieces designed to hold them steady. I saw the video—it was like Peloton for rodents!" The arrogant student erupted in laughter.

Dr. Clark thought it was funny, too, but he had enough experience with lab rats to know that when rewarded, they keep coming back. His eyes remained locked on the neurosurgery suite below. He watched as the anesthesiologist gently placed a small, transparent oxygen mask over Emma's nose. As the anesthesia took effect, her breathing slowed; her eyelids appeared heavy. Within moments, she had slipped into a state of deep sedation.

"Can anyone tell me why I am injecting the microglia via intra-cerebral injection instead of using a different method, say encapsulation?" Dr. Vedurmudi asked.

A student rushed to the podium. "An intra-cerebral injection allows for the immediate release of microglia into a targeted region of the brain, whereas encapsulation allows for slow-release overtime."

"Right again," Dr. Vedurmudi replied. "With the help of an MRI and three-dimensional coordinate system, we can reach the target injection site with extreme precision." He turned to the neurosurgical nurse. "Clean and sterilize the part of the head around the temporal lobe, please."

"This is revolutionary," a student commented from the operation theater. Although the student was not at the podium, the microphone picked up their comment.

"Indeed, it is," Dr. Vedurmudi replied. "Intra-cerebral injections are nothing new, but our ability to develop synthetic microglia is a modern miracle that will affect patients suffering from Alzheimer's to amnesia to posttraumatic stress disorder and more."

"She's ready," the neurosurgical nurse said.

Dr. Vedurmudi leaned over Emma's bedside and marked the location of the incision on her scalp using a marker. "I'll be making a small incision on the medial temporal lobe." He extended his hand; "Scalpel, please." Dr. Vedurmudi's gloved hand hovered steadily over Emma's scalp as he focused on the marked area.

Dr. Clark watched as he made the cut with calculated precision.

"Now I'll be drilling a burr hole." He extended his hand again. "Drill," he said. The neurosurgical nurse handed him a cranial drill that resembled a hardware drill with a thin bit at the end. He drilled a small circular opening into her skull.

"Now I will insert the injection needle through the burr hole and into the brain tissue," Dr. Vedurmudi said. No longer stopping to entertain questions, his focus was fully dedicated to the task at hand. He inserted a long needle into the opening in Emma's skull.

Although Dr. Clark fully trusted Dr. Vedurmudi's abilities as a neurosurgeon, he couldn't deny the element of risk involved with even the most routine of procedures, let alone one of this caliber. He held his breath, knowing that the following moments would be critical to the procedure's success.

Dr. Vedurmudi guided the needle to the target location. "Bingo. I've injected the microglia." He carefully pulled back the needle from her skull.

"Let's get her cleaned up," he said. The neurosurgical nurse rushed to clean and sterilize the site of the injection.

"I'll be using a suture to close up the burr hole." He inserted a needle with the suture thread from one part of the skin through the tissue on the other side. "Now we do the same on the other side of the wound." He tied a knot and trimmed the excess thread. "Finally, we apply a sterile dressing to protect the wound and pro-mote healing."

"Vitals look good. Patient is showing no sign of distress," the neurosurgical nurse said.

"We'll monitor her for a few hours before she's released. I don't want to get ahead of myself, but all in all, I'd call this procedure a success," Dr. Vedurmudi said with a smile.

The operation theater erupted in applause. Dr. Clark breathed a heavy sigh of relief; his shoulders dropped as they released the tension he was unaware he was carrying. He looked down at Emma; she appeared to be sleeping peacefully. *Now we wait.*

22

THE SUN HAD NOT YET RISEN over the Department of Psychiatry and Behavioral Neuroscience building at the University of Chicago. His chest expanded; the cold crisp early-morning air filled his lungs. As he approached, he couldn't help but stop to look at the dense fog that clung to the building through the darkness like a haunted medieval castle. He proceeded onward. There was a loud click as he thrust the glass door open at the building's entrance. Inside the building, the sound of a loud clatter echoed through the dim empty hallway. There was an audible gasp.

"Good morning, Sunny, I hope I didn't scare you," Dr. Clark said.

"Good morning, Dr. Clark," Sunny replied, kneeling to pick up his mop. "Maybe just a little." He swirled the mop in the bucket.

"I'm sorry about that. I imagine you don't get much building traffic this early," Dr. Clark said with a smile. "Have a good day, Sunny."

He nodded. "You too, Dr. Clark."

He charged toward his office, eager for solitary time to focus. Although he was optimistic that the procedure had worked, several questions weighed heavily on his mind. He was compelled to investigate further for the sake of science and his own good conscience. Science had to explain why Emma was having these dreams. Science had to explain what triggered her dreams to begin with. He thought that Noah's death alone couldn't have triggered her dreams. *Or could it have?*

He stepped into his office and switched on the lights; he squinted at the jarring bright white artificial fluorescent lighting that suddenly filled the room. "Locking the door." He spoke aloud.

At his desk, he picked up his notebook. "What's the connection between Herod and John?" He stared at the notebook before opening it, as if he could sense the answers were at his fingertips. It was just a matter of finding them.

He read aloud from the notebook. "Emma met John in college while in Austin." He thumbed through the pages. "She met Herod after several years of working at her firm in Chicago."

He continued to thumb back and forth between the pages. He shook his head as he struggled to piece the information together. The flapping and fluttering of paper as he moved back and forth between pages served only as a distraction. "This isn't working," he said.

With a face set in intense determination, he gripped the edge of the notebook with one hand and pulled the pages out with the other. The sound of paper being ripped filled the quiet room.

He grouped the pages by the names of the men in Emma's dreams, in the order they discussed them. "Where's the tape? I can never find the tape." He fumbled through his desk drawer. "There it is." He taped the ripped pages to the whiteboard on the wall.

He stepped back and read the names. *John. Rico. Zack. Noah. Jonah. Herod. Davis.*

"I need a timeline." He examined the names, looking from

right to left, then right again. "Noah was her first boyfriend. He goes to the front of the line." He stepped up and moved a grouping of notes to the far-right side of the whiteboard.

"She met John right before her college graduation, after Noah. And she met Rico when she had just moved back home from college." He rearranged the groupings behind Noah.

Noah, John, Rico.

Three down, four to go.

"Davis was her last relationship. She met him on the cruise after breaking up with Herod."

He looked at the groupings for Herod and Davis, already taped on the far-right side of the whiteboard. They were the last two men Emma talked about. He imagined she reserved speaking about them until the end because of the difficulty and rawness of the topics and her emotions.

"That just leaves Zack and Jonah." He reviewed his notes, looking for any detail that might reveal who she met first. He recalled her saying that they assigned her to a special assignment in the early part of her career. *They called her a 'rising star.'*

"Zack had to come before Jonah."

He read the names again. *Noah. John. Rico. Zack. Jonah. Herod. Davis.* "I don't know what I'm looking for yet, but so far, so good."

He picked up a dry erase marker and wrote under the groupings on the whiteboard. "This is looking like a crime board, which is ironic because some of these guys belong in prison." He scoffed.

He stepped back. "That's much better." His notes were now organized and in full view in front of him.

He paced back and forth, arms folded, his gaze fixed on the whiteboard. "What's the connection?"

He observed the distance between John and Herod on the whiteboard. From left to right, John was second. Herod was second to last. "How do two people she met twelve hundred miles apart just run into each other seven years apart?"

As he stared at the whiteboard, Emma's words from a visit earlier in the week echoed in his mind. *You're focusing on the wrong thing.*

He took another step back. Keywords from his notes jumped out at him as if sending a message from the beyond. "What on earth?"

He stared at the makeshift crime board in front of him. "There's nothing scientific about this." He paced back and forth across the room, his steps rapid and unsteady as he maintained his gaze on the whiteboard. In his years as a clinical professor of psychiatry, he had witnessed nothing science couldn't explain. Unlike a few people he knew, he had never witnessed a supernatural or religious phenomenon. But years ago, a colleague told him of an experience he claimed to have had involving a spirit in a home he had just purchased. His wife claimed to have seen the spirit first. She said it was the spirit of a young child. His wife claimed she was not afraid, outside of the initial fear she experienced when the spirit revealed itself. She said there was nothing malicious about the spirit. It appeared to be lonely, to be seeking company. Then his colleague's two children claimed to have seen the spirit. Again, they claimed they were not afraid. It was as if the spirit was slowly revealing itself as it got more comfortable with the new tenants. It wasn't until his colleague saw the alleged spirit with his own eyes, day after day, night after night, again and again, that he could not deny what he had witnessed. His colleague told him he struggled with his experience because it went against everything he had studied. Everything he knew to be true. Dr. Clark considered himself fortunate to never have experienced what his colleague referred to as 'an existential crisis.'

He knew all too well that there were things that science couldn't *prove*. But science could always, always *explain*. Science aims to make sense of the natural world through evidence and observation. It's what drew him into the field to begin with.

But he had just uncovered a pattern unlike one he had ever seen before. And although he couldn't explain it, he couldn't ignore it. He brought his palms together and held his hands to his chin as he stared at the finding before him. As he searched for an explanation, only two words came to mind. "Holy. Shit."

23

THE THUD OF MAGAZINES being shuffled against the coffee table was amplified by the still quiet of the room. Across the lobby, a man sighed audibly. Clearly agitated, he lowered his newspaper and shot Brianna a cold, piercing glare. "Sorry," Brianna whispered. She laid the magazines down on the coffee table.

The silence in the waiting room was oppressive, as if time itself had stopped. She pulled her phone out of her backpack in search of a distraction, but the clock on its screen only brought her attention back to her nervous thoughts. *What's taking so long? She should be out by now.*

The hospital corridor door swung open; a cool draft filled the room. She looked up. Emma was being wheeled out by a nurse.

She rushed to her side. "Em, how are you feeling?" she asked. She gently stroked her hair, careful not to disrupt the white sterile dressing on her scalp.

"It's not as bad as it looks."

"You can pull your car around; I'll wheel her outside," the nurse said.

"I'll be right back," Brianna replied, clutching her keys in her hand. She rushed out into the parking lot.

"Just breathe," she said aloud as she reached her vehicle.

In the car, she looked at her rear-view mirror. *I can't let her see me like this,* she thought. She exhaled deeply and focused on keeping her composure.

Unbeknownst to Emma, Brianna's mother, a neonatal nurse, had a special interest in neurology ever since she could remember. Her mother was especially interested in new developments in cutting-edge medical technology. She often spoke of her interests and findings over dinner and, in large part, inspired Brianna to go into nursing. As a result, she was keenly aware of the risks involved with Emma's procedure. And, although worrying was not in her nature, she couldn't help but be concerned for her friend.

But she would keep her concerns to herself. She had witnessed what Emma, practically a sister to her, had gone through... The pain, the tears, the manifestations of her suffering. She had watched her best friend's physical and mental health deteriorate before her eyes. And as much as she wanted help, it was out of her hands. So, she would do nothing, say nothing that might interfere in the slightest with Emma getting the help she desperately needed.

It's over, she's OK, she thought. She looked in the rearview mirror and rehearsed a fabricated smile as she pulled up to the front of the hospital where Emma and the nurse awaited. The nurse opened the passenger's side door and assisted Emma in.

"Should we go straight to my place?" Brianna asked.

"Yes, please," Emma replied, her voice just a little louder than a whisper. "Dr. Clark said I should continue with the dream training I told you about."

As she looked at Emma, she tried not to stare at the bandage on her scalp. "When will you know if the procedure worked?" she asked.

"My microglia levels are much higher than they were before the procedure. I should start seeing results over the next eight to twelve hours."

"What method did they use to measure your microglia levels?"

She turned to Brianna with squinted eyes. "How should I know?"

Brianna's eyes widened. She searched for what to say. "I couldn't help but imagine a nurse measuring your levels by putting a dipstick in your ear."

There was silence.

Emma erupted in quiet laughter.

Brianna laughed too; her laughter triggered the emotions she had been repressing.

"Are you crying?" Emma asked with a puzzled look. She leaned in. "I've never seen you cry in my entire life."

"I guess I was worried," she replied, her emotions on full display. "I'm just happy everything went as planned."

The drive home was quiet. She drove more conservatively than usual, careful to avoid bumps and sharp movements.

She pulled into her driveway.

"Where's my car?" Emma asked.

"I parked it in the alley behind my house," Brianna replied. She sensed Emma was concerned. "Don't worry; it will be safe there."

Brianna lived in a quaint neighborhood of contemporary garden homes. The yards of each home were small and perfectly manicured. The small close-knit community prided itself on its reputation for low crime rates driven by attentive neighbors and an active neighborhood watch program. Emma's car being stolen was of no worry, as far as she was concerned. In fact, she thought parking Emma's car in the back, tucked in a quiet alley visible from her backyard fence, would be even safer.

She got out of the car. Her dark curly hair was pulled up into a tall ponytail, like a crown on her head. She wore sneakers, leggings, and a tank top, yet there was a style about her that made her stand out. Despite being similar in height and build to Emma, her athletic physique was the result of lifelong dedication to good nutrition and regular exercise. *The holy trinity of health*, she called it.

She rushed around the car to help Emma out.

"I was talking to Dr. Clark about how strict my father was when I was growing up. That got me wondering, given how you've always been so focused on health and fitness, why didn't you participate in sports?"

She shrugged her shoulders. "I don't know, it was just never my thing," she replied. She did not wish to share more. She put her arm around Emma's waist. "It's cold. Let's hurry inside."

They approached the front door to the sound of mechanical whirring.

"What's that noise?" Emma asked.

Brianna pushed the door open. "Keyless entry," she replied. Their steps echoed across the foyer as they entered the home.

"OK, first things first. I'm going to need your phone," Brianna said, extending her palm, face up toward Emma.

Emma rolled her eyes. "Is that really necessary?"

She suspected Emma wouldn't turn over her phone willingly. She reached for Emma's purse. Before Emma could react, she fished out her phone. "Yes," she replied.

"Ugh, I forgot how fast you are. But I'm serious. I need my phone to set alarms for my sleep training."

Does she really think I'm giving her this phone? She was prepared to find out. "I'll make you a deal. I'll give you your phone if you repeat after me: Brianna is the best. No other person in the universe comes close."

She scoffed. "You're joking, right?"

"Not joking." She crossed her arms tightly in front of her chest and glared at her. "My house, my rules."

Emma rolled her eyes again.

"You know, if you keep doing that, your eyes are going to stay like that."

She scoffed again. "You know what, fine. I'll feed your ego for a few seconds if it means I get my phone back. Brianna is the best. No other person in the universe comes close."

"Got it. I have added user to Brianna's voice recognition account," an electronic voice announced.

"Thanks, Dharma!" Brianna exclaimed.

"What was that?"

"That's Dharma. It's been a while since you've come by. Most of the things in this house are voice-activated. Now you can use all the features."

"Oh yeah? Dharma, make me a sandwich," Emma asked with a mischievous smile.

"Got it. Ordering from TriBecca's Sandwich Shop," Dharma announced.

Emma gasped. "Oh crap," she said, covering her mouth.

"Dharma, cancel," Brianna said, looking unamused.

"OK. I have canceled the order," Dharma announced.

"If you need to set an alarm, just ask Dharma." She removed the cushions from her couch, then pulled on the bar underneath to transform the couch into a bed. "Where's the recording for your dream training?"

Emma reached into her purse; she pulled out a CD. "Here."

Brianna stared at the CD as if it were a relic. "I didn't know they still made these. Fortunately, I'm prepared for anything." She inserted the CD into her sound system. "Dharma, dim the lights and play the CD," she said. Instantly, the lights dimmed, and Dr. Clark's soothing voice projected throughout the house. "Do you think the dream training will work on me?" she asked.

"Ha! As if you need it!" Emma exclaimed.

Emma was right. Although Brianna lived an easy-going life,

she never hesitated to stand up for herself, her family, or Emma when push came to shove. Her instinct to protect her loved ones fueled any underlying fear she might possess. Fear fueled her to act. To stand up. To speak up. And she welcomed it.

She prepared the bare sofa bed with linens and pillows. "Let's get you started with a nap," she said.

Emma removed her coat and shoes. She laid down on the sofa bed and rested her head on a pillow.

"Dharma, set a sleep timer for two hours," Brianna said. She watched as Emma quickly drifted off to sleep. Although Brianna had not been completely honest with her about what she knew about the procedure and the worry that ensued, she convinced herself it was better this way. *She's OK—nothing else matters*, she thought.

24

THE BEEPING FROM DHARMA'S alarm awoke Emma from her slumber. She rubbed her eyes. For a moment, she had forgotten where she was.

"Dharma, stop," she commanded.

The beeping went silent.

"Yes, Dr. Clark, she's awake now," Brianna said. "I'll hand her the phone."

Emma took the phone from her. "Hello?"

"Hello Emma, this is Dr. Clark. I was just leaving a message with your friend. How are you feeling?"

She rubbed her eyes again, still drowsy from her nap. "I feel fine."

"Any changes to your dreams so far?"

"No, other than I slept deeper just now, but I imagine that has to do with the anesthesia."

"You're probably right. Listen, Emma, I have something I need to talk to you about."

Emma sensed concern coming from his voice. Her eyes widened. "Did the procedure go as you expected?"

"It's too early to tell, but this has nothing to do with the procedure."

"What is it then?"

"I was reviewing my notes from our sessions. At first, I was looking for a connection between Herod and John. But when I stepped back, I noticed an unusual pattern that I'd like you to examine."

"What kind of pattern?"

There was silence.

"Dr. Clark?"

"It's challenging to describe over the phone," he replied. "I'd like to send you an image of my notes for you to look at."

"OK."

"I'll be honest. I don't completely know what to make of it," he said. "It's not exactly within my field of expertise, but I recall you talking about your father being a pastor. It may be worth getting his opinion on this."

Why would I want my father's opinion? "OK, please send me the image. I'll reach out to my father if I think it will help."

"OK, Emma. Goodbye now."

She clutched her phone and stared at its screen.

"Alright Emma, give me your phone back," Brianna said.

"No, wait!" she exclaimed. "I'm waiting for Dr. Clark to send me something."

The phone chimed.

"That must be it." She opened the notification. As expected, it was an image of Dr. Clark's notes. She read the notes to herself.

She shook her head. *I don't get it.*

She read it again.

Her eyes bulged; she let out an audible gasp.

"What is it?" Brianna asked. She rushed to look over Emma's shoulder.

Noah–Excessive drinking–Gluttony

John—Sexual predator—Lust

Rico—Heartbreak/envy/relationship with Leah —Envy

Zack—Distracted by money—Greed

Jonah—Unemployed; walls of filth closing in—Sloth

Herod—Break up attributed to pridefulness/shame—Pride

Davis—Jealousy, anger management issues, violent—Wrath?

Emma stood up, stunned by the connection Dr. Clark made. "It can't be a coincidence."

"He must have organized the list in chronological order," Brianna said.

"He did," Emma replied.

"Why do you think he has a question mark next to the word wrath?" Brianna asked.

Emma brought the phone closer to her face and leaned in as she inspected the image further. "We talked about my past with Davis at length, but we haven't discussed my dreams of him yet. I would guess that's why."

"You haven't discussed your dreams of him?" Brianna asked with a raised brow.

Emma sensed there was something more to her look. "Yes, why?"

"I didn't know you were dreaming of him."

Emma's eyes narrowed in disbelief. "I must have told you."

She shrugged her shoulders. "If you ask me, Davis resonates with all seven of these themes." In a defensive posture, she retreated slowly and raised her hands over her chest. "But who am I to judge?" She folded her arms. "That does make me wonder though…could there be more to it?"

"What do you mean?"

Her eyes squinted, and she looked contemplative while staring at the image. "If Herod and John knew each other, could there be others?"

Emma reached into her purse and pulled out her planner; she

turned to a blank page. "Let's think about this." She entered the dining room and sat at the dining table. "I'm going to note where I met each of them…Maybe we can find a pattern."

She wrote the names of each of the men. Next to the names, she wrote the name of a city:

Noah–Austin

John–Austin

Rico–Chicago

Zack–Chicago

Jonah–Chicago

Herod–Chicago

Davis–Chicago

Brianna sat next to her. "That's not right," she said. "You met Davis in Galveston."

Emma shook her head. *How could I forget?*

"And wasn't he there visiting family from Houston?"

Emma's eyes sparkled with inspiration.

Brianna pushed herself away from the table; her chair scuffed the marble flooring as she stood up from her seat in a hurry.

"Where are you going? I need your help!" Emma exclaimed. Hours had passed since the procedure. She worried she could lose her memories at any moment. When she did, Brianna would be their sole custodian. If she was to partake in this investigation, she would have to act fast.

"I'm just getting my laptop!" Brianna shouted from the living room. She rushed back and took a seat across from Emma. "Got it. In case we need to do any research."

Emma's attention returned to her notes. "OK, Noah…I met him in Austin, but he was from Houston," she said. "Rico, I met in Chicago."

Brianna interrupted, "But he went to school in Bloomington." She rolled her eyes. "What an ass."

"Jonah is from Chicago. I don't know of any other place where he's lived," Emma said. She couldn't fathom him moving. At least not far. Moving would take effort. Moving would take away from his sleep. Moving would take him away from his loyal customers. It was all too unlikely. "Zack is from Chicago, and he works here as well." She wrote *Chicago* next to Zack's name.

Brianna double tapped on the page. "You should write Chicago for John since he ran into Herod here."

"Right."

"Do you remember anything else about John?" Brianna asked.

"I remember he told me he was visiting from out of town."

She paused.

"I don't remember where he said he was visiting from."

"Do you recall *anything* about your conversation with him?" Brianna asked.

She straightened her posture. "He said the town was three hours from Austin. The town's name was unique, like it was an emotion."

"What do you mean?"

"Happy, sad, hungry, angry, I don't know exactly. It was such a long time ago." She tried to remember, but she had done the best she could. Now she questioned if she had lost the memory over time, or whether her memories were becoming extinct because of the procedure.

Brianna's eyes were fixed on the laptop's screen. She searched the Internet. "Could he be from a town called Humble?"

Emma slapped her palms together. "That's it!" she exclaimed.

Brianna stood up, her mouth agape. "You're not going to believe this," she said.

"What is it?"

"Humble is a city in the Houston metropolitan area."

"You're kidding."

She turned the laptop to face Emma. "Not kidding. Write it down."

Noah–Austin, Houston

John—Austin, Humble/Houston, Chicago
Rico—Chicago, Bloomington
Zack—Chicago
Jonah—Chicago
Herod—Chicago
Davis—Chicago, Galveston, Houston

"There's a lot of overlap," Brianna said. "But do you see a connection?"

Emma shook her head. "The only thing that comes to mind is the time Davis and I ran into Rico at the Rumba Room. But even then, they didn't know each other—I'm sure of it."

Brianna pressed her lips together. "Is there any way Noah and John may have known each other?" she asked. "They were both in Austin around the same time."

Emma shrugged her shoulders. "I have no idea; I don't even know John's last name."

Brianna's fingers moved swiftly over her keyboard, tapping out a series of keystrokes.

"What are you searching for?"

"I'm searching Noah's social media accounts," Brianna replied. "But they've all been shut down."

Emma lowered her head; her shoulders drooped.

"There has to be something out there with Noah's digital footprint." As she continued her search, her movements became more fluid. Her eyes widened. "Emma, look at this! Look at this comment on Noah's obituary site."

Emma rushed to stand; her chair scuffed the floor loudly.

She read silently from the screen. *You left us too soon, brother. I'll never forget all the fun times we had on 6th Street. RIP. -John Romo, Humble, Texas*

She glared at the profile photo next to the comment. "It's John for sure." Although she had only met John once, her dreams were vivid enough to recognize him, without a doubt.

"John and Noah were brothers?"

Emma shook her head. "They were fraternity brothers."

Although Emma didn't think, or even care, to ask John if he was in a fraternity, it was common for fraternities from other colleges to visit Austin, mostly because of the thrill of the big campus and the bustling Austin nightlife. But there was something else that stood out about John's comment.

"Romo? Looks like Herod and John were more than just friends," Brianna said. Her eyes widened; she turned to Emma. "Do you think they targeted you?"

She took a step back; her nose flared up, and she looked at Brianna gravely. "How could I possibly know that?!" she erupted. She had never considered the possibility that there was any connection between any of the people in her past, let alone that they were plotting against her.

Brianna raised her shoulders. "I'm sorry! It just seems like too big of a coincidence!"

Unwilling to continue playing detective, Emma reached for her phone. "I'm calling my mom." She placed the phone against her ear and listened as it rang.

And rang.

And rang.

Come on, Mom...Pick. Up.

"Hello, angel," her mother answered.

"Hi, Mom."

"I wasn't expecting a call from you at this time of day. Is everything OK?"

"I'm fine, but I don't have a lot of time to talk. Listen, you know I've been seeing a doctor about my dreams."

"Yes, I know."

"We've been talking about some people that keep showing up in my dreams, and my doctor thinks there might be a pattern.

He thought it might be a good idea to run it by Dad," she said. "I think it's biblical."

There was silence.

"Mom, are you there?"

"You should talk to your father."

"OK, is he with you?"

She listened on as her mother primed her father for the conversation.

"¡Emma, mija!" her father exclaimed. He spoke in a mix of Spanish and English. "¿Todo bien?" he asked.

"Unfortunately, no, Dad. I'm having bad dreams, and my doctor thinks there's a pattern... I think it's biblical."

Again, there was silence.

"What's going on, Dad?"

There was a heavy sigh on the phone. "I prayed this day would never come."

"What is it, Dad?" she asked, her stomach sinking with worry.

"I would prefer this conversation in person."

What could he possibly have to tell me? "Dad, I'm not a child anymore. We've been through this. Please, just tell me whatever you have to say."

There was silence.

More silence.

"Fine. I'm at Brianna's house. Please, just get here as soon as you can," she conceded.

She turned to Brianna. "I hope you don't mind them coming over."

"Of course, I don't mind." Her eyes fixed on Emma's head.

"What are you looking at?" Emma asked.

"You're going to need a hat."

25

"HELLO, MIJA!" EMMANUEL exclaimed from the door, holding two tall brown grocery bags. His wife, Josephine, stood closely next to him.

"Come in! It's so nice to see you; it's been such a long time," Brianna replied.

They stepped inside.

Emmanuel leaned in and, with a gentle tilt of the head, planted a soft paternal kiss on her cheek.

"Oh, I've missed you, sweetheart," Josephine said, firmly embracing Brianna. "It really has been too long! How are you?"

She shrugged her shoulders. "I'm great, just, you know, busy...with work."

Josephine raised an eyebrow. "Is that why we haven't seen much of you lately?"

She cleared her throat and looked away. "Uh, yeah. Yes. I've been...putting in a lot of overtime," she replied without making eye contact. She paused and returned her gaze to Josephine. "I hope that will change soon though." She smiled. "Please, make yourself at home."

"Should I take my shoes off?" Emmanuel asked.

"No, don't worry about it," she replied, waving off his offer.

He looked down at his white sneakers. "Good, because it's not often I get to wear my comfy shoes."

He looked over Brianna's shoulder. Emma sat on the sofa bed, stretching her arms fully. "Mija, is everything OK? What are you doing sleeping in the middle of the day?"

She rubbed her eyes. "My doctor told me I needed to catch up on sleep, so I'm squeezing in as many naps as possible."

He tilted his head. "Why are you wearing a beanie?"

"My head is cold," she replied.

He nodded slowly; his eyes narrowed in a skeptical gaze. He thought there was more to the story, but he had become skilled at respecting Emma's boundaries and knowing when to back off. So back off he did.

"Angel, you look so thin!" Josephine exclaimed. "Are you sure you're OK?"

"Yes, Mom. Except for the dreams, I'm fine."

"Well, it's a good thing we brought lunch. You know your dad loves to cook your abuela's famous Mexican recipes any chance he gets."

"Yay!" Brianna squealed, pumping her fist. Emmanuel passed her the grocery bags.

"Thanks, Dad." Emma stood up from the sofa bed, extending her arms toward him. He wrapped his arms around her with a tender squeeze. "Let's talk in the dining room," she said.

Emmanuel unpacked the food containers as the others sat around the table. The aroma of garlic, cumin, and oregano filled the room.

Emma sat across from Josephine. "Why did you bring your Bible?" she asked.

"I never leave home without it," Josephine replied, holding

the Bible tightly. She placed the Bible on the table. "Brianna, any chance you have some coffee?"

"Coming right up!" she exclaimed.

"Will Brianna be joining us?" Emmanuel asked.

"Of course," Emma replied.

"For the meal or the conversation?"

"Both," she replied with a look of confusion.

He carefully pried open the lid from the plastic butter tub he repurposed to transport the rice and skillfully concealed his discontent. Although he loved Brianna like family, he would prefer not to have an audience for this conversation. "OK, let's get started." He brought his palms together in a resounding clap. "I cooked up some chile relleno, topped with queso fresco, and stuffed with papas and picadillo. Sides of arroz, frijoles refritos, and, of course, fresh homemade tortillas de maíz."

Emma's eyes widened as she gazed at the feast before her. "It smells great, Dad, thank you."

His attention turned to Brianna. "No need to raise your hand, mija. What's your question?"

"Can you translate, please?"

"Yes, of course. How rude of me. I cooked some delicious fried poblano peppers stuffed with seasoned ground meat and potatoes and topped with fresh cheese," he said. "And, of course, no authentic Mexican meal would be complete without sides of Mexican rice, refried beans, and fresh homemade corn tortillas."

"That sounds incredible!" Brianna exclaimed. She closed her eyes and inhaled deeply. "And it smells incredible."

"This is the reason I come home to visit," Emma said with a smile.

"Everyone, dig in!" Emmanuel said as he took a seat next to Josephine. His eyes darted around the table. "Brianna, do you have any Tabasco sauce?"

"No, sorry."

His shoulders drooped. *Surely, she must have something spicy,* he thought. "How about Salsa Valentina?"

"No, sorry," she said again.

"Salsa verde?"

"No."

"Fresh serrano pepper?"

"No."

"Fresh or jarred jalapeño pepper?"

"Nope."

"Chili pepper flakes?"

"Dad, enough!" Emma exclaimed.

"Actually, yes, I have chili pepper flakes," Brianna replied.

He breathed a sigh of relief. Emma shot him an incredulous look. "Chili pepper flakes, Dad?"

He shrugged his shoulders. "It's better than nothing."

She shook her head. "OK, Dad. What was so important that you couldn't tell me over the phone?"

He exhaled deeply and, with a firm grip, pulled his chair closer to the table. "I wouldn't exactly call this a lunchtime conversation topic, but here we are...When I was young, I made some mistakes."

She rolled her eyes. "Dad, we've been over this."

"This has nothing to do with my parenting skills, or lack thereof. I'm talking about some mistakes I made *before* you were born."

She crossed her arms tightly over her chest and gazed at him. "I'm listening."

He had never spoken to Emma about life, his marriage to Josephine before she was born. Perhaps it was because he was ashamed of the mistakes he had made. Perhaps it was because he didn't want to shed more light on his imperfections. Revealing his past mistakes would surely result in another chink in his armor. And he only wanted what every father does...To be his daughter's hero.

He took a deep breath. "Before you were born, I made some horrible mistakes, mija. I was young and stupid. You know I love your mother more than anything, but we went through a period in our marriage where I was terrible to her."

"Coffee?" Brianna asked.

"No, mija, thank you...

"I drank, and it got out of control. Every night I would leave your mother at home and go to the cantina down the road from the house. Before I knew it, I was cheating on your mother."

He paused.

"Well, not sexually."

"Dad!" she exclaimed with a look of disgust.

"I said *not* sexually. Your mother's instincts kicked in before it could get that far. Anyway, one day, she grew suspicious, and she went looking for me at the cantina. That's where she caught me with another woman."

Emma's eyes widened.

Josephine crossed her arms and gave a slow nod.

"You would think I would have fallen to my knees and begged your mother for forgiveness, but instead, I lashed out at her in front of everyone. I yelled at her as if she was the one wrong for being there and forced her to leave. I made a fool of us both."

"You didn't even ask for forgiveness? I mean, after?" Emma asked.

He shook his head with a look of self-disappointment. "My drinking got worse, and they fired me from my job for showing up late, or not showing up at all. I grew depressed and kept drinking. I didn't care enough to find a new job, leaving us with no income. Your mother wanted to get a job, but I was so jealous, I could not bear the possibility that she might find a better man than me at work. With no income and no job, your mother made candied apples she sold on the street corner so that we could get by." He turned to Josephine. "You're an amazing woman. You still figured out a way, even when I left us with no options,." She patted him delicately on his back.

"Is that what you needed to tell me in person?" Emma asked.

He shook his head; his gaze became distant and hollow. "I wish that was it."

26

EMMANUEL WOULD COME TO make many mistakes throughout his life. He was not perfect; he never claimed to be. He lived, and learned, and owned up to his mistakes. But there was one mistake that haunted him, followed him, taunted him. It was a mistake that came with an insidious consequence. He gazed at Emma from across the table; his eyes filled with a haunting sadness. "One night, after leaving the cantina, I came home to an empty house. I searched every room. I even looked under the bed. I thought your mother was playing games. Then it occurred to me to check her drawers. All her clothes were gone. She had left me.

"It mortified me; I did not know where she could be. Night after night, I searched for her aimlessly. I thought I had lost her forever. Not knowing what else to do, I went to see your abuela. I told her what happened, and she gave me a glimpse of hope."

"What did abuela say?"

"She told me about a curandera."

Brianna raised her hand. "What's a curandera?" she asked.

"It's pronounced coo-rrran-de-rrra." His tongue flicked back and forth as he effortlessly rolled the *r*'s in the word. "It means woman healer. Many people in my culture believe that illness is linked with evil spirits and thus seek remedies from curanderas, who use simple herbs and holy water to cure physical, psychological, and even spiritual ailments.

I had dark and sunken bags under my eyes and my mother said I had been cursed. She said it explained my dramatic change in looks and horrible behavior. She gave me the address of a curandera that she said could break the curse.

"That night, I sought the home of the curandera. Along the way, I came across an old tiendita, a little corner store. The tiendita's rusty tin roof and blue wooden siding gave it a sort of authentic Mexican charm that drew me to it. In my drunken stupor, I abandoned looking for the address my mother gave me and stumbled up the cement steps that led to the tiendita's porch. Its rusty screen door was closed but not locked, and the door behind it was wide open. Through the screen door, I saw an old woman sweeping the floors. She looked at me as if she had been expecting me. 'Are you the curandera?' I asked.

"'Yes,' she replied. Her hair was long and unkempt, mostly white, peppered with a few strands of black. She wore a long, tattered dress. It was crimson red, like the color of old blood.

"I pulled the screen door open to let myself in. Candles flickered over the windowsills.

"'What brings you here?' she asked.

"I fell to my knees and told her I wanted my wife back. 'I would give anything for a second chance with her,' I pleaded.

"She wiped a tear from my face. Her fingers were rough like sandpaper and as cold as ice. She put her finger in her mouth, as if savoring my tears. 'I want to help you, but I can't get rid of a curse that easy,' she said. 'The curse needs a new home.'

"'What do you mean?' I asked.

"'Your wife will bear a daughter,' she replied. 'This unborn child must carry the burden of your sins if you want a chance with your wife.'

"Like a fool, I accepted her terms."

An eerie silence cloaked the room. Emma and Brianna exchanged looks.

He continued, "I thought the curandera's words couldn't possibly come to fruition. And yet they haunted me, so I returned with my mother the next night. *Surely there was something she could do*, I thought. We pulled up to the tiendita.

"'What are we doing?' my mother asked.

"'This is the place,' I replied.

"I'll never forget the deep stare my mother gave me. 'No, it isn't,' she said.

"I hung my head down. I failed again.

"'There is nothing we can do now. Let's go inside,' she said.

"The building didn't have the same charm it had the previous night. The tiendita was cloaked in darkness. Weeds had taken over the front porch through its cracks. Its screen door nailed shut. My mother ordered me to break it down.

"You broke down the door?" Emma asked.

"I didn't need to. The frame around the door was rotted. With just one pull, the screen door opened. The door let out a high-pitched squeak that seemed to drag on forever as I pushed it open. The smell of mold and mildew filled our nostrils when we stepped in. The room was pitch black except for a small beam of light that shone through a crack in the boarded windows in the back. I lit a match.

"A shiver ran down my spine. It looked nothing like it did the night before. Overgrown weeds covered in thorns crept in from the backyard through more cracks in the boarded windows giving it an eerie, haunted appearance. I looked up; the roof was sagging, the ceiling crumbling. It was a shell of what I remembered. I looked down; the floor was covered in dust, rat-droppings, and cobwebs—evidence that the building had long been abandoned. I could not believe my eyes. 'I saw her sweeping; she was sweeping the whole time,' I told my mother.

"I noticed my mother kneeling on the floor. She was holding something. 'What is it?' I asked.

"'Let's go,' she replied. 'Now.' She rushed to the car so fast that I struggled to keep up. In the car, she revealed what she had found."

He paused.

"It was a wedding photo of me and your mother. There were X's scratched over my eyes and over your mother's womb. My mother told me that the woman I saw was no curandera. She was a bruja."

Emma let out an audible gasp; her eyes bulged with disbelief.

He turned to Brianna. "Bruja is Spanish for witch. Brujas pray to spirits and practice witchcraft and black magic known as brujería, or witchery. But not all brujas are bad. Some practice white magic, a type of magic used for good or selfless purposes," he explained.

"Where did she get the photo?" Brianna asked. She appeared captivated by his story.

"I can only assume that I brought it to her, but I was drunk, and I truly don't remember. I don't think it matters much.

"My mother and I said nothing to each other the entire way back to her home. When we arrived, she ripped the photo into tiny pieces and ordered me to bring her a tin can. I sifted through a garbage bin outside, searching for a tin can, and brought it to her. She put the pieces of photo in the tin can. Then she lit a match, tossed it in the can, and burned the photo to ashes."

Emma and Brianna sat silently, their mouths agape.

"When I got home that night, your mother was waiting in the dining room. I told her what happened. I never went back to look for the curandera. Instead, from that day forward, we put all our faith in God and committed to serving him together for the rest of our lives."

To this day, he whole-heartedly believed it was God who brought Josephine back to him, and that it was God who transformed him into a new man, a better man, not the brujería. Josephine believed it, too. And when their first and only daughter was born, as the bruja predicted, they prayed every day and night of Emma's life that the curse would be broken. "From the day your mother and I welcomed you into the world, I promised I would do everything in my power to protect you." He bowed his head and wiped away his tears. "But I failed again. I'm so sorry, mija."

There was silence.

"I don't think I would have done anything differently," Emma said.

Emmanuel lifted his head.

"Me neither," Brianna added.

His eyes widened. "What do you mean?"

"You loved Mom so much that you were willing to do anything for a second chance. In some dark way, you just shared your love story with us."

He was still, his eyes wide open.

"Besides, I'm not here to judge you," Emma said. "That's what you always taught me, right?"

He could not believe his ears. He held on to this secret for so long. If this day ever came, he had imagined losing Emma forever. The argument he had with Josephine about her desire to move away for college came to mind. *She was right; we raised her right.* "Thank you, mija," he said.

Emma stood up and came around the table; she extended her arms toward him. He stood up and embraced her firmly. "You do not know what this means to me," he said, his eyes welling up with tears. He sniffled. "I know you're not as comfortable talking to me as you are with your mother, but she told me all about your dreams."

"Do you really think my dreams have anything to do with the bruja?"

He looked into her eyes. Although she wore makeup, he noticed her eyes appeared dark and sunken from the moment he walked in. He remembered his mother made the same observation about him, but he didn't have the heart to point it out to Emma. "I'm sure of it," he replied.

He also knew how stubborn Emma was. He knew because he recognized that she got the trait from him. No matter how much she needed it or what she was going through, he knew she wouldn't ask him for help. He reached for her hand and bestowed on it a gentle kiss. "Mija, please, let me help."

27

SHE GLOWERED AT BRIANNA with the same look an angry prisoner might give his prison guard. "May I have my phone, please?" Emma asked.

Brianna placed Emma's phone on the table.

"Why does Brianna have your phone?" Emma's mother asked.

"I lost a bet; it's not important." Although she knew her mother was no fool, she would say anything to keep her from worrying. "This is the image my doctor sent me today…This is what I wanted to talk to you about." She handed the phone to her father.

He stared at the image on the phone with squinted eyes. "Your doctor. Is he a religious counselor?"

She shook her head. "No, far from it. He's a clinical psychiatrist."

He furrowed his brow. "And it was him that made this connection with your dreams?"

"Yes, do you think it's a coincidence?"

"The seven deadly sins," he responded with no expression and heaved a heavy sigh. "It's no coincidence…you're dealing with a demon. Maybe more than one."

Emma's eyes grew wide, her mouth agape.

"It's the bruja's curse," he said with anger in his eyes. "I had suspected it when your mother told me you were seeing a doctor for your dreams. Now I'm certain of it."

"How can you be so sure?" she asked.

"Demons take pleasure in mocking and corrupting humans," he replied. "Their names... It's no coincidence."

"What do you mean? What about their names?"

He crossed his arms and leaned back in his seat. "Noah was the first farmer to plant a vineyard. He drank from its wine, got drunk, and passed out, naked, in his tent. That's gluttony.

"There is no mention of a 'Rico' in the Bible, but Rachel and Leah were sisters. Rachel was very envious of Leah for having children. That's envy.

"The book of Proverbs speaks of the lazy. They want much but get little, but those who work hard will prosper. At first Jonah fled to avoid doing the work that God had asked of him." His words flowed effortlessly, as if each one was carefully chosen and expertly delivered.

"What about Zack? I don't remember a Zack in the Bible," Emma said, hoping that her father was wrong.

"Zacchaeus was a chief tax collector. He was a rich man who was guilty of the love of money," he said.

Brianna turned to Emma. "You said he was literally counting money in your dream."

"Shall I continue?" he asked.

"Yes, of course," Emma replied nervously, fearing what he might reveal about John.

"In the book of John, John wrote of lust."

Instantly Emma recalled a Bible verse she memorized as a child. *For everything in the world — the lust of the flesh, the lust of the eyes, and the pride of life — comes not from the Father, but from the world.*

"Herod was a royal king. His heart became arrogant and

hardened with pride when he was deposed from his throne and stripped of his glory. That's pride.

"And last, the book of Samuel speaks of how David burned with anger against another a man. David said, 'As surely as the LORD lives, the man who did this must die!'"

She recalled the fire she saw in Davis's eyes that night at the Rumba Room, and at the fast-food restaurant, and many other times. "Wrath," she said with wide eyes.

"Does this mean there are seven demons?" Brianna asked.

"Based on the information in front of me, I believe so," he replied.

Emma fixated on his words. *I believe so.* "You really can't be certain, can you?"

"Short of witnessing them for myself, no. But it is my professional opinion—for what it's worth."

"How do you know all this?" Brianna asked, seemingly captivated by his extensive knowledge.

"I guess you can say I've had a lot of practice."

Emma recognized his words were an understatement. He had more than a lot of practice. He was highly respected in theological studies for both his experience and his credentials. While she was away at college, she often spoke to her mother on the phone. Her mother told her that her father was working on obtaining a higher education of his own. While she was away, he earned a bachelor's degree in theology. But when her mother told her he was pursuing a master's degree in theological studies, she chalked it up to her father trying to fill a hole left by her leaving. She never inquired about it, maybe even downplayed it. Even after he earned a PhD in theological studies, she never fully acknowledged his accomplishments. Perhaps it was time. She turned to Brianna. "Did you know my dad has a PhD in theological studies?"

His eyes grew wide; he appeared surprised by the acknowledgement. He straightened his posture.

"Wow, that's impressive!" Brianna exclaimed. "How did I not know that?"

Emma shrugged her shoulders. "I don't know, but you know now," she replied. She looked at her father, a smile tugged at the corners of her lips.

In that moment, his features transformed; a mixture of surprise and delight, a proud smile played on his lips in a humble yet gratified expression.

"OK, Dr. Dad, what should we do?" she asked light-heartedly to mask how utterly daunted she was by what her father had just revealed.

"We pray," he said instantly. He spoke firmly and with no hesitation.

She rolled her eyes. *Prayer hadn't worked for the last twenty-nine years. Why would it work now?* "Dad, think bigger!"

"More prayer!" he exclaimed.

She shook her head. "Dad!" Her patience was wearing thin.

"I'm serious, mija. Until today, we've kept the bruja's curse a secret. Your mother and I have been praying about this all alone. But the power of God is great, and His authority knows no boundaries." She gazed deep into his eyes, like windows to the soul. They revealed an unmistakable sincerity.

She sat quietly with her thoughts. It had been over a decade since she stepped foot in her father's church. She feared if she went back, her father would attempt to exert control over her life like he did when she was growing up. Going to her father's church was a boundary she was unwilling to cross. She turned to him. "I need to focus on my doctor's orders. I need to stay here and rest."

He nodded. "OK, I will organize a cadena de oración, a prayer chain." He stood up from his seat. "Ya nos vamos."

"We're leaving already?" her mother asked.

"Yes, I need to prepare," he replied. "We will start the prayer chain early Sunday morning." He turned to Emma. "Mija, just keep doing what your doctor ordered and stay strong in your faith. I'll take care of the prayer chain."

"You hardly touched your food, angel."

She looked down at her plate as she searched for an excuse to appease her mother. "It got cold. I'll re-heat it and eat after you leave." It was an excuse that even *she* wouldn't buy. She stood from the table. "I'll walk you to the door."

"Angel, can I just ask you for one thing?"

She nodded. "Yes, Mom. What is it?"

Her mother held out her Bible. "Can you hold on to this for me?"

"Why?" she asked.

"Because I'll feel better if I know you have it," her mother replied.

The boundaries Emma had established applied to her father's church, but never to her faith. At no point did she hold a grudge against religion, biblical teachings, or God. She only resented how her father used it to control her growing up. She smiled, her expression adorned with a subtle hint of home, and took the Bible.

28

IS HAND EMERGED FROM the glass, waving goodbye. "Get some rest and don't worry about a thing!" Emmanuel shouted.

"It's freezing," Josephine said. "Close the window."

"Sorry," he replied. With the swift press of a button, the window glided upwards, shielding them from the world outside. There was silence as he stared off at the road ahead.

"What's wrong?" Josephine asked.

He glanced at her before returning his gaze to the road. "The demons…They could still be after her."

"You mean in her dreams?"

"No." He glanced at her again. "I mean in real life. Demons don't have direct access to the minds, thoughts, or dreams of believers." His words rang with an air of absolute certainty. Since learning about Emma's dreams, he had given much thought and time researching demons and dreams in theology. There were no examples in the Bible of a believer whose dreams were the working of a demon or demons. And, in his years of experience, he had witnessed demonic powers play out in countless ways, but never had he seen a demon act through a dream. "But that doesn't mean demons can't affect our thoughts and dreams through secondary means."

She shook her head. "That's not possible. Emma doesn't have any contact with them anymore, and half of them live on the other side of the country."

The car came to a halt at a traffic light. He turned to her. "You know demons can move from one host to another. All they need to do is to be in the same room together."

She shot him an incredulous look. "What, do you think they all booked a one-way ticket to Chicago?" She scoffed. "Even if they somehow crossed paths, Emma doesn't have contact with any of them."

"What about Davis?"

"They broke up."

"When?"

"I don't know—maybe two or three months ago, before the dreams started. Besides, you remember Davis. He was so sweet, such a gentleman, and he was a police officer. Emma is not in danger from him."

He let out a deep sigh. "I'm sure you're right. That's why I didn't bring it up with Emma. No need for unnecessary worry. She's going through enough." He returned his gaze to the road.

She reached for his hand. "So, what's your plan?"

"It's my turn to host the Vision meeting. I'll lead the prayer chain there…I'll call the pastors today to prepare them." Emmanuel, a senior pastor, was a member of a group called Pastors of Vision International that met once a month. Their monthly agenda consisted of pastor testimonials, special speakers, and special topics. It was an exclusive group. Only affiliated pastors were welcome. Anyone not directly affiliated with the group could come as a special guest of an affiliated pastor under the condition that the guest was spiritually strong.

"Will it be enough?" Josephine asked with a tone of concern. "Not everyone always shows up, right?"

"I'm going to confess to them. I will call them individually. They will come." He thought about the fragile state he saw his daughter in. He had never seen her look so thin. And he saw the suffering in her eyes. Although he and Josephine had always prayed for the curse to be lifted, he always wondered if the curse ever really existed. Except for having a single daughter, he had no concrete evidence of the curse's existence. But he had now witnessed it for himself. It was written all over Emma. He could see the evil at play. It was the curse; he was certain of it. And he was just as certain that, with an army of God's soldiers behind him, he could help. He had no doubt that his fellowship of pastors would be there for him in his time of need, just as he had been for them many times before.

"What will you be praying for, exactly?" Josephine asked. "Emma's health?"

"We will pray for an end to this generational curse," he replied. "Our prayers will be for Emma's every step and thought to be guided by God. We're going to attack this demonio from all sides!" he exclaimed in a raised voice. With the push of a button, the window glided down.

"Emmanuel, it's freezing! What are you doing?"

He extended one arm out the window, pumping his fist in the air as his other hand maintained a steady grip on the steering wheel. The adrenaline rushing through his body acted as a layer of protection against the frigid air. He shouted at the top of his lungs, his voice booming with commanding authority, "¡En el santo nombre de Jesucristo, Satanás no ganará!"

29

THE AROMA OF BASIL, ROSEMARY, garlic, and oregano filled the air, captivating Emma's senses. She lifted her nose, inhaled deeply, and followed the enchanting fragrance to the kitchen. A bouquet of fresh basil lay atop the kitchen island. She picked up a stem and gently pressed the bright green leaves against her nose to breathe in the plant's sweet and pungent aroma. "I can't believe it's dinnertime already."

"Well, that's what happens when you spend your whole day napping," Brianna replied with a closed-lip smile. "Go get comfortable. I placed some pajamas in the powder room for you to change into."

"Thank you. I can't believe I didn't pack any."

"No worries. You've got a lot going on."

She stepped into the powder room; a crystal pendant hung over the sink glimmering like a rare gemstone. It wasn't there before. But then again, it had been some time since she had been over. A pair of meticulously folded pajamas lay atop the sink counter. Although she preferred pajama pants and a long-sleeved top over pajama shorts and a short-sleeved top, it would have to do. She lifted her arms to remove her turtleneck blouse, careful not to disrupt the bandage on her scalp.

She stepped out of the powder room. A lot changed in the home, besides the crystal pendant, since she had been over. They both lived busy lives, she told herself. And although they didn't spend as much time together as they used to, their friendship was as solid as ever.

She looked over her shoulder at the front door, constructed of four panels of frosted glass in a black steel frame. It was one thing that hadn't changed. Brianna designed it herself.

Emma strode through the dining room, where a crystal vase containing a dozen fresh pink roses took center stage on the dining room table. She had celebrated more than enough occasions with Brianna over the years to know that pink roses were her favorite. On the wall hung two white photo frames. In one photo, Brianna and her parents stood in front of a grand piano, dressed in formal wear under an elegant chandelier. It was one of many formal photos Brianna had taken with her parents during their time vacationing on cruises over the years. In the other photo, Brianna wore a black cap and gown and held a bouquet of pink roses. Next to her stood Emma, arms over shoulders with Brianna, the teeth from their wide smiles in full display.

She stepped through the dining room and looked into the kitchen. There was no sign of Brianna. She opened the back door. "Brie, where are you?" she shouted.

"I'm in the pantry!"

She shut the door and headed towards the kitchen. The pantry door next to the refrigerator blended seamlessly into the cabinets. She stepped toward the pantry. "I didn't know there was a door here." She grazed her hand over the door. "I thought it was part of the cabinetry."

"It's new...Neat, huh?" Brianna replied. "And I can use it as a panic room if I ever need to."

Panic room? That's strange, Emma thought. Brianna never mentioned wanting a panic room before. She lived in a safe neighborhood, after all. It's her home, though. She chose not to question it. She turned to the sound of rumbling; a large pot filled with water boiled on the stovetop. "What's for dinner?"

"We're having angel hair pasta with made-from-scratch spicy marinara, meatballs, and garlic bread," Brianna replied. "And yes, this meal fully intends to put you into a food coma."

"Can I help?"

Brianna pointed to a pan simmering on the stovetop. "The marinara sauce could use some more fresh tomatoes."

Her eyes darted around the kitchen. She spotted the tomatoes on the cutting board on top of the kitchen island but no knife. "What happened to the knife block?" she asked.

"Knife blocks are for amateurs; they dull your knives. Grab the knife from the top drawer," she pointed toward the lower cabinets. "If you invest in one good knife, you'll never need a second."

"Duly noted." She pulled the knife from the drawer. *They practically slice themselves*, she thought as the knife cut through the tomato.

"When you're done, don't put the knife in the dishwasher. Rinse it off and put it back in the drawer, please."

Emma turned to her. "Let me guess...because it dulls the knife?"

"Exactly."

She rinsed the knife and returned it to the drawer. As Brianna plated the meals, Emma poured them each a glass of white wine before taking a seat at the dining table.

Brianna placed Emma's dish in front of her.

Her eyes grew large; her mouth watered at the sight and smell of the steamy bowl of angel hair noodles. "This looks amazing. Shall we dig in?" Emma asked.

There was silence.

Although her question was mostly rhetorical, she expected a response. She turned to Brianna; she had a look of concern. "What's the matter?"

"I have something I need to tell you."

Emma examined Brianna's expressionless face. She had seen it before and could predict that whatever she had to say would not be good. She crossed her arms tightly over her chest and braced herself for the worst.

30

ER BODY SHOOK, STARTLED from the clanking that came from her ceramic bowl slamming down atop the marble top dining table. The bowl shattered; steam rose from the marble tabletop covered in angel hair pasta. "I'm sorry, I'll clean that up," Brianna said.

Emma stood up.

"Sit, I got it," Brianna ordered. She stepped toward the back door and lifted the shade to look outside.

"What's the matter?" Emma asked. "What startled you?"

"I thought I saw a shadow," Brianna replied, still looking outside. "There's nothing there." She turned and pulled a chair out across from Emma. "Listen, I ran into Herod a few days ago. Does that name ring a bell?" she asked, scooting in her chair.

Emma's face went pale. She pushed her bowl away. "I'm not hungry anymore."

As much as Brianna's encounter with Herod weighed on her, she immediately regretted her decision to tell Emma. "Em, please eat. You really should eat." She pushed the bowl of pasta back toward Emma.

She stared at the steam rising from the pasta in front of her. Her eyes suddenly widened at the realization of yet another decision she regretted that night. *Scuzzi's*. She slapped her forehead with a groan, cursing herself for forgetting the significance of the meal she prepared. "I'm a jackass, Em. Here I am, serving you Italian food like an idiot."

Emma sat quietly with her arms folded. "Did you speak to him?"

Her shoulders drooped as the weight of the conversation she started descended upon her. "At first, no. I acted as though I didn't see him, but he approached me."

"What did he say?"

"He asked how you were doing. I said you were well and that you had moved on." It was what she thought Emma would want her to say. But from her perspective, it was a half-truth. Emma had indeed moved on but wasn't well by any stretch of her imagination. Before Emma's dreams started, she had become withdrawn. Quiet. In her eyes, she was a shell of her former strong, independent self. She missed the old Emma, the one she could talk openly with. The one she could be real with. The one she didn't have to tip-toe around. The one that didn't shy away from constructive criticism because she knew it was coming from a place of love because she knew it would make her better. She missed their frequent dinners, their check-ins, their girl's nights. But Emma had become distant. And over time, Brianna learned not to question her because questioning her just made things worse.

"I can always count on you to say the right things," Emma said, the corners of her lips lifting to reveal a bittersweet smile tinged with sorrow.

Aware of Emma's fragile state, she carefully considered how much more she should reveal about the encounter. She exhaled audibly. "I wish that were all…He told me he left his job at your firm a year ago because, even after all that time, seeing you in the office was still too painful."

She paused.

"He looked so sad."

There was silence.

She looked at Emma. Her eyes were closed, and her face was as white as a sheet. Her hands shook even as she clutched the edge of the table with a tremendous grip. "I'm here, Em. Take all the time you need," she said.

More silence.

Emma opened her eyes. "I didn't know he left the firm. I hadn't seen him in ages, but I just figured we were both avoiding running into each other."

Brianna stood up and walked around the table; she placed her hand on Emma's shoulder. "I'm sorry I didn't tell you sooner. I didn't want to add to your stress."

She dropped her head. "I know you were just looking out for me, like you always do."

Brianna leaned forward, extending her arms, surrounding her in a tender embrace. "I'll love you forever, my friend," she said, fighting back tears. "OK, enough of this. Let's eat!" she exclaimed releasing Emma from her embrace. She had seen her cry once today. She had no intention of letting it happen again.

"Did he say where he's working now?"

Brianna tilted her head and exhaled as she contemplated what good could come from her knowing that information. "He said he was working in the technology department at Global Public Relations."

Emma leaned in, her glass bumped into the table and teetered precariously before tumbling over. She stared off into the distance without blinking.

"What's wrong?" Brianna asked.

She held her trembling hand to her face. "That's where Zack went to work," she whispered.

Brianna's eyes grew wide. "Are you sure?" she asked.

Emma bobbed her head at a snail's pace.

Perhaps it was a coincidence, but the revelation was too much for her to process for one night. She looked at her phone. "It's almost 9…You need to rest. Let's talk about this tomorrow." She reached to clear Emma's untouched plate. "Not even a bite?"

"I'm not hungry. It's not your fault. I'm just not."

Brianna exhaled deeply. "OK, let's get you to bed." She reached for Emma's hand.

"Wait, there's something I've been meaning to mention. I should tell you now, in case I forget."

"What is it?" Brianna asked.

"I was talking to Dr. Clark about how you showed up in some of my dreams. He helped me realize that the parts of my dream where you show up were likely based on memories."

Brianna raised her brow, her curiosity peaked. "OK."

"He also said my dreams might be trying to warn me about something."

She nodded. "Makes sense."

"I got to wondering if maybe you were showing up in my dreams because you were trying to warn me about something?"

Brianna's eyes widened.

"You know, given your magical empathetic powers that transcend distance and what not."

Brianna cleared her throat. "I need to use the bathroom. I'll be right back."

She stepped into the powder room and locked the door behind her. To say that she was surprised by Emma's question would be an understatement. She needed to think. Fast. She crossed her arms tightly on her chest and paced the short length of the room. She could always be honest with Emma in the past. Why not now? It was Emma who had asked, after all. It wasn't like she had brought it up on her own. Still, she had caused Emma enough stress for one night. Was this really the right time? And if the procedure worked, would what she had to say even matter? Or, in the long run, would it hurt more than help? She opened the door, stepped out of the powder room, and inhaled deeply; her mind scrambled, tangled with what she should or should not say.

Emma faced her. "What is it?"

31

SHE DIDN'T EXPECT ANYONE but wasn't completely surprised when Dharma announced someone's arrival. Brianna watched her home's security footage on her phone. Someone was in the front yard. Although she could not see the visitor's face through the darkness of the night, she recognized the visitor's silhouette and posture. "Shit," she muttered. She hoped it would not come to this, but given past recent events, she had prepared for it, at least to some extent. She had made some preparations but knew she could never be fully ready. Whatever her plan, she knew she had to act fast. *I need to hide her,* she thought.

"Are you expecting anyone?" Emma asked.

"Go into the pantry and wait there until I come back to tell you it's OK to come out," she said. Her words were quick and deliberate.

"Why?"

She reached for Emma's hand.

Emma dug her heels into the ground like a child being dragged away from a playground.

"I don't have time to explain right now, but I promise I'll

explain later." She summoned her physical strength to force Emma into the pantry.

"Brie, if you want this person to leave, if you plan on opening that door, I should be with you."

"Don't worry; I have no intention of opening that door." On her tiptoes, she reached up to the top shelf of the pantry. She handed Emma her phone. "Just in case you need it. I'll take it back after I deal with this."

Emma glowered at her as she took her phone.

"If I need you, I'll let you know." She closed the pantry door behind her and inhaled deeply. *You got this,* she thought.

"Open up! Let me in!" a male voice shouted.

"Go away!" she exclaimed through the intercom.

"I know she's in there! Parking her car in the back alley was a rookie move! I just want to talk to her!"

"You are not welcome here!" she fired back. She paced the length of the room, her movements measured and rhythmic as she deliberated her next steps. The pounding on the door intensified. "This is a quiet neighborhood. Someone is bound to call the cops! Please, leave!" she exclaimed.

She watched from her phone as the unwelcome visitor leaned in to stare directly into the doorbell camera. He placed his index finger over his lips. "Oh, you're right, I better get inside then," he whispered with an eerie hiss.

She watched from her phone as he picked up a landscape rock from the ground; her eyes widened. She braced herself for what he would inevitably do next. She covered her head with her hands and looked away from the door. The crackling sound of glass shattering masked her instinctive scream.

"Problem solved," he said with a wide, sinister grin. He stumbled into the home. The scent of alcohol and marijuana consumed the room.

In a flash, the matter escalated from one involving an

unwelcome guest to one involving an intruder. She looked out into her front yard through the shattered glass of the front door. The intruder parked on her perfectly manicured grass, adding insult to injury after the destruction he caused to her home.

Her eyes filled with deep loathing as they narrowed in on him. "Get. Out. You are not welcome here." She spoke in a no-nonsense tone that she had used with him before.

He looked over her shoulder.

She turned to see what had caught his attention—*the sofa bed.*

"Aw, are you having a sleepover? That's adorable!" he exclaimed. His grin was like a predator's—full of sharp edges and evil intent.

"Come on, Em, did you really think I wouldn't find you?!" he shouted as he crept across the room; his words dripped with malice. "Where else would you be? You have no one!"

She leaned in toward him; her nostrils flared as anger ran through her veins. "She has me," she said as she tapped on her puffed-out chest. "And I won't allow you to put a finger on her!" Her voice boomed with authority.

He rolled his eyes and slithered toward the dining room. "Brie, I know you never liked me," he said as his eyes darted around the room like a predator searching for its prey.

That wasn't true. She *loathed* him. And not because he had come between her and Emma. She could accept never speaking to Emma again if she knew she was happy. She loathed him for the destruction he had caused Emma, mentally, emotionally, and physically. Everyone has at least one thing they wish they could change about their past. Hers was getting Emma on that cruise ship.

He continued, "But that's OK, because I never liked you, either."

Her eyes bore into his with a seething anger, unable to contain her hatred. "Don't call me Brie." Her hands clenched and unclenched by her side. "You haven't earned that privilege."

He grinned an unsettling grin, stretching all too wide as if it belonged to something inhuman.

He turned to the dining room and locked eyes on something. She couldn't tell what. "Nice vase," he said with a menacing smirk.

She knew him well enough to know he wasn't one to pay compliments. "Davis, don't!"

32

SHE DRUMMED HER FINGERS on the cool marble floor as time dragged on. She tried to remain calm, but her mind raced with worry. *I should have heard from her by now. What if she's in trouble?* A part of her resented Brianna for asking her to wait when she could be out there with her, but she could think of countless times in recent years when Brianna respected her wishes to stand down. The least she could do was respect Brianna's wishes in return.

Her ears perked up at the sound of muffled voices coming from outside the pantry door. *Who is that? Is she dating someone I don't know about?* She pressed her ear to the door. The sound of a loud crash interrupted her thoughts.

She cracked the door open and peeked outside. Her eyes widened at the sight before her. *I must be dreaming*, she thought. She looked up at the solid white ceiling. Her eyes darted back and forth as she thought about her next move. *I need to call the police.* She dialed 9-1-1 and held the phone to her ear.

There was silence.

Her gaze fixed on the phone's screen. Her eyes widened. *No signal.*

She peeked out the door as Davis continued to make his way through the dining room.

"That's enough! Not another step!" Brianna shouted.

He grinned in pure delight. "Oh, I must be getting warmer!" he exclaimed, rubbing his palms together as if preparing for a feast.

"I'm calling the police," Brianna said. She pulled out her phone.

He turned around and faced her. "You'll do no such thing," he said in a deep and venomous whisper. With a forceful blow, he knocked the phone out of her hand, causing it to shatter on the marble floor.

Emma peeked out the door. His back was to her. She crawled out of the pantry, being cautious not to be noticed, and positioned herself behind the kitchen island. From there, she observed Brianna step back and touch the corner of a photo frame on the wall. *What is she doing?* Emma thought. She observed Brianna lift the frame by its edge while the sound of mechanical whirring filled the air. She watched Brianna pull a gun from a safe concealed in the wall behind the photo frame.

She pointed the gun at Davis, her hands trembling. "Leave," she said in a firm and commanding tone.

He raised his hands. "OK, all you had to do was ask," he replied. He stepped back through the dining room in the same direction he entered.

Her gaze fixed on him as he crossed her path, her gun pointing at him, following his every move.

Hands still raised, he stopped with his back to her.

"Keep movi—"

In a quick motion, he leaned forward in a bow and kicked his leg out from behind, knocking the gun from her hand. It may have seemed like an impossible move for an intoxicated person to pull off had she not seen him execute it, even in his most inebriated state, many times before. At its core, it was a modified version of a basic salsa move.

The gun slid across the marble floor, deep under the dining room table. Brianna fell to her knees, groaning as if she had the wind knocked out of her. He stood over her. "That was cute," he said, petting her head. Using his index finger, he pushed her to the ground and narrowly missed hitting her head against the edge of the dining table.

"Em! Come out, come out, wherever you are!" he shouted. As if trying to stifle laughter, he put his hand over his mouth and said, "Your friend needs you…" He stepped toward the kitchen.

Emma army crawled across the kitchen floor, her knees no longer able to withstand the direct contact with the hard marble floor. She opened the cabinet drawer and reached for Brianna's signature knife. Holding the knife in her hand, she emerged from behind the kitchen island.

Surprise flickered across his face. "Oh shit, where the fuck did you come from?" He spoke slurred and slow, making his words muddled and difficult to understand.

"Get out, Davis." She spoke in a commanding tone. Her words rang out clearly and forcefully as she gripped the knife within sight.

"Awe, come on, Em. How many times have we been through this?" he asked in a melodic tone; its sinister cadence echoed through the room.

She locked eyes with him, unshaken.

He paced the length of the dining room, stepping over Brianna's motionless body. "Nothing's going to change. You're going to cry, then leave, then come running right back, just like you always do. As you should, because you're mine. You've belonged to me since the day we met; you know that."

He paused.

"Remember? I made that clear when we were on the ship." He smiled and blinked a slow blink. "But you caught me by surprise this time. I wasn't expecting to come drag you back on my own."

She looked to the floor at Brianna; her chest rose and fell in shallow heaves. She looked back at him. "You're nothing but a bully," she said. Her gaze filled with a smoldering resentment that carried over into her tone.

He cackled. "What are we, in grade school?" He took a step toward her.

"We may as well be," she replied. Her voice grew increasingly louder and firmer. "I won't allow you or anyone else to hurt me or my friends."

"That's ENOUGH, Emma!"

With her head tilted, she gazed at him as if he were a baby deer. "You don't intimidate me. And you for damn sure can't force me to do anything I don't want to do." Her voice was steady and unwavering. "Now. Get. OUT."

His jaw clenched; his brows narrowed together, forming a deep clench on his forehead. "What is your dysfunction!?!" he shouted.

Dysfunction.

Dysfunction.

Dysfunction.

The word echoed in her mind. She shot him a withering look, her eyes filled with a deep-seated resentment. "It was you," she said. "It was you in the car that nearly ran me over outside of Dr. Clark's office."

He scoffed.

"You were chasing me." She shook her head in disbelief.

She looked through him. "It was you inside the building. It was you outside the building. It was you this whole time."

He shook his head. "There she is again, delusional Emma. That's my girl."

A silence hung in the air as Emma glared at him.

He covered his face with his hands as he expelled a deep, growl-like moan. "OK, fine!" he shouted. "Guilty as charged!"

"You made me think I was going insane!"

He stepped toward her. "Don't act surprised." He shook his head. "What, did you really think I wasn't going to be watching you?"

She held up the knife and stepped toward him. "Leave!" she shouted.

"Or what? You're going to attack me with your big knife?" He placed his palms on his cheeks. "Ooh, I'm so scared." He scoffed. "Come on, you know you could never hurt me."

"If only I could say the same." Her eyes narrowed into angry slits with a cold and unforgiving expression. "I'm in control, Davis. Leave, or I'm calling the police."

He continued to pace, his steps quick and agitated. "And you wonder why I don't listen? Enough with the empty threats, Emma!" His eyes homed in on the gun underneath the table.

"Dharma, send the police and the paramedics," Emma commanded.

"OK, got it. Sending the police and emergency services to 4679 Virginia Street," Dharma announced.

He looked at her with a cold, unamused stare. "Dharma, cancel!" he shouted. He reached under the table, his body just halfway under.

"Sorry, but your voice is not associated with this account," Dharma announced.

He slammed his head under the table; it shook in his haste to get back up.

He glowered at Emma. "Dharma, CANCEL!" He bellowed at the top of his lungs.

"Sorry, but your voice is not associated with this account," Dharma announced again.

Emma took a deep breath to prevent her laughter from

escaping. "Try repeating it, but this time try even louder. Maybe that will get Dharma to recognize your voice."

With a piercing gaze, he locked eyes with her. She had seen that gaze many times before. It was fierce, his eyes flashing with anger and outrage. "You fucked up for the last time, Emma!" he shouted. He turned to run.

"Coward!" she fired back.

As he fled in his vehicle, an eerily familiar sound of tires screeching pierced through her ears. It triggered another realization. *It was him in the parking garage, too.* Her attention turned to Brianna. Glass from the shattered vase and pink roses surrounded the area of the floor where she lay. "Brianna! Are you OK?"

She opened her eyes. They appeared glassy and unfocused. "Yes, I think so, it's just my head, it hurts…it hurts a lot," she replied in a soft whisper.

She breathed a heavy sigh of relief. *Thank God, she's responsive.* "Don't move; an ambulance is on the way." She reached for her hand.

"Did the police get Davis?"

"You were knocked unconscious before you could dial 9-1-1, but I got him to leave." She stroked Brianna's hair. A warm, wet sensation clung to her fingertips. She examined her bloody hand and forced herself to appear calm.

The paramedics stormed in.

"How did you get him to leave?" Brianna asked.

"I'll tell you all about it later. Right now, let's focus on you, OK?" She leaned in and kissed her gently on her forehead. "You're all that matters right now."

The paramedics delicately placed her on the stretcher. The floor beneath where she lay revealed a pool of blood.

"What happened?" the paramedic asked.

"She fell; she was pushed, and she hit her head on the floor," Emma responded, her voice quivering with sadness.

"We're transporting her to Northwestern Memorial Hospital," the paramedic said. "You can check up on her there."

A police officer entered just as the paramedics left. He stopped at the foyer. "It looks like someone came in here and made some major damage." He looked at Emma. "What happened?"

"My ex-boyfriend came here uninvited," Emma replied. "My friend and I tried to get him to leave, and he became violent."

He pulled his phone from his pant pocket and aimed its camera lens at the shattered glass in the foyer. There was a click. He turned and paced the length of the living room. His movements were measured and deliberate as he assessed the scene. At the far end of the living room, he picked up two pieces of shard and held them up to the light. The shard had fractured cleanly in a geometric shape. "It's not glass. Where did these come from?" he asked.

He followed the trail of shards to the dining room as he maintained his gaze on the floor.

Suddenly, he stopped.

His eyes widened at the gruesome sight of blood pooled on the floor.

He unclipped a hand-held police radio from his holster belt. "I'm going to need a crime scene unit," he ordered. His attention turned to Emma. "I know your friend is being taken care of. What about you? Are you OK?" He spoke slowly and calmly.

She nodded. "I'm fine. It was only my friend who was hurt. Are we done here? I'd like to get to the hospital to be with her." Her words tumbled out in a torrent.

"Are you sure you're OK?" He held up his phone and positioned its camera lens toward her. There was a click. He turned the phone screen and extended it towards her. "Does this look like a picture of someone who's OK?" the officer asked.

She looked at the image on the phone. Her eyebrows raised; her mouth cracked.

"Looks like you've sustained several injuries over various periods of time," the officer said.

"How could you know that?"

"I can tell by the colors of your bruises." He pointed at her wrists. "Purple, black." He pointed at her left arm. "Blue, yellow." He pointed at her collarbone. "Green, red." He shook his head. "That doesn't happen all at once. Your bruises are in various stages of the healing process."

She inspected her arms. *How could I have been so blinded?* She recalled Dr. Clark asking her to wipe the makeup from under her eye back in his office. "I'll be right back," she said.

She stepped into the powder room. In a rush, she dampened a tissue and wiped her face. She leaned into her reflection in the mirror. The skin below her eyes had a yellow-green tinge to it. *They're bruises.*

She returned to the living room.

The officer flashed his phone in front of her again. "Is this your ex-boyfriend?" he asked.

"Yes, that's him." She glanced at the officer. "Do you know him?"

He nodded. "I know of him. It's not like we're best buds or anything."

He paused.

"Alright, I think he's an arrogant asshole. But keep that between us. Anyway, he was just pulled over near the area for speeding and suspicion of drunk driving."

She exhaled a sigh of relief, but her thoughts remained with Brianna.

"Go with your friend," the officer said. "Just call me when you get a minute. I'll need a statement from you to file a separate report for the injuries you sustained." He handed her his card.

"I will. Thank you," she replied.

"And don't worry about your ex-boyfriend. No one is above the law, not even law enforcement."

33

A S SHE RAN FROM her car to the parking lot, she pushed her body to its absolute limits, feeling her lungs burn with each shallow breath. She didn't stop running until she reached the nurse's station inside the hospital. She gasped for air. "I'm looking for my friend, Brianna Brown. She came in with a head injury," Emma said as she struggled to catch her breath.

There was silence.

A nurse sat hunched over her computer screen; her fingers flew over her keyboard at lightning speed.

"Hello, can you hear me?"

"Eighth floor," the nurse replied.

Eighth floor? The intensive care unit is on the eighth floor, she thought. Her mind raced with worry. She sprinted toward the elevator. Her heart raced and her palms grew sweaty, a sign of her growing anxiety. She tapped her toes incessantly as she waited for the elevator to arrive.

From the corner of her eye, she spotted the stairwell. Ignoring the throbbing incision on her scalp, she sprinted up the stairs without stopping to rest.

On the eighth floor, she spotted a nurse and strategically placed herself in her path. "Hi, excuse me, I'm looking for Brianna Brown," she panted.

The nurse smiled. "I'm headed to her room now. Follow me."

She followed the nurse through a corridor to a set of steel double doors. Above the doors was a sign the read *Neurosurgery Unit*. Emma surveyed the familiar area.

"She's right in there," the nurse said. She pointed to the room just ahead of them. "You can go in as soon I'm done checking in on her."

Emma wiped the sweat from her brow and placed her hands on her knees as she tried to catch her breath. A woman in a white lab coat stood just a few feet away, her gaze fixed on an electronic tablet.

"How is she?" Emma asked.

She tilted her head in Emma's direction. "She's in good condition. Fortunately, her blood clotted as expected, which prevented her from sustaining severe blood loss from her fall," the doctor said. "We're keeping her overnight for observation."

Her blood clotted as expected? Emma's brow furrowed in confusion. "But there was so much blood."

"Well, over twenty percent of the blood flowing from the heart goes up to the cerebrum," she explained. "Even minor injuries to the scalp and face can make for a gruesome scene."

Emma closed her eyes. A look of relief washed over her. *It looked worse than it was.*

"Do her parents know she's here?" Emma asked.

"They've been contacted. They are out of town but are arranging a flight back and should be here in the morning."

Emma peeked through the window of the room door.

"She's going to be asleep for a while, but you're welcome to pull up a chair and stay with her overnight," the doctor said. "Someone will be in later to check in on her."

As Emma stood outside the hospital room, she surveyed her surroundings with a mix of familiarity and confusion. Having been there just the day before, she knew they reserved the eighth floor for the neurosurgery and intensive care unit. They treated most head injuries in the emergency room, on the first floor. *If her condition isn't serious, why did they bring her up to neurosurgery?* she thought.

The nurse emerged from the room. "You're welcome to go on in," she said, holding the door open.

Emma stepped inside and laid eyes on Brianna; she was sleeping. Her body appeared frail, not the fit, muscular appearance she usually displayed. The needles piercing through her wrists and arms were a stark reminder of the events that had just unfolded.

She spotted a blue upholstered chair in the corner of the room. She sighed. *That must be where I'm sleeping.* She took a seat and placed her thumb and index finger on the bridge of her nose as she sobbed, consumed with guilt.

Time stood still as she waited for her to awaken. With each passing moment, her eyelids grew heavier, her head bobbing and snapping back up as she fought to stay awake.

She heard a faint whisper. "Em."

Assuming she had succumbed to her exhaustion, she looked up at the bright fluorescent hospital room ceiling lights.

"Em," the voice whispered again.

She opened her eyes fully and turned to Brianna. "You're awake!" She rushed to her bedside and gently reached for her hand. "Can you move your fingers?" she asked.

Brianna tapped her fingers on Emma's palm. "Yes, why?" she whispered.

"I don't know. That's what people ask when they are in this type of situation."

Brianna giggled, her laugh barely audible.

She's going to be OK. Thank God, she thought. "I'm so sorry, Brie. This is all my fault."

She scoffed. "You know I'm tough. I would do it all over again. It's no big deal."

She paused.

"But—"

She paused again.

"Is it really over with you and him? I mean, is it going to stick this time?"

Emma dropped her head. Memories of her attempts to break up with Davis and the brief moments of joy that convinced her to stay flooded her mind. She knew she deserved better. So, occasionally, she built up the courage to leave him. But as hard as she tried, he wouldn't let go. Tragically, a part of her didn't want to let go, either. So, for reasons she could not understand or explain, she stayed until she could build up enough courage to leave him again. And the cycle continued. She thought back to a conversation with Dr. Clark; she lifted her head. "I talked to Dr. Clark about the abuse I endured from Davis. I questioned how I could allow myself to stay in such a dangerous situation. Dr. Clark told me I was in the FOG, and that it was possible to get out of it. I couldn't fathom what he meant, but I get it now."

"What did he mean?"

"Remember that time we drove to Utica to celebrate your twenty-fifth birthday? It was late, and the fog was so thick, we couldn't see, and we had to pull over."

She nodded.

"As hard as we tried, we couldn't even see what was right in front of us."

"I remember; it was terrifying."

"I was *living* in the FOG, the fear, obligation, and guilt that Davis used to manipulate me, and control me. And I got so used to it I lost sight of who I was and everything that was important to me." Emma watched as Brianna lay silent with her gaze on the ceiling. She didn't say anything, but the tears in her eyes revealed her overwhelming joy. She continued, "Remember when we were in middle school, and I got my first pair of prescription glasses?"

"Yes, I remember threatening to beat up anyone who made fun of you," she replied with a smile. "And I remember you singing 'A Whole New World' from *Aladdin* on repeat."

Emma chuckled. "Anyway, before I got my glasses, I didn't know it was humanly possible to see things so clearly. With glasses, I could see things far away that I had never seen before. Even things near me became clearer. It's surreal, but that's how I feel now."

Her lips curved upward into a smile. "I can see your light again," she said unable to contain her tears. "I've missed it."

"I know; I'm sorry. But I assure you, I will never dim my light again."

"I believe you. You're such a good person, Em. You deserve the best." She wiped away her tears. "I'm so happy for you." She looked at Emma, her eyes radiating a soft glow of warmth and unconditional love.

Emma met her gaze with a silent look of understanding. "Looks like someone is getting softer with age, after all." She glanced at her phone. "You should get some rest; the doctor insisted on keeping you overnight for observation, but we can go home first thing in the morning." She crossed the room and took a seat on her makeshift bed.

Brianna turned to her side, facing her. "Hey, Em," she whispered.

"Yes, Brie?"

"Have you thought more about whether any of the other guys in your dreams are connected?"

"No. Why?" Emma asked.

Brianna lay in silence, her eyes fixed on Emma.

"What is it?"

"Davis reeked of weed," Brianna said.

"Don't remind me." She inhaled deeply. "I can still smell it. I'm going to have your entire house deodorized."

She raised herself into a seated position on the bed. "You don't get it."

"Get what?" Emma asked, her head tilted.

"What if Jonah is White Whale?"

Her eyes widened; she hadn't considered it but fought back the urge to discuss the possibility. "Interesting. I'll look into it. Now get some rest," she said, masking her interest.

Brianna reclined on her back and closed her eyes.

Emma reached for her phone, her eyes still wide and thoughts racing from the possibility Brianna had planted. She swiftly scrolled through Jonah's social media, searching for anything that might confirm Brianna's suspicion. She didn't know Jonah as White Whale, but could this be another example of demons using biblical names as mockery? Or just another coincidence?

There's nothing here, she thought. In fact, there wasn't much activity on his social media account at all. She continued to search and came across a familiar face. *Jonah's roommate.* She clicked on his profile and browsed through his posts. Unlike Jonah, he was very active on social media, posting photos of everything from his dog to his lunch. Her eyes grew wide as she homed in on a photo of him and Jonah and the caption underneath. *#Roomies #Whitewhale.* She covered her mouth to mask her gasp.

She sat motionless, her mind struggling to comprehend the significance of what she had just learned. She recalled her father telling her that demons can move from one host to another. *What if Noah had a demon and it was passed to John somewhere along the way, then to Herod?* She imagined the demons jumping from host to host as they encountered one another. Could they all have come in contact with one another? She wrote in her daily planner:

Noah knew John –> John is related to Herod –>Herod works with Zack.

Under that she wrote:

Jonah knew Davis–>Davis shook hands with Rico.

She studied her notes intently, her eyes darting back and forth as she absorbed every detail of her current and previous notes. *Something's still missing,* she thought.

34

EMMA AWOKE TO THE glimmer of morning sunlight peeking through the curtains in the hospital room. She cracked her neck and raised her arms in full stretch as she stepped toward the window. With a firm grip, she tugged at the heavy curtain; it remained stubbornly in position. Undeterred, she inspected the fabric for instructions. *Maybe it's voice-activated*, she thought. "Open curtain," she said, staring at the unmoving drapery. She crossed her arms; her eyes landed on Brianna, still asleep, and the bedside remote next to her. She picked up the remote and brought it close to her face, her gaze fixed on the array of buttons. She leaned in closer, as if deciphering a secret code. Her eyes widened. *Elite.* The curtains pulled back at the push of a button; the sun's natural light shone into the room. Gazing at the sky, she took a deep breath and basked in the beauty of sunrise's pink and purple hues.

She turned to Brianna, eager to share the revelation she just made. "Brie, wake up. You'll never believe what I just realized. Zack and Rico must go to the same gym!" she exclaimed.

There was a knock at the door.

A woman wearing pink scrubs entered the room. "Good

morning, Ms. Brown. I'm your nurse; my name is Amy. I came in to take your vitals. How are you feeling this morning?" she asked.

Brianna awoke slowly. "My head hurts," she whispered.

"OK, I'll get you something for that, but first, I'll be taking your blood pressure." She leaned in and gently wrapped the blood pressure cuff around her arm.

Emma stepped back and watched as the blood pressure cuff inflated. The nurse recorded the measurement on a tablet and turned to her. "Her blood pressure is a little low. I'm going to call my charge nurse for support." She picked up the phone.

Within moments, the charge nurse entered the room. She pumped hand sanitizer on her hands, rubbing them together vigorously. "Hi, what's going on?" the charge nurse asked.

"This is Ms. Brown. She says her head hurts. Last night she was feeling fine. Her systolic is in the eighties," Nurse Amy said.

The charge nurse stepped closer to the bedside, her eyes scanning Brianna from top to bottom. "I do not like how she's looking. I'm calling a RAPID."

Emma stepped forward. "What's a RAPID?" she asked.

The charge nurse held her hand up to Emma as she spoke on the phone. "Hi, I'm in 834, I have a RAPID."

Emma turned to Nurse Amy. "What's a RAPID?" she asked again.

"I'll call the primary team." She picked up the phone. "Hi, this is Amy. I'm calling about a patient in 834, Ms. Brown. Can someone come in and look at her? RAPID response is on their way."

"I need a monitor!" the charge nurse shouted.

"What's happening?" Emma asked.

"You need to wait outside," the charge nurse replied.

She stepped to the side.

"You need to wait outside," the charge nurse repeated with a stern look.

She stepped toward the door, moving aside to avoid colliding with a cart being pushed through her path.

She stepped outside. A woman wearing a red t-shirt that read *Rapid Response Team* rushed in behind her. "Excuse me," a doctor said, pushing her aside.

"Ma'am, please step away from the door," a male voice said.

She took a step back and gazed at the man. He wore varying shades of blue from head to toe.

"Why are you here?" she asked, looking at his badge.

"It's standard protocol," the security guard replied, crossing his arms.

His presence confused her. Surely, security wasn't called to be there because of her. He was the least of her worries, anyway. She stepped back and peeked in the window from afar. The security guard watched her every move. "Can I stand here?" she asked incredulously.

The door opened with a gentle groan; the sound was barely audible in the moment's stillness. Emma rushed to the doctor. "How is she?" she asked.

The doctor sighed heavily. "I'm sorry, but Ms. Brown passed away."

Her eyes fixed on the doctor, unblinking. The color drained from her face, leaving behind a pale mask of disbelief. Her mouth opened, but no words escaped. She shook her head, her confusion clear by the look of her furrowed brow and down-turned mouth. *That's not possible,* she thought.

Finally, the words came. "I don't understand. We were supposed to go home."

"I'm not at liberty to share any further details," the doctor replied. "I'll be calling her parents now to inform them. They can provide you with further details if they wish to do so."

A somber aura surrounded her as she stared off blankly into the distance.

The doctor leaned in and squeezed her arm gently. "I'm sorry for your loss."

She stood motionless. Her gaze wandered aimlessly as her mind was consumed with questions. *Why would the doctor tell me they would release her after a night of observation? She hit her head. What other details about her death could the doctor possibly have?*

Her phone rang. She fumbled to pull it from her purse, her hands trembling. She looked at the phone screen. Her eyes widened. "Hello, Mrs. Brown, I'm so sorry."

"Hi Emma, I was just calling to check up on you," Mrs. Brown replied. There was a calmness in her tone.

"If it wasn't for me, she would still be here," Emma sobbed, her words running together in her frantic effort to get them out.

"Emma, that's not true."

She must not know what happened; she must not know the entire story, she thought. The weight of her guilt was suffocating. She couldn't hold on to it. "Davis pushed her, and she hit her head on the floor. Davis wouldn't have been there if it wasn't for me." She spoke in a hushed, apologetic tone.

"Emma, listen to me. The police called. I know exactly what happened. Mr. Brown and I won't be able to rest if you think for one moment that you are to blame for any of this."

She paced nervously; her footsteps echoed through the hall as she fretted over what to make of the situation. She wiped her tears. "Aren't you angry?"

"It upsets me to know that Davis pushed her, but we don't blame him for her passing, and we most certainly don't blame you."

"I don't understand. How do you have the strength to forgive so soon?"

There was silence.

"Hello? Mrs. Brown?"

"The doctor told me you were looking for answers,"

Mrs. Brown replied. "There's something you don't know about Brianna."

What could I possibly not know? Her eyes widened. *I didn't know she owned a gun.*

"Brianna was born with a cerebral cavernous malformation, a brain cavernoma."

"What's a brain cavernoma?"

"It's a cluster of abnormally formed blood vessels in the brain. Over the years, Mr. Brown, Brianna, and I have become experts on the subject."

Emma listened intently.

"Most people with brain cavernoma live their entire lives without knowing they have one. Most brain cavernomas are tiny, about the size of a mulberry. But the cavernoma in Brianna's brain was larger than the size of a golf ball."

Her eyes widened, her mouth agape. "What?"

"We discovered it when Brianna was young and often complained of headaches. We saw several neurologists. They told us the same thing…Given the location of the cavernoma, if we operated, she might not survive, or come out of it worse off. We decided it was too risky."

She blinked rapidly; her mind struggled to process the new information. "Why didn't she tell me?"

"She didn't want to be treated differently. You know Brianna, she's tough. The last thing she wanted was to be treated as if she were anything but that."

"So, you're saying you were prepared for this?"

"Emma, we knew this day would come. We knew that a car accident, hit, or fall could cause a major brain bleed, yet nothing could have prepared us for the pain of losing our—" Her voice cracked, and she paused mid-sentence, sniffling audibly. Emma could only imagine the pain in her eyes.

She continued, "Our only child." A deep breath followed, as if the weight of the conversation was exhausting. Still, she resumed speaking. "Mr. Brown and I are hurting deeply. But we have no choice but to find peace in believing that this was her time, and that she is in a better place where she is free to roam and play and do as she pleases without worry, without holding back."

As she spoke, Emma pieced together the answers to the questions she had been asking herself. *This is why she never played sports. This is why they brought her into the neurosurgery unit. This is why she was so worried about me having my procedure.*

"I pray that knowing what you know now that it's nothing short of a miracle that Brianna lived as long as she did, brings you some peace."

It's nothing short of a miracle that Brianna lived as long as she did. Mrs. Brown's words echoed in her mind but did nothing to bring her peace. Her gaze became intense and furious; her anger simmered just below the surface. *Jail isn't enough. Davis is going to pay for this.*

35

Day 6, The University of Chicago
10:15 a.m.

THE DOOR BURST OPEN. Papers swirled in the air, their edges flapping wildly as the sudden updraft created by the momentum behind its swing lifted them off the desk. Dr. Clark looked up. Emma was glaring at him from the door. He saw her chest heaving as if her lungs were filled with fury. "Emma, are you OK?"

She stomped into the room without regard to who or what she might be interrupting.

A student sitting in the office turned to Dr. Clark with a look of concern.

"We're going to have to pick this up another day," Dr. Clark said. He ushered the student out of the office.

"Emma, what happened?"

She panted heavily; her breaths came in short, quick bursts. "I was at Brianna's house...Davis found me."

Davis? He thought back to his last session with Emma. They didn't have the opportunity to finish talking about Davis. "I thought he was in your past?"

"Not far enough in my past." She sunk her head into her hands. "Before I got him to leave, he pushed Brianna. She hit her head on the floor, and now she's dead." Her gaze dropped to the floor. A visible tension gripped her body; her muscles seemingly coiled with guilt.

In an instant, his eyebrows shot up; his eyes bulging with utter astonishment. A sense of unease settled upon him. "Emma, you can't blame yourself for this," he said. He paced nervously. "What happened to Davis? Did you call the police?"

"Davis went to jail."

Finally, some good news, he thought. His mind raced with questions, but given Emma's condition, he treaded lightly. He stared at the yellow discoloration under Emma's eyes. "Is that where the bruises came from?"

"Yes, I filed a police report. But it's up to the prosecutor at the district attorney's office to determine if there's enough evidence to press charges."

Her phone chirped. "Hello?"

"This is she."

She shook her head; her shoulders slumped forward. "Is there anything I can do? Is there an appeal I can file?"

Her hand trembled as she massaged her temple, the pulsing pressure through her forehead evident from the visible throbbing of her protruding vein. "OK. Thank you for calling."

She placed the phone down on the coffee table and stared at it with discontent.

"What just happened?"

She inhaled deeply. "It was the police officer I filed the police report with. He thought I should know that Davis got out of jail on his own personal recognizance."

A look of utter disbelief washed over his face, his eyes

narrowing in confusion. "How was he released so quickly?" His eyes widened at his own realization. "He has connections in law enforcement." His brow furrowed in worry as his mind raced with potential scenarios of what Davis could do next, especially considering his position of power.

"No one is above the law, my ass," she said, folding her arms.

"You're not safe, Emma."

She turned to him with a look of intense sorrow. "I don't have anywhere to go. Either way, he will find me," she whimpered as tears streamed down her cheeks.

He paced back and forth, his steps quick and agitated as he worked out his thoughts. Surely, there was something he could offer to help Emma. He turned to her; his eyes sparkled with inspiration. "Emma, the dream training you have been doing affects beyond the sleep state. It's affecting your psyche while you're awake."

She cocked her head to the side with a look of puzzlement. "Is that why I could stand up to Davis?"

He bobbed his head. "Yes, I'm sure of it. Did you recognize him when you saw him?"

She nodded. "I recognized him instantly."

It wasn't the answer he had hoped for. "Do you remember any *fearful* memories involving Davis?" he asked, looking for evidence suggesting the procedure was successful.

"Davis, Noah, John, and the others… I remember every scary detail," she replied.

He clenched his fists tight, his knuckles turned white with the force of his frustration as he struggled to contain his disappointment. "Damn it," he said, unclenching his fist. "Damn it!" he exclaimed with a sudden burst of frustration, his palm colliding with the desk, sending a jolt of energy through the room. He looked at her. "What about your father? Did he offer any solutions?"

She shook her head. "Nothing...except for prayer."

"Prayer?"

She nodded.

He continued to pace and inhaled deeply as he focused on collecting his composure. "I'm sorry, Emma. The good news is that the dream training worked." He lifted his hand to his neck, kneading his tight muscles with his fingers. "I'm just not sure how that can help protect you from Davis right now."

There was silence.

Dr. Clark looked at Emma. She appeared deep in thought.

More silence.

She stood up. "We need to get him here," she said.

His eyes narrowed, studying her intently, as if he was noticing something suddenly different about her. Her posture was different, her shoulders back; she held her chin high. She exuded an aura of confidence. "You want to bring him here? It's a little late for couple's therapy," he scoffed.

She looked away and shook her head, showing her annoyance. "I'm going to make sure he never hurts me or anyone else ever again." She spoke with a sense of purpose; her words conveyed a strong sense of determination. "Are you willing to help?"

Under normal circumstances, he wouldn't give a second thought to helping a patient outside of a therapy session. But these were far from normal circumstances. He was certain Emma was in imminent danger. He gazed at her intently with a resolute expression that said he was ready to fulfill his duty. "Just tell me what you need me to do."

36

SHE WAS PREPARED TO UNLEASH a side of her Dr. Clark had never seen before. It was the side of her that Davis had slowly chipped away at until it was unrecognizable, buried deep within but not gone. It was the side of her Davis put out to pasture, locked up, never to be accessed again. She looked at him with intense focus. "You have a sleep study underway, don't you?" she asked.

"Yes, of course," Dr. Clark replied.

"Sign me up," she said, smiling inwardly. She spoke with firmness and confidence. It was more than just a side of her, it was her complete and authentic self back in full control. "Davis knows I've been coming here and knows I have nowhere else to go."

"You plan on luring him here by having him sign up for the sleep study?"

"That's exactly what I plan on doing. He'll be excited by the notion that he has me cornered and come running."

He scratched his chin; his eyes narrowed. "How do you plan on getting him to sign up?"

She reached for her purse. "Take me to the sleep laboratory. I'll explain there."

She stepped out of the office. Dr. Clark rushed to follow her out. They strode purposefully forward, their steps long and determined as they walked toward the sleep laboratory.

"Are we close?" she asked. Her notably shorter legs moved quickly to keep pace with him.

"It's just over in the next building." They walked through the elevated walkway that adjoined the buildings.

In the next building, high-pitched squeals echoed through the hallway. She stopped to peek into a research lab, her curiosity getting the best of her. The walls in the lab were shelved with metal cages. In each cage was a single white rat. Their tails were long and pale pink, a sharp contrast to their bright fluorescent pink eyes that appeared to glow. "Are those your pets?" she asked with a playful smirk.

Dr. Clark laughed. "Those are lab rats. They're used for sleep experiments. Although they make for company on late nights when I'm here alone."

"Why on earth would you use a rat for a sleep experiment?" Emma asked.

"We use them all the time. Fun fact: through sleep experimentation, we learned rats can survive an average of twenty-one days without sleep."

She looked at him with a flat, unamused expression. "You call that a fun fact?"

They continued toward the sleep lab. Emma spotted a pair of white metal doors tucked within a short corridor. They were unlike the wooden doors that lined the offices and classrooms throughout the building. *That must be it*, she thought. Above the double doors was a sign stenciled with paint directly on the wall.

Sleep Disorders Center / Clinic

"Is this it?" she asked, her head cocked to the side.

"This is it," he replied.

She furrowed her brow. "I thought you were taking me to the sleep laboratory."

He pointed to the wall to their left. Installed on the wall was a massive sign made of wood and engraved with white letters.

THE UNIVERSITY OF

CHICAGO

DIVISION OF BIOLOGICAL SCIENCES

SLEEP DISORDERS CENTER

AND

SLEEP RESEARCH LABORATORY

The top of the sign bore the coat of arms of the University of Chicago, a phoenix emerging from flames and the Latin motto Crescat scientia; vita excolatur. *Let knowledge grow from more to more; and so be human life enriched.*

"That's hard to miss," she said.

Dr. Clark pulled the door open. "After you."

She entered the laboratory. Her eyes darted around the space as she surveyed the area. The state-of-the-art facility's bright, open, and modern design was in stark contrast to the dim and aging Psychiatry and Behavioral Neuroscience building. Not a soul was in sight. "Is anyone here?" she asked.

"No, we don't have anyone coming in until Monday."

Although she had never taken part in a sleep study, the layout of the sleep laboratory was very familiar, like that of a hospital wing. Wooden double doors lined the walls, each leading directly into a sleep study room. The sleep study rooms looked like typical bedrooms. Each room came equipped with a television, queen-sized bed, adjustable lighting, and monitoring equipment.

"What is the monitoring equipment used for?" she asked.

"It's used to collect data on patients sleeping patterns and behaviors," he replied.

A large reception-like area comprising two long desks that resembled a nurse's station was at the center of the sleep laboratory. One desk faced the wall. The wall above it was lined with cabinets and inserts for storing patient files. The second desk faced the sleep study rooms that surrounded it.

"That's the observation area," Dr. Clark said. "That's where we remotely monitor the patients and review the polysomnography recordings."

"What is poly-somno-graphy?" she asked, sounding out the word.

"It records brain waves, blood oxygen level, heart rate, and breathing data," he replied.

"May I leave my things here?" she asked.

"Yes, of course."

She placed her purse on the observation area desk, then pulled her phone from her purse, angling the screen towards her face. Tilting her head slightly, she held the phone up to her best side, ensuring the monitoring equipment behind her was visible. After a few quick taps on the phone's screen, she reviewed the photos to ensure they satisfied her.

"What are you doing?" he asked.

"I'm posting photos to my social media accounts along with a link to sign up for the sleep study." Although Emma used social media frequently for work, she grew to loathe it when Davis began using it to monitor her every move. For this, she would gladly make an exception.

He shot her a sidelong glance, his eyes flickering with doubt. "Do you really think that's enough to get him here?"

She looked up from her phone. "Yes," she said matter-of-factly. She returned her gaze to her phone. "It's just a matter of time."

"What if someone else sees the link you posted and signs up?" he asked.

"I'll only keep the link up for an hour," she said with an incredulous look. Something was telling her people wouldn't exactly be lining up for a last-minute sleep study. "That will be more than enough time for Davis to see the post."

Her attention turned to a machine she spotted through an open door. "What's that?" She pointed to a device with multiple wires and sensors attached to it.

"That's a polysomnography monitor," Dr. Clark replied. "Once we have connected the patient to the electrodes and belts, we can determine all sorts of information about the patient's sleep, including what stage of sleep they are in and any disruptions to breathing."

She held up her phone and snapped another photo with the polysomnography monitor in her background. "Can it detect REM sleep?" she asked.

He scoffed. "Of course it can. It uses eye electrodes to detect movement of the eyes that work together with chin electrodes to identify the onset of REM sleep."

Bingo, she thought. She paced the length of the observation area. "Can you give him something to fall asleep?" she asked, her tone laced with a tinge of concern.

"Yes, it's not uncommon to administer a sedative-hypnotic drug to induce and/or maintain sleep," he replied. "We use them in sleep studies often."

She let out a sigh of relief. Getting Davis to fall asleep would be of utmost importance. "How do the sedatives work?" she asked.

"They work by increasing the activity of gamma-aminobutyric acid, a neurotransmitter in the brain to produce drowsiness that can facilitate or maintain sleep."

Although she listened intently to his explanation, she only registered two words: *maintain sleep,* and she clung to them. "Does that mean we can use the same drug to keep him asleep?"

"Most certainly," he replied.

His response was magic to her ears.

"I'm going to sleep in that room for the night." She pointed at the sleep study room directly across from the observation desk. "But I'm going to need a few of those sleep sedatives."

Dr. Clark opened a locked cabinet above the observation desk and pulled a bottle of pills from it. "Here you go." He handed her a single pill.

That won't do. "May I have a few extra?" she asked; she held out her hand with wide eyes.

He looked at her with squinted eyes, seemingly reluctant to fulfill her request.

"Please?" she asked, gazing at him.

The bottle rattled as he dispensed three more pills. "Consider this a sample. Anymore, and I'll need to write you a prescription," he said with an icy, penetrating stare.

She nodded. "Yes, of course. Absolutely," she said, smiling inwardly. "Davis will show up tomorrow," she said with certainty. "And when he does, check him in as you would any other patient, hook him up to the polysomnography monitor, and administer the sedative."

"So, I should do what I would with any other patient. That's the plan?" His forehead creased with lines of confusion, his furrowed brow a clear sign of his puzzlement.

Keenly aware that Dr. Clark was sticking his neck out for her, she was unwilling to ask him to do anything that might put his career in jeopardy. She smiled. "That's the plan."

She stepped into the sleep study room; Dr. Clark followed behind.

"Put him in the room next to mine and make sure he gets a good look at me through the window on the door before he goes in," she said, removing her shoes. "I'll count on you to monitor his vitals and to alert me when he is entering REM sleep."

"Put him in the room next to mine and make sure he gets a good look at me through the window on the door before he goes in," she said, removing her shoes. "I'll count on you to monitor his vitals and to alert me when he is entering REM sleep."

"Is that all?" he asked.

"That's all…I'll take care of everything else."

"It's probably best if I don't know the details, anyway. I'll be in my office if you need anything… I plan on sleeping there tonight." He turned to step out of the room.

She settled beneath the sheets and nestled into her pillows. She jolted upright, her body springing from the mattress. "Dr. Clark, there's one more thing."

He turned to her. "Yes? he asked.

Her lips curled up in a subtle smile. "Can I have some of your powdered sugar donuts?"

37

Day 7, Nations for Christ Pentecostal Church
8:00 a.m.

"**B**IENVENIDOS HERMANOS. WELCOME. Please come in," Emmanuel said, greeting a steady stream of pastors into the church with a firm handshake at the door. The exterior of the church resembled a small home. The area surrounding it once comprised a yard of grass was now paved with asphalt for parking. One might not even be able to tell the building was a church if not for the sign installed on the exterior wall that bore a giant cross. To the right of the cross, the sign read *Naciones Para Cristo*. To the left, it read *Nations for Christ*. Pastor Emmanuel's mission was to honor his mother's legacy and his heritage by catering to both English- and Spanish-speaking families.

Not much in the church had changed since he opened it thirty years ago. It was timeless, in a sense. Inside the church were ten rows of wooden pews separated into two sections. An aisle ran down the middle, leading up to the altar and podium. Thin, gray commercial-grade carpeting covered the floor. The church's interior walls were white and bare except for a dark wood donation box that hung on the wall and a black felt letter board with the number 52 used to display the attendance count from the last service.

He walked up to the podium at the front of the church with his Bible in hand as the pastors took their seats in the pews.

He placed his Bible on the podium, its frequent use evident from its worn binding and dog-eared pages. "Thank you all for being here today," he said. "I consider it an honor and a sign from God that, when my family needs your prayers the most, I have the privilege of hosting this month's gathering." His face was serene, a look of peace that radiated from within.

He looked around the room as though taking inventory of each pastor present. There were at least thirty of them. He had called most of them personally over the last two days to confess his sins and to ask for their help in what he knew would be a tough battle.

"So many of you showed up," he said. "I see some of you even brought friends." His emotions fought to seep through the cracks in his voice. "I want to thank you all for your support… Emma, my wife, and I need all the help we can get." He blinked back tears of gratitude, his eyes misty with emotion.

"We're here for you, hermano!" a pastor exclaimed from the pews.

"Que Dios te bendiga, hermano. Muchísimas gracias," he replied. "I know we normally use this time to share testimonies of healing and salvation, but today will be a spiritually draining day," he said. "There is just no sugar-coating it."

Pastors throughout the church nodded in unison.

"Now it's time to begin the cadena de oración, the prayer chain, para mi hija, Emma."

Without further instruction, each of the pastors walked to the front of the altar like soldiers preparing for war.

Emmanuel reached for the bottle of anointed holy oil sitting on the podium. He poured the oil on his fingertips and prayed out loud. "Heavenly Father, we are here today to pray for my daughter, my only child, Emma." He walked up to each pastor. Using the holy oil from his fingertips, he marked a cross on each of their foreheads. One by one, they raised their hands and began praying their own prayers. Some prayed silently, some quietly, some loudly. Some prayed on their knees, some on their feet, but all prayed with at least one arm raised toward the heavens.

"We rebuke you, Satan!" a pastor shouted. "You have no power over us! You have no power over our kingdom!" His language was forceful and assertive, his tone brooking no argument.

As the others prayed, Emmanuel got down on his knees and prayed on his own. He raised his hands in the air in surrender. "Heavenly Father, I come before you, asking that you lift this generational curse that I have brought upon my family," he said. "I know I have prayed before. Perhaps my prayer was not loud enough." He inhaled deeply. "I claim and proclaim, in the name of Jesus Christ my Savior, that you can hear me now." His voice was steady and unwavering, his words spoken with steadfast conviction.

He continued to pray silently to himself. "Espíritu Santo, por favor, ayuda a mi hija. No es su culpa." He sighed heavily; his shoulders slumped with the weight of his burden.

Hours passed. With each passing hour, their voices got stronger.

"Satan, you have been defeated!" a pastor shouted. He articulated his words with precision, each syllable enunciated with conviction.

Emmanuel looked up to see the pastor standing with one arm raised.

"Do you hear me, Satan?" the pastor asked. "I REBUKE you in the name of Jesus Christ and the Father! You have been defeated!" He shouted with authority. His words carried heavy weight and innate power.

Emmanuel felt the urge to get on his feet, as if called to do so by a supernatural presence in the room. As he stood, his body rocked from right to left, back and forth, right to left, back and forth.

The pastors swarmed around him, as if they sensed the presence, the Holy Ghost, was with him. With their arms raised, they prayed mostly in tongues.

"You have no power here!" a pastor shouted. "Emma is a child of God; I command you to release her!" The pastor's knees collapsed from under him. Another pastor was prepared to catch him as he fell.

The prayers grew louder and louder. Then, quieted as, one by one, each pastor lost consciousness and collapsed.

Eventually, there was silence.

Breathless and exhausted, Emmanuel fell to his knees. "I'm not done," he whispered. "Lord, almighty heavenly Father, I know you have been preparing me for this battle before Emma was even born, and I am grateful." A sense of peace and solace settled over him like a warm blanket, soothing his worries. "Lord, thank you for what you are doing here today." He clasped his hands together in front of his chest, displaying a gesture of gratitude and thankfulness. He blinked rapidly, trying to clear his vision. The edges of the world around him seemed to darken as he swayed back and forth on his knees. He continued, "Thank you for preparing me for this battle. I'm ready." He closed his eyes.

A loud thump echoed in the room's still. His body collapsed. He lay motionless on the floor.

More silence.

His eyes jolted wide open, as if his heart was defibrillated, shocking him back to life. The black of his pupils widened, almost entirely eclipsing the irises of his light-brown eyes. His mouth opened slowly, as though he was attempting to speak. Although he uttered no words, his thoughts blared like a trumpet cutting through the quiet of the room. *Tell me your names, demons!*

38

The University of Chicago
7:30 a.m.

WITH EACH BLOWING STRIKE, the pounding on the door grew louder and louder. "I'm up! I'm up!" Dr. Clark exclaimed. "One moment, please!" He reached for his glasses and looked up at the clock. *It can't be him,* he thought. *It's too early.* He pulled himself up from the couch and rushed to slip on his loafers. "I'll be right there!" he shouted. He cleared his throat and composed his posture as he turned the doorknob, pulling it open. "Good morning. How can I help you?" he asked, fighting to contain a yawn.

"Hey, I'm here for the sleep study!" the man exclaimed enthusiastically. He was tall and clean-shaven, and wore a black puffer jacket, a button-up shirt, and jeans.

His eyes homed in on the man's hazel eyes. *I wouldn't describe them as mesmerizing, but OK,* he thought. His doubts were extinguished. He looked nothing like he imagined. *Where are his horns?* he thought, scoffing inwardly. "Ah, I wasn't expecting you so early," he said. "Follow me this way." He stepped out of his office, his steps deliberate and his expression serious, as Davis followed. Dr. Clark chose not to say more than he needed to.

"Not much for chit-chat, are you?" Davis asked.

Dr. Clark looked back at him with a muted, humorless smile, his expression showing his annoyance.

"That's OK; neither am I," Davis said.

They approached the entrance to the sleep laboratory. Dr. Clark was not good at acting, and he was even worse at lying. Fortunately, he didn't have to do either. "Thank you for volunteering in this study," he said. He maintained steady eye contact as he spoke, conveying a sense of authority. "I'll take you to your room," he said. He opened the door, gesturing for Davis to enter ahead of him. As Davis entered the sleep laboratory, Dr. Clark stood behind and observed as he turned his head from right to left, then left to right. He was surveying every inch of the area, like a police officer assessing a crime scene or a lion hunting its prey.

Having seen enough, Dr. Clark stepped ahead of him. "Follow me this way," he said. As he crossed the sleep laboratory, he glanced back occasionally to find Davis still stalking the area. He stopped directly in front of Emma's room and peeked into the narrow glass window on the upper right side of the door. Emma appeared to be sound asleep. "It's a quiet morning," Dr. Clark said. "We only have one other person in the sleep laboratory today." He turned his head toward the door again, in a subtle gesture to get Davis to do the same.

Davis looked through the observation window. His eyes widened. A sinister grin flashed across his face, as though revealing his underlying intentions.

"Is something funny?" Dr. Clark asked, head tilted.

"No, no. I, I…I was just thinking of something that happened to me earlier," he replied, stuttering as if he had been caught off guard.

Dr. Clark shot him a withering look; his unamused expression conveyed his displeasure. "If this isn't a good time, we can certainly reschedule," he said.

"No, no, this is good. I'm just easily distracted because, you know, I'm not getting any sleep," he replied, running his fingers through his hair.

Liar, liar, pants on fire, Dr. Clark thought. He gestured to the door next to Emma's room. "This is where you'll be sleeping."

Davis entered the room. His eyes locked on the white pastry box of donuts on the nightstand. "Are those for me?" he asked, pointing at the pastry box.

Dr. Clark turned to the pastry box; his head tilted. *What are those doing here?* He brought them down and placed them in Emma's room. He was sure of it.

There was silence.

He stepped slowly towards the nightstand. *Surely, they must be here for a reason,* he thought. He looked down at the pastry box; his eyes widened at the sight of the hand-written note on the box's lid.

Davis, thank you for participating in our sleep study. Enjoy!

He picked up the box and turned to Davis. "Yes, we give them to all of our sleep study participants as a token of our appreciation." He handed Davis the box.

"Awesome," Davis replied. He opened the pastry box and picked up a donut, sprinkling the powdered sugar that remained in the box on it before bringing it to his mouth.

Dr. Clark watched as he devoured one donut after another. Powdered sugar cloaked his fingertips. *Why would Emma want him to have the donuts? I would never load a patient up with sugary food before I expected them to sleep,* he thought. He watched as Davis swallowed the last donut whole. *Unbelievable.*

"I've had better," Davis muttered, sucking the powdered sugar from his fingers, one by one.

Could have fooled me, Dr. Clark thought. He reached into the nightstand and pulled out a pale-blue hospital gown made of thin cotton. "When you are ready, change into this gown. I'll be back in a few minutes."

He stepped out of Davis's room and approached Emma's closed door. Through the window it appeared the bed was empty. *Where is she?* he thought.

He opened the door and switched on the lights for a better look.

There was no sign of her.

He scratched his head. Suddenly, he spotted something from the corner of his eye. He turned around and looked out the door.

There she was.

Emma stood in the observation area wearing a laboratory coat, her face covered with a surgical mask. Even though her mouth was covered by the mask, her wide smile was evident from the crinkles at the edges of her eyes.

Well, I'll be damned, he thought.

They exchanged nods.

He peeked into the observation window of the sleep study room. Davis was dressed in the hospital gown, seated on the bed. He stepped back into the room. "I'm going to start by connecting you to the polysomnography monitor." Dr. Clark pulled the polysomnography monitor near Davis's bedside and pulled out a wire basket containing electrodes and belts from under the cart.

Davis's shoulders hunched; his body instantly recoiled. "Are you going to use needles?"

Dr. Clark shook his head. "No, of course not. I'll be using electrodes and belts to connect you to the monitor. Don't worry, they won't hurt you. They'll simply help us collect information about your sleep patterns and breathing."

He fidgeted nervously, his hands twisting and turning; he appeared to struggle to keep still. "OK, because I don't do needles," he said.

Dr. Clark sensed his apprehension. "Would you like me to explain what each electrode does?"

He bobbed his head, like a nervous young child at a doctor's appointment.

"I'm going to place six electrodes on your scalp," Dr. Clark explained. "I will use these to determine if you are awake or asleep and to identify the different stages of sleep you are in."

Davis watched as Dr. Clark removed the electrodes from their packaging, closely following his every move.

He placed the first electrode. "Not so bad, right?"

He shook his head.

Disaster averted, Dr. Clark thought as he affixed the remaining electrodes to his scalp. "Next, I will place electrodes near your eyes."

"What are those for?"

"They sense eye movement. Eye movements help us identify specific sleep stages." He placed an electrode next to his right eye, then his left. "Still doing OK?" Dr. Clark asked.

"Yes," he replied, shifting impatiently in his seat. "Let's just get this part over with."

Dr. Clark continued with the electrode placement, placing an electrode on his upper lip and then on his ear. He placed two electrodes on his chin, three on his chest, and two on his lower legs. "We are done with the electrode placement," Dr. Clark announced. "Now for the belts."

Davis's eyes widened. "What belts?"

He turned his back to reach for a belt. *I guess he's not so tough after all,* he thought, rolling his eyes. "They won't hurt you." He placed a belt loosely around Davis's chest, then a second around his abdomen. "They measure how much effort you are making to breathe."

"Just one more step," he said, placing cuffs around each ankle. "These will record your leg movements." The electrode and belt placement were complete. "Now, I'll be administering a sleep sedative." He handed him a pill and a cup of water.

Davis raised his hands in protest. "No, I don't do pills."

Dr. Clark looked through the observation window. Emma was shaking her head. *Her plan is unraveling*, he thought. "There's no need to worry, this will simply help with—"

Davis clenched his fist and struck the nightstand with a fierce blow; his eyes narrowed into angry slits. "I don't do pills!" he shouted. A cloud of powdered sugar rose from the nightstand.

He had now witnessed Davis's violent temperament firsthand. *There's nothing more I can do,* he thought. He dropped his head; his shoulders drooped with a sense of defeat.

"Can I go to bed now?" he said with a muffled sigh.

Dr. Clark looked up. *He's yawning.* His eyes were heavy-lidded and droopy; it appeared as though he was struggling to keep them open. Before he could make sense of his sudden drowsiness, Davis reclined on his bed and drifted fast asleep. *What just happened?* he thought. His eyes darted around the room. *How did he fall asleep so quickly without the sedative? He was wide awake when he came in.* His attention turned to the pastry box still sitting on the nightstand. He stepped up and looked through the pastry box's clear window; only remnants of powdered sugar remained.

He turned to look through the observation window at Emma. There was a mischievous sparkle in her eyes. He turned to the pastry box again. His eyes widened at his sudden realization. *I'll be damned...She laced the donuts.*

39

THE DOOR EXPELLED a long, drawn-out creak, breaking the silence in the room. The wheels of the tray table being rolled in emitted a sharp, high-pitched squeaking sound that pierced through the calm of the atmosphere. Emma positioned the tray table by Davis's bedside. With the excitement of a young child setting up a tea party, she picked up the plastic water pitcher from its place on the nightstand and moved it to the tray table. Next to the water pitcher, she placed her phone. She carefully planned the events that led up to this moment, leaving nothing to chance. Davis behaved precisely as she predicted. With her arms behind her back, she paced the length of the room and watched him sleep.

She turned to the sound of a single knock on the observation window. Dr. Clark flashed a thumbs up, signaling Davis was in REM sleep. They exchanged a silent nod of understanding.

She picked up her phone and brought up its voice recorder with a few deft taps before placing it back on the tray table.

"Hello, Davis," she said in a gentle whisper. "I want you to imagine a situation where you are abusing someone; you are tormenting them, or maybe they are tormenting you…"

His lips curled into a sinister grin, belying his true nature, making it clear that the sheer thought of tormenting another person triggered a sense of deep satisfaction within him. But somehow, Emma already knew that. She shook her head. *Pure evil*, she thought.

She climbed onto the bed and swung her leg over Davis's abdomen in a straddled position. She turned to look out the observation window for Dr. Clark's reaction. *Surely, he didn't expect this*, she thought. As she suspected, his mouth was agape, his eyes widened.

She turned her attention back to Davis. "As hard as you may try, you cannot move," she said, her words laced with an unyielding resolve and in deep conflict with Davis's psyche. His body flinched, but knowing he was experiencing sleep paralysis, she was not concerned. She smirked, knowing he couldn't hurt her if he tried.

She leaned forward, placing her body weight fully on his chest as she reached over to the tray table and picked up the water pitcher. His muted squirming reassured her that her plan was working. "The more you struggle, the more you will drown in your fear," she said.

In a deep slumber, his body began to wriggle and squirm with an otherworldly grace.

You're so predictable, she thought as she poured water from the pitcher directly over his nose and mouth.

He gasped for air.

"The more you struggle, the more you will drown in your fear," she repeated. She continued with every intention of pushing her actions to the limits. "You are no longer capable of instilling fear in others. And the thought of *Em-ma* brings you intense, paralyzing fear," she said, emphasizing the syllables in her name.

He flashed a twisted and malevolent grin.

She shook her head. *Again, so predictable*, she thought as she poured water over his mouth and nose.

His head turned from left to right, no longer grinning.

She followed his every movement as she continued to pour the water over his face.

He wasn't moving.

She put the water pitcher back down on the tray table and stared at his motionless body. Her brow furrowed with confusion. In a panic, she hurried off the bed. Dr. Clark should have alerted her if his vitals were approaching the danger zone. She held her hand up to her mouth as she stared at him. *Why isn't he moving?*

There was silence.

The door opened with a gentle sigh; the sound was barely audible in the room's stillness. Or perhaps it was the noise in Emma's mind that made everything around her seem quieter. She turned to Dr. Clark. "Is he OK?"

"He's fine," he replied.

"Why did he stop moving?"

"Maybe you got through to him."

She shook her head. "I hope you aren't upset," she said, bracing herself for what he might have to say after just witnessing her act out the folklore he told her about.

"A real-life mare; I didn't know you had it in you."

She shrugged her shoulders. "What can I say? Hell hath no fury like a woman scorned."

His eyes widened. "I thought you despised clichés."

She laughed. "Well, if the shoe fits," she replied. Her eyes crinkled with delight; she savored the light-hearted moment with him, even if it was fleeting.

"Leave. Now."

She turned to Dr. Clark. "Excuse me?"

"It wasn't me," he replied. "It had to have been him." He pointed to Davis.

She turned to him. He was sound asleep.

"Somniloquy," Dr. Clark said.

She stared at him blankly. "What?"

"Somniloquy," he repeated. "Also known as sleep talking."

She raised her brow. "I've never heard him talk in his sleep before. But then again, I've never observed him sleep like this."

"There are various reasons for sleep talking in healthy adults, including high levels of stress and nightmares." He crossed his arms as he turned to her. "The dream training may really be getting through to him."

She smiled. "I hope so."

He stepped toward the door. "I'll let you know when he's ready again." He dimmed the lights and stepped out of the room, closing the door behind him.

She stepped back and stared at Davis as she rubbed her hands together briskly, trying to generate some heat in her frigid fingers. As she watched him, she thought of the destruction he had caused. She wondered how many people he had hurt before her. While they were together? And if dream training could impact his behavior, even in the slightest way, how many people would benefit from the positive behavior of a single man? But not just any man, a police officer? Someone whose actions could either help or hurt countless people every single day. She had to find a purpose in Brianna's passing. She had to believe the greater good would come from this. She had to believe so that she could keep going.

She heard a knock on the observation window.

They exchanged nods.

She crouched down and whispered softly in Davis's ear. "Imagine a situation where you are hurting someone, or maybe you are thinking about hurting someone."

As was now expected, a sinister grin flashed across his face.

"As you imagine the situation, you are overcome with fear; you are suffocated by fear." She picked up a pillow. "As hard as you try, you cannot breathe." She gently placed the pillow over his face.

He flinched in response.

She held the pillow just over his head.

His breaths came in short, ragged gasps as he fought for air.

"The more you struggle, the more you will be suffocated by your fear," she said, watching for a reaction.

He flinched again.

She brought the pillow down to his face and turned her attention to the polysomnography monitor by his bedside. Although she knew Dr. Clark was monitoring his vitals from the observation area, her mind raced with worry that his oxygen levels would dip too low. *I'm not a monster*, she thought. She pulled the pillow away. *Even if you are.*

She turned to the sound of an urgent knock on the observation window. Dr. Clark gestured for her to come out.

She reached for her phone. *I'd better leave it*, she thought. She tapped on the phone's screen. The sound of her recorded voice filled the quiet room.

She stepped out of the room, toward the observation area. The lines on her forehead deepened with worry. *Maybe I went too far*, she thought. As she walked across the sleep laboratory to the observation desk, she mentally prepared herself for the kind of scolding she received as a child.

"Emma, you need to see this," Dr. Clark said; his breath formed into a fog. He pointed to the polysomnography monitor.

She tilted her head, unsure of what she was looking at.

He folded his arms and took a step back. "This is unlike anything I've ever seen before. He's no longer following the normal stages of sleep."

She folded her arms tightly across her chest. "Why is it so cold in here?" she asked.

"I don't know, but look." He pointed to the polysomnography readings. "He's switching back and forth between sleep stages three and four. He should have cycled back to stage one by now."

She shook her head. "I don't understand. Is that a problem?"

"Let me show you." He reached for a notepad and pen from atop the observation desk.

She looked over his shoulder as he wrote.

"This is what the sleep stages should look like, in this order:

Stage 1: 1 to 7 mins

Stage 2: 10 to 25 mins

Stage 3: 20 to 40 mins

Stage 4: 10 to 60 mins

"The last stage, stage four, is REM sleep. REM can also occur in stage 3. But he's not cycling through the other sleep stages. He appears to be stuck in a loop between stages three and four."

Emma's mind raced as she searched for an explanation. "Did we administer too much of the sedative?" She turned to the video monitor, watching Davis sound asleep.

"That's not possible. That amount of sedative doesn't explain what we're seeing here." He stared at the polysomnography monitor.

"Oh my God," she whispered. Her eyes bulged and nostrils flared as her breathing intensified.

He turned to her. "What is it?"

She pointed to the video monitor, too stunned to explain.

His eyes widened; he brought his hand to his mouth. "OH. MY. GOD."

40

THE FAINT SOUND OF FOOTSTEPS echoed through the seemingly impenetrable darkness from a distance. With each footstep, the echoes grew louder; the air grew thicker with haunting whispers and guttural growls. The room exuded an otherworldly malevolence, a place where nightmares thrived —a place of pure terror.

The sound of the footsteps halted. A loud ripping sound cut through the momentary silence and a glimmer of light emerged from the depths, as if a sword had sliced through it. The glimmer was faint at first, but with each passing moment, it grew stronger. It expanded, pushing back the darkness and illuminating even the deepest corners of the room.

The echo of footsteps resumed, grew louder. Emmanuel stepped forward. "I'm ready," he said.

"¿Quién te mandó?"

"Who sent you?"

"Who sent you?"

"¿Quién te mandó?"

"¿Quién te mandó?"

"Who sent you?"

"¿Quién te mandó?"

The deep and menacing voices growled.

He looked around the room in search of the source of the voices. They seemed to come from nowhere and everywhere all at once.

"Who sent you?"

"¿Quién te mandó?"

"Who sent you?"

"¿Quién te mandó?"

"Who sent you?"

"¿Quién te mandó?"

"¿Quién te mandó?"

They growled again.

"The authority of Jesus Christ sent me!" he exclaimed. He stood tall like a knight ready for battle and strode forward as if in familiar territory.

"He has no authority here," a single malevolent voice growled. The voice came through as if distorted by a mangled loudspeaker.

Emmanuel laughed with a sharp bark that held a note of incredulity. "There are no limits to my God's authority!" he shouted. "My authority comes from the blood of Christ!"

A woman crawled out from the depths of a corner, like a cockroach, seemingly out of nowhere. Her skin hung loosely on her face. She stood slowly; her bones cracked, her posture slumped as if she had not been upright in years.

He examined her from top to bottom, never imagining he would be face-to-face with her again. "You haven't changed, bruja," he said with a look of disdain. After thirty years, he imagined she would be dead. Then again, a part of him wasn't surprised to see her still in some form of existence. As the saying goes, the good die young, pero hierba mala nunca muere.

She looked at him, her eyes devoid of any trace of humanity.

"Does this place look familiar to you?" she asked, extending her arms in the air as though delighted by the very existence of her personal hell. "Don't you recognize it?" she asked.

He did not acknowledge her question, but he recognized it. He never forgot it. But this time, he could see more clearly. The light he brought with him revealed every crack, hole, and blemish in the room and the dust and cobwebs that cloaked it. And unlike what he remembered, the musty scent of mold and decay assaulted his senses.

"It's the tiendita," she said. She had a crooked grin that stretched unnaturally wide across her face. "You thought it was so charming before, no?"

The voices growled hauntingly and eerily; their sound echoed through the room.

"What are you doing here?"

"¿Qué estás haciendo aquí?"

"¿Qué estás haciendo aquí?"

"What are you doing here?"

"¿Qué estás haciendo aquí?"

"What are you doing here?"

"¿Qué estas haciendo aquí?"

"I'm here to rebuke you, demons!" Emmanuel exclaimed.

The voices laughed maliciously.

"Tell me your names, demons," he ordered.

Her eyes grew into a wide, lifeless stare. "My name is Rodrigo," a voice growled through her.

Her posture jerked; chest puffed out, shoulders askew. "Yo soy Juan," she said in a distinctly different, yet equally malevolent, voice.

Her eyes rolled back; head tilted parallel to the floor. "Mi nombre es Lucia," she said, laughing hysterically, with a grin filled with malice.

One by one, each demon revealed themselves through her. As he suspected, there were seven of them.

"You are outnumbered!" a voice shouted. "Now leave us!"

"Leave!"

"¡Vete!"

"¡Vete!"

"Leave us!"

"¡Vete!"

"¡Vete!"

"Leave us!"

He took a step forward. "There may as well be a million of you. You are no match for my God!" He shouted in a commanding tone and raised his hands high toward the bruja. "I REBUKE YOU DEMONS!"

"¡Vete!"

"¡Vete!"

"Get out!"

"Get out!"

"Get out!"

"¡Vete!"

"¡Vete!"

"Demons, in the name of Jesus, I bind you, and I cast you out!" he shouted with a deep, resonant voice that carried the weight and authority of his convictions.

The sinister laughter grew louder.

He continued, his voice steady and unwavering. "Satan, I command you to leave! I bind you in the name of Jesus Christ!"

"He is empty-handed!" a voice growled as the others cackled.

The bruja took a single step toward him and looked at him with a stare that carried the weight of pure evil. "You have no power here." She laughed in a high-pitched cackle that pierced through his eardrums like a thousand needles. "You are just a sheriff without a gun!"

41

THEY WATCHED THE VIDEO monitor in utter disbelief. Had she been alone, she would be certain she was
dreaming. But she wasn't alone. And for the first time since
her nightmares started, she had absolutely no doubt that she was
awake.

"He's levitating," Emma said.

"I can't believe my eyes," Dr. Clark replied.

She turned to him. His eyes bulged, mouth agape. From the
look on his face, she suspected that, for once, he would be of no
help to her. Fortunately, she could rely on her father's knowledge
and experience. She reached for her phone.

"Shit!" she exclaimed.

"What is it?" he asked.

"My phone—I left it in the room with Davis." Her eyes darted,
scanning the observation desk. Her eyes widened. She lunged to
pick up the desk phone and dialed. Hand trembling, she brought
the phone receiver to her ear and listened as the line rang. "Come
on, Dad, I need you," she said aloud.

But there was no answer.

"It's Sunday. He must be at church," she said in a disheartened tone.

They looked on as Davis's body hovered over the bed, still connected to the polysomnography monitor, electrodes, and belts. His eyes were closed, and his body was still. It appeared as though he was sound asleep.

"I've seen nothing like this in my entire life." He turned to her. "Have you?"

"Not exactly," she replied. She recalled how her father always told her there was evil in the world and that demons walked among us. He told her that, inevitably, the time would come when she would be in the presence of evil and that she should be prepared for battle like a soldier of God. She would never have believed him if it had not been for something she experienced as a child. She gasped; her eyes grew wide. *The prayer chain…it must be working.*

❧

She stood next to her father at the entrance of the church as the congregation trickled in for Sunday evening service. It was her job to greet the congregation with a handshake alongside her father.

A visitor stepped up to enter the church.

"Welcome, sister. Please, sit anywhere you'd like," Emma's father said, shaking the woman's hand.

"Thank you, Pastor," she replied.

Emma extended her hand. Her father swiftly intercepted and picked her up. "Let's go inside, sweetheart. Service is about to begin."

Emma watched the visitor take a seat at the back of the church. She came alone.

The service began with worship and praise music, as it always did. Emma's father stepped up to the podium to begin the sermon. He opened his Bible to the book of Corinthians. "For the word of the cross is folly to those who are perishing, but to us who are being saved, it is the power of God," he read. He looked up at the congregation. "That's a powerful message."

His attention turned to a loud, sinister cackle coming from the back.

"Sister? Is something funny?" he asked.

It was the visitor. She laughed again, mouth closed, her smile all too wide.

"Do you need prayer?" he asked.

"No hablo inglés," the woman said in a deep and raspy voice, not the same voice she came in with.

"¿Cómo te llamas?" he asked.

"¡No, cabrón!" she growled. She spit as she spoke, her mouth overflowing with saliva.

He pointed at her. "Come here, demon!" he demanded.

The woman cackled as she remained firmly planted in her seat.

He turned to a group of men sitting at the front of the church. "Bring her to me." He spoke in a commanding tone.

The men approached the woman and lifted her from her seat. The woman kicked and screamed intensely; her limbs contorted in ways Emma didn't know possible as she fought to escape.

"She's very strong," one of the men said, his voice quivering.

She swung her head from right to left. Her teeth were clenched but visible, like a dog about to bite. Her fangs appeared to descend from her gums.

Emma's eyes widened in disbelief.

"¡Saca a los niños! Remove the children!" her father ordered.

Her mother grabbed her hand. "Let's go, now," she said.

"Mommy, what's happening? Where are we going?"

"We're going to the car," her mother replied. "We need to run."

"Why?"

She looked down at her. "Because you're too young to see this."

❧

Something should have happened by now, she thought. She leaned in closer to view the video monitor. Davis's body hovered horizontally in the air, several feet above his bed. "Why is nothing happening?" she said in a frustrated tone.

"What do you mean?" He shot her an incredulous look. "He's levitating!"

She shook her head. "The prayer chain…it's not working."

Dr. Clark's brow furrowed in confusion. "What's a prayer chain?" he asked.

Something told her that her father needed help. She paced the length of the observation desk, her movements fast and jerky as she tried to find a way through the thicket of the problem.

"Emma!" he exclaimed. He stepped in front of her.

She stopped.

They locked eyes; he squeezed her arms in a tight grip. "What's a prayer chain?" he asked.

The lights flickered.

"I don't have time to explain," she replied.

The lights flickered again.

"What happens if we lose power?" she asked.

He released her from his grip. "The video cameras are equipped with night vision, and we have a fully battery-powered backup grid in place," he replied.

Her eyes widened. "That's it!" she exclaimed.

"My father has no power!"

He shook his head. "Emma, what are you talking about?"

She looked at him. "My father, he's a pastor, a man of God."

"Yes, I know."

"He has the authority to exorcise the demon, but he's powerless in Davis's psyche."

Her eyes darted across the expanse of the observation desk,

scanning for the Bible her mother had given her. Her hands moved with urgency as she searched high and low, the air thickening with tension. "Where is it?!" she shouted.

Her eyes fixed on her purse and planner; blinking slowed; her shoulders slumped forward. "I left it at Brianna's house." She dropped her head.

"Emma, talk to me. I want to help." He lifted her chin with one finger and looked her in the eyes. "What did you leave at Brianna's house?" He spoke in a tone that was firm yet gentle.

"The Bible my mother gave me," she said, pushing his hand away from under her chin. "I don't know what else to do."

His eyes widened. "I have one in my office," he replied.

She looked up at him with a look of puzzlement. "What? Since when?"

"I used it for research. Should I go get it?"

"Yes!" she exclaimed. "Hurry! Like your life depends on it!!!" She rushed her speech and punctuated her words with exclamations of excitement.

He lunged toward the sleep laboratory's exit, nearly slipping. His arms flailed wildly as he tried to regain his balance.

She gazed intently at the video monitor and prepared for what she would do next.

42

HE GRIPPED THE BIBLE, gazing at it, in awe of the supernatural power she knew it possessed. "Stay here," Emma said.

"What are you going to do?" Dr. Clark asked.

"I'm going to place it on his stomach."

He flashed her a look of disbelief. "Are you insane? You can't go in there!"

"Just watch me." She stepped toward Davis's room with intense purpose. The door let out a high-pitched creak as she pushed it open. Instantly, Davis's body recoiled in horror, as though aware of the power of the weapon she brought with her. She stepped toward him and carefully positioned the Bible atop his abdomen. Maintaining her gaze on the holy book, she stepped back. It was firmly in place, unmoved by his sharp jerking, as if defying gravity.

Davis hissed and snarled, like a fuse had been lit on a bomb atop him.

She rushed out of the room to the observation area.

"He's reacting to the Bible," Dr. Clark said.

She stepped behind the observation desk. They watched as

Davis's back arched. His eyes opened, revealing his eyes glowing with a fiery red light. His body flinched and jerked as it tried ridding itself of the holy book.

Dr. Clark turned to her. "How did you know to put the Bible on his stomach?"

"My dad told me stories of exorcisms he performed," she replied.

He stepped back. "Why haven't you brought this up before?" he asked with a look of disbelief.

She shrugged her shoulders. "I didn't think it was pertinent."

They looked on as Davis's head jerked from left to right, then up and down. His eyes were wide open, still glowing with fiery red light. His teeth were clenched. He stared ferociously at the video camera as if he knew he was being watched.

"Is he awake?" she asked.

"Not according to the polysomnography readings," he replied.

A chilly draft cut through the air. Emma brought her hands to her arms and rubbed them vigorously to generate heat. She gasped, turning her head to a sound in the distance. "Did you hear that?" she asked. Her heart raced as she tried to figure out what had caused the noise that seemed to come out of nowhere.

"Hear what? There's no audio coming from the monitor," Dr. Clark replied.

She gasped, turning her head again. "It sounds like a voice," she whispered.

"That's impossible. We're the only ones here."

They turned their heads; their gasps filled the air with an unmistakable aura of terror.

"I hear it now," he said.

They inched closer to each other, their breaths shallow and erratic.

"Leave!"

"¡Vete!"

"¡Vete!"

"Leave!"

"¡Vete!"

"¡Vete!"

"Leave!" the voices growled loudly.

They stepped back.

"Is that an echo?" he asked.

"No." She turned to the video monitor. "It's coming from Davis's room."

She paused.

"They're demons."

Dr. Clark's eyes, once filled with curiosity and wonder, were now filled with a look of fear that penetrated his very soul. As fear gripped him, he swallowed, his throat seemingly constricted. "There's more than one?" he asked, his voice trembling ever so slightly.

"There are seven," she said with a look of certainty.

He took another step back as he stared at the monitor, seemingly transfixed by the haunting image in front of him. "What? How?" he asked.

She heaved a heavy sigh. "Each of the men from my dreams crossed paths and are hosted within Davis. I'm sure of it now."

His eyes widened. "What do they want?"

She turned to him. "They want me."

43

FLICKERS OF LIGHT PIERCED through the depths of eerie darkness. Each flicker brought with it a pulse of anxiety and a sense of unease that lingered in the room like a heavy fog.

"I thought you said the power was backed up," Emma said.

"It is...I don't know what's happening." Dr. Clark reached for his phone, tapping on its screen. A flashlight shone from it. "That's better."

"At least the video equipment is still working," she said. Shades of green and black displayed on the video monitor. They watched as the electrodes and belts connected to Davis were stripped from his body by an unseen force. His body contorted in agony as he struggled to escape the burning of the holy book.

"I'm going to kill you!"

"¡Te voy a matar!"

"I'm going to kill you!"

"¡Te voy a matar!"

"¡Te voy a matar!"

"I'm going to kill you!"

"¡Te voy a matar!" the verminous voices shouted.

The tray table levitated and violently slammed into the door, as though an unseen force was looking for a way out.

"Lock the door!" Emma shouted.

Dr. Clark pulled a king ring from the observation desk drawer. "Why is it trying to break through the door? Why doesn't it just go through the door?"

She shook her head. "The demons are tied to Davis. He's asleep, so they can't go far. But that won't keep them from trying to inflict as much damage as possible from where they are. Now hurry!" she shouted.

He pointed his flashlight at the key ring and examined each key one by one. "Here it is!" he exclaimed. With the key in hand, he ran towards Davis's door. He positioned the key over the keyhole, his hand trembling with intensity. He gripped his right hand with his left to steady his hand and turned the key.

As Emma looked on, a Bible scripture she memorized as a child flashed across her mind as if being broadcasted by an emergency alert system. She closed her eyes. *"He said to them, 'Go!' So, they came out and went into the pigs, and the whole herd rushed down the steep bank into the lake and died in the water."*

Dr. Clark returned to the observation area. "It's locked. Now what do we do?" he asked, hands still trembling.

She opened her eyes. "The demons will need something to attach to when they leave Davis's body. They need a new host."

"We can use the lab rats," Dr. Clark replied.

They exchanged nods. He sprinted out of the sleep laboratory. Emma followed the light that shone from his phone to navigate through the dark, hollow halls of the building.

They entered a research lab.

"Let's get them in a single cage," she said. She pulled a cage from the shelf and placed it on the floor.

Dr. Clark opened the cages; one by one, he passed the rats to Emma.

"How many do we need?" he asked.

"Seven," she replied in a bold and unwavering tone.

"Right—of course." He placed the final rat in the cage. "Let's go," he said as he picked up the cage.

They ran out of the research lab. The echo of malevolent voices boomed through the halls.

"Leave!

"¡Vete!"

"¡Vete!"

"Leave!"

"¡Vete!"

"¡Vete!"

"Leave!" the voices shouted with a thunderous sound.

They entered the sleep laboratory and sprinted back to the observation area.

Emma looked at the video monitor. "He's foaming at the mouth. I need to get in there before it's too late."

He handed her the key.

"Before I go, I need you to repeat after me, 'I plead the blood of Jesus,'" she said.

"I plead the blood of Jesus?"

She nodded. "I need you to keep repeating that. The words act like a shield. The demons won't attack you if you're pleading the blood of Christ. Do you understand?"

He nodded. "I plead the blood of Jesus."

As she stepped toward Davis's room, a feeling of tension consumed every muscle in her body. After a month of little food, sleep, and mounting anxiety, her body was prepared to give up, whether she wanted it to or not. Her shoulders hunched forward, her body bent over.

"Emma!" Dr. Clark shouted. He stepped toward her.

She turned to him. "Stay there!" she ordered. "Just do what I told you and stay where you are, no matter what!" She placed her hand over her stomach and winced, her face contorted with pain from the now life-threatening effects of stress on her body. Still, she persisted forward.

She looked through the observation window; a cloak of darkness blanketed the room, illuminated only by the smoldering embers of Davis's eyes. She yelled out in pain as she fought against her body's pleas to lie down. *Just a little farther, Emma. You can do this.* Her quivering legs betrayed her will to keep going. She grunted and moaned as she fought to take just one more step. Unable to move any farther, she planted her trembling hand on the frigid metal surface of the door and fell to her knees. "It can't end like this…God help me," she whispered. Her body jolted with an electrifying surge as she rested her forehead on the door, resuscitating her near-lifeless body. Her head pulled back as she fell to the floor.

"Emma!" Dr. Clark shouted.

The voices growled louder, as if trying to interfere with outside efforts to communicate.

She lifted her head. "Stay there and do as I said!" she shouted in a commanding voice. She examined her hands and legs, no longer quivering or in pain. With steady hands, she lifted herself from the floor, picked up the cage, and inserted the key; a tremor of energy pulsed through her body.

The lights powered on as she opened the door. A deafening crash reverberated through the walls as the flying objects fell to the floor in unison the moment she stepped foot in. Davis's body remained suspended in the air, showcasing a captivating demonstration of supernatural ability. He lifted his head and turned to her. "Emma, sweetheart, please help me," he said. He spoke gently, as if conveying sincerity and remorse for his actions.

She hadn't heard that tone of voice from him since their time on the cruise ship. It was the voice of the man she fell in love with. She looked into his hazel eyes, devoid of the once-fiery red glow. They seemed kind, as though trying to convey it was him again. She smiled, but was not fooled. She placed the cage on the floor by his bedside and looked at him with an unwavering gaze. "You no longer have any power over me, and you never will again," she said.

His eyes, no longer hazel, blazed with a fiery intensity as he growled demonically; his shoulders lunged forward like a rabid animal trying to attack.

She stepped out of the room and returned to the observation area, reaching for Dr. Clark's hand.

"We plead the blood of Jesus," they said together. Their breaths formed a cloud of fog with every exhale.

She looked at the video monitor. Davis was foaming at the mouth.

"Should we do something?" Dr. Clark asked.

"Keep pleading!" she shouted.

He nodded.

She got on her knees and bowed her head.

Dr. Clark followed her lead.

"We plead the blood of Jesus," they continued.

A gentle stillness settled upon the room. She lifted her head and turned to the video monitor. They watched as Davis's body fell to the bed as though released from the grip of evil forces.

She opened her mouth lightly and exhaled. There was no more fog.

Dr. Clark turned to her. "Does this mean it's over?"

She nodded slowly. "I think so." She stared at the video monitor. His body was still. "How long do we have before he wakes up?"

He returned his gaze to the video monitor. "He's not moving. That tells me we have some time." They stood up. "But we need to hurry; we still need to clean up and bring the rats back out before he wakes up."

They stepped into Davis's room.

"Ugh, it stinks in here," she said, waving off the ammonia-like smell in front of her nose. "I'll clean up here. You take the rats back to the observation area."

Dr. Clark surveyed the room. "No, you're going to need some help."

The two worked quickly to put the room back in order. Emma stared at Dr. Clark as he picked up items from the floor.

"What is it?" he asked.

"I'm just curious. Were you raised in a religious home?"

He shrugged his shoulders. "Religious enough that I can identify the seven deadly sins when I see them." He picked up the cage. "I'm going to walk the rats back to the research lab."

He took a single step toward the door, then stopped.

"What's wrong?" Emma asked.

The cage rattled violently, as if an unseen predator was causing the rats to thrash back and forth.

She stepped toward him. They observed the rats leaping and jumping, like tiny acrobats buzzing with uncontainable energy.

"Rats are nocturnal; I expected them to be sleeping, but they're probably riled up because they're not accustomed to sharing a cage," he said. "I'll place them on the observation desk to monitor them for the time being."

She looked around the room. Everything had to be back in order. "Oh, I almost forgot." She picked up the Bible still atop Davis's abdomen and placed it on the nightstand.

Dr. Clark observed Davis turn to his side. "He's moving. He could wake up at any moment. We need to go. Now."

44

DAVIS AWOKE TO THE PUNGENT stench of urine that permeated the air, its acrid and noxious fumes making it impossible to ignore; his nostrils flared instinctively. With a furrowed brow, his eyes darted around the room as he attempted to pinpoint the source of the foul scent that seemed to come from all around. He lifted his bed sheet; his eyes watered as the overpowering odor reached his nostrils. "What the fuck?" he said.

There was a knock on the door.

Dr. Clark stepped into the room. "Knock. Knock," he said. "Rise and shine, sleepyhead."

"How long was I out?" he asked.

"Not long. I suspect those sugary donuts you had interrupted your sleep. Next time, maybe eat them after…unless you'd like to stay and cont—"

"No!" he shouted in a thunderous voice.

Dr. Clark cocked his head back. "OK, maybe another time." He pointed to the nightstand. "Your clothes are over there."

"Why does the room reek of urine?" he asked. "Was that really me?"

"Yes, it seems you were very hydrated when you came in. We have pee pads and adult diapers for our bedwetters. I would have set those out for you had I known it would be a problem."

His face went red with embarrassment.

Dr. Clark stepped back toward the door. "I'll give you a few minutes to change. I'll be back shortly to escort you out."

"What the fuck? How does this work? Where are the strings?" He spoke out loud as he battled with the urine-soaked gown. The gown rustled with every movement. His efforts yielded no progress; the gown tightened around him as his chest ballooned with anxiety. He heaved out a long, exasperated groan as he grabbed the collar of the gown and tore it away from his body.

There was a knock on the door; it opened just a crack. "Are you OK in there?" Dr. Clark asked.

"Yes, I'm fine!" he exclaimed.

"OK, just checking," he replied, closing the door.

He reached for his clothes on the nightstand, his movement languid and heavy. His eyelids, normally alert and wide after a nap, were heavy-lidded, drooping with the weight of his exhaustion. He slapped his face to bring life back to himself and bent down to put on his pants. He hopped on one foot while he wrestled with them, his movements quick and erratic.

He reached for his white V-neck t-shirt. Its tag was facing out, but he would waste no time adjusting it, instead slipping it on as it was.

He glowered at his button-up shirt with disdain.

There was a knock at the door. Dr. Clark entered the room. "Are you ready?" he asked.

He nodded his head vigorously. "I'm ready." He reached for his socks, stuffing them in his pant pockets.

Dr. Clark looked down at Davis's feet. His tennis shoes were halfway on, like make-shift slippers. "Aren't you going to tie your shoes?" he asked.

He looked down at his shoelaces and weighed the risk of

tripping against spending another moment in that room. "No. Can I leave now? I have somewhere I need to be."

Dr. Clark tilted his head and pursed his lips. "Yes, you may leave. I'll walk you out." He stepped out of the room.

Davis followed.

He stopped; Davis nearly bumped into him from behind. "Aren't you going to put your jacket on?"

Davis held his jacket in his arms. "No."

Dr. Clark shrugged his shoulders. "It's cold out," he muttered as he proceeded down the hallway.

He stopped again. "I'd just like to thank you again for participating in the study," Dr. Clark said.

But Davis had no interest in his pleasantries. "No problem, bye," he blurted as he turned to leave.

"Wait. Before you leave, I have a message for you," Dr. Clark said.

Davis turned to him. *A message?* He hadn't told anyone he would be participating in the sleep study. No one knew he was there. "From who?"

"There was a participant here yesterday, a young lady named Emma."

He stood motionless and rigid, as if his legs had fallen asleep.

"She said to tell you hello," Dr. Clark said with a smile.

He turned to the exit, holding his arms close to his chest as he stepped forward. With each step, he felt a tingling and numbness in his legs. He leaned on the wall for support.

"Are you OK?" Dr. Clark asked. "Was it something I said? Was it Em-ma?"

He stared blankly into the distance. He knew he had gone there to get Emma. But now, he questioned why. For reasons he couldn't understand, he didn't even want to hear her name, let alone see her. There was one thing he was certain of…He wanted nothing to do with her.

The sound of footsteps echoed from afar.

It's her, he thought. "I...I have to go," he stuttered. His face contorted in pain as he struggled to lift his legs. Each footfall seemed to echo in weariness.

"Bye now," Dr. Clark said as he held the exit door open.

Outside of the building, he wiped the sweat off his brow. Now, it was only a matter of getting to his car. He took a step, his legs still enveloped by a numbing sensation. He spotted a ramp, but the stairs directly in front of him were the more direct route to the parking garage just ahead. *Just four steps down.* He gripped the banister tightly and used his hips to propel his legs carefully down each step.

He had just one more step to go.

"Are you OK?" Dr. Clark shouted from the top of the steps.

He turned; momentarily distracted, he tripped on his shoelace and tumbled down the last step.

"Can I help?" Dr. Clark shouted again.

His limbs trembled as he struggled to pull himself up, his muscles weak from exhaustion. He looked from right to left, surveying his surroundings. The campus was empty, not a soul in sight. Although he didn't want to accept Dr. Clark's offer, it became apparent that he didn't have a choice.

"Yes, help me up," he shouted.

There was silence.

He looked up. Dr. Clark was gone. With a deep scowl etched on his face, he shouted at the top of his lungs. "FUCK!!!"

≈

"Are you OK?" Emma asked.

Dr. Clark strode purposefully in her direction. He appeared visibly stunned. His eyes were wide. He placed his hands on his head. "Did you see that? Did you see how he reacted to your name?"

She nodded. "I saw the whole thing."

His body buzzed with energy. He removed his hands from his head, leaned forward, and placed them on his knees, looking up at her. "He should have tied his shoelaces."

His posture straightened; he swung his arms back and forth at his side. "He left so fast he didn't even have time to turn his T-shirt right-side out!" he exclaimed, placing his hand on his stomach as he erupted in laughter.

She smiled.

"Every part of your plan worked, even the powdered donuts!" He extended his hand in the air, gesturing for a high-five.

She brought her hand to his. "I told you I was a good planner," she replied.

"I never doubted you, Emma. I knew there was a brilliant fighter in there."

She smiled again. "Thanks for your help, Dr. Clark."

He shrugged his shoulders as he placed his hands in his pockets. "What help? All I did was conduct a sleep study. Just another day at the office, if you ask me," he replied sheepishly.

Dr. Clark wasn't the only one Emma felt compelled to thank. She placed her palms together and looked up at the heavens. *Thank you both.*

She looked at him. He had a smile on his face like none she had seen on him before. She, too, was satisfied with the outcome of the day's events. And although she couldn't prove it yet, she knew her nightmares were over, in every sense of the word. She wanted to laugh and enjoy the moment with Dr. Clark, and under different circumstances, she might have. But her joy was overshadowed by the reality of Brianna's death. She bowed her head, closed her eyes, and heaved a heavy sigh.

"You know, I have a rule against hugging my patients, but if it helps, I'm here."

She looked at him with intense sadness. Outside of her

immediate reaction to Brianna's death, she had not yet stopped to grieve.

He extended his arms toward her. "It's OK," he said.

Wary of crossing the boundaries between doctor and patient, she gazed at him as she considered his offer. The tears she had been repressing welled up in her eyes. She inhaled deeply. *There are no boundaries to human decency,* she thought. She stepped toward him. Arms extended. She sobbed uncontrollably as she sank into his chest. Her body shook with each deep, guttural cry. "It hurts, Dr. Clark. It hurts so much…"

45

THE AIR WAS HEAVY with sadness and grief, soft sobs punctuating the stillness of the atmosphere. The walls were adorned with drapes of pink velvet placed at Mrs. Brown's request in an attempt to soften up the room, a stark contrast to the brutal reality before them. From her reserved seat in the front row of the church, Emma stared at the glossy white coffin cloaked in bright, fresh pink roses not far from her, lost in thought. Her thoughts drifted to the countless memories she shared with Brianna. She could still hear her voice, her laugh, her sneeze. Several formal portraits of Brianna were on display, taken throughout the years on her various voyages. Every now and again, she glanced at one and Brianna's wide, toothy grin to remind herself that the moment was real.

Her father approached her, leaning in for a gentle embrace.

"Thank you, Dad," she said. "For everything."

"I wish I could have done more," her father replied. Her mother stood behind him.

"I'm so sorry, angel," her mother said, unable to hold back her tears.

"It's OK, Mom," she replied, consoling her mother, gently rubbing her back.

Between the two of them, she always considered Brianna to be the stronger one. Perhaps they were both incredibly strong, and perhaps that's what gravitated them to each other to begin with. Or perhaps Brianna had rubbed off on her over the years. Regardless, Emma's strength and love for Brianna would be on full display today. Today, she would use her pain to fuel her strength and deliver the eulogy Brianna deserved. And she wouldn't be alone. But then again, she was never alone. She had her parents. She had Jim. She had Jaden. She had her closest friends, sorority sisters, there with her. She had countless people, many who never knew Brianna, surrounding and supporting her. And although she was grateful, she had little to say. At least for today.

"Are you sure you want to do this?" Jaden asked.

"Yes," Emma replied.

Jaden embraced her firmly. "We're here for you. Hermanas por vida," she whispered in her ear.

"Sisters for life," Emma replied.

Mrs. Brown approached her. She leaned in. "It's time," she said, gently squeezing Emma's arm.

She nodded and took a deep breath before standing. The ushers directed people to take their seats as she approached the podium.

At the podium, she looked down at the program that bore Brianna's picture and obituary. *Brianna Rose Brown*, it read. She took another deep breath and looked up, prepared to speak from her heart. Unscripted, she addressed the attendees.

"From the first day I met Brianna, I knew she was a fighter and a protector with a heart of gold. I knew, not because she told me, but because I witnessed it firsthand, time after time, again and again. She was like a big sister to me, and not because she was older. Technically, I was older by a couple of months."

She paused, acknowledging the quiet laughter in the room.

"She was the first person I would call in my happiest of times, and in my most difficult ones. Overtime we became so close that it was *her* that would call *me* when she sensed something was wrong." With a heavy heart, she exhaled deeply, as if releasing the weight of her sorrow from her breath.

She looked at her mother for comfort but found none. Her mother's eyes were dripping with tears.

She looked at her father. His muted closed lip smile and slow nod served as a gentle encouraging pat on the back. *I can do this*, she thought.

"When we were in the third grade, Brianna came to my house for a playdate. I was so excited to have her over, and to introduce her to the chickens and ducks my family was raising in the backyard. But when she saw the ducks, she said they looked sad. Before I knew it, she picked up a shovel my dad left in the yard and started digging. 'What are you doing?!' I shouted in a panic. She said the ducks needed a place to get their feet wet. I pleaded with her to stop. If my dad found out, I was sure he would never let her come over again...

"But she persisted.

"Later, when my dad came out to check on us, he saw what Brianna was doing and headed straight to the garage. I feared the worst until he emerged holding two shovels. He handed me one, but I stood there, stunned. 'Aren't you going to help?' he asked.

Laughter emerged as soft giggles.

"She was right...The ducks did need a place to get their feet wet. I didn't know ducks could look so happy."

The atmosphere in the room became lighter; laughter became intertwined with tears.

"She came over every weekend that summer, and over time, the hole we dug became the most beautiful pond," she said, her face adorned with a heartfelt smile.

She paused.

"I'll never know exactly why she chose me to be in her life, but I'll always cherish every sleepover, every conversation, every girl's night, and every single moment we shared. I'll always remember her smile. Her laugh. Her pouty face and her sad face. And yet, it will never, ever be enough to fill the void that her passing has left. I will forever regret not snapping one more photo, not getting one more hug, not getting one more look.

She paused again. The sound of sniffling and quiet crying filled the room.

"We are here today because Brianna touched our lives. I know I'm not alone when I say that I will forever be grateful to her for her unconditional love and friendship," she said, her eyes welling up with tears. She looked up at the heavens. "I pray God gives us the strength to move forward while we hang on to the precious memories our beautiful friend left us with. That's what Brie's parents want. And that's what Brie would have wanted."

She smiled and turned her attention to Jaden. "I'll never forget one of the last things she told me. She said, 'You're such a good person. You deserve the best.'"

She turned her gaze to the Browns. "Since her passing, those words have played in my mind repeatedly. And I can't help but believe that if, by Brianna's standards, I'm a good person, then heaven just received its newest saint."

She returned her gaze to the heavens. "I'll end with this. Brie, I know you're listening. Brianna is the best. No other person in the universe comes close. I'll love you forever, my dear friend." She dropped her head, inhaling deeply. "Until I see you again."

46

S HE STOOD OUTSIDE THE door; her brow furrowed with confusion as she reviewed her daily planner. *It's today, alright,* Emma thought. She knocked on the door.

The door swung open. "Sorry about that, Emma. I was just reviewing a patient's file. Come on in," Dr. Clark said.

She stepped into his office. It seemed smaller.

"How are you doing?" he asked. "No makeup today, I see. It's a great look on you."

She took her usual seat on the couch. "Thanks, I've been resting well. My nightmares stopped, and my appetite is back...mostly." Her eyes welled up. "Things are mostly back to normal. Of course, memories of Brianna will come seemingly out of nowhere. Mostly when it's quiet and I'm alone. I still cry most days, but I know that's to be expected."

"I'm so sorry for your loss," he replied. He handed her a box of tissues. "Grieving is a brutal process. I wish I could prescribe it away."

She nodded. "I know."

She paused.

"Can I ask you something?" she asked.

"Sure, anything," he replied.

"When did you figure out my dreams were more than just dreams?"

He leaned back in his chair, seemingly reflecting on Emma's question. "I think you figured that out before I did."

Her eyes widened. "What do you mean?"

"You followed your instincts, and came to see me when the other doctors couldn't give you answers. I think it was your sub-conscious warning you, telling you something was wrong all along."

She nodded. "I guess you're right."

He continued, "But the bruises on your arms and neck were the clearest signal to me that something was off."

She looked down at her clothing. Like most bitter days, she donned a long-sleeved turtleneck blouse and pants. "When did you see the bruises?" she asked with a look of puzzlement.

"It was on your second visit," he replied.

She reached for her planner.

"I'll save you the trouble; it was the day the heating wouldn't shut off."

She thought back to that day and recalled him acting strangely, but she had chalked it up to him ogling over her. His behavior made perfect sense now. "That's why you were staring at me. Why didn't you say anything?"

"I was waiting to see if you brought it up on your own. When you didn't, it made dream training much more important."

"Why?"

"Because whether your experiences occurred in your dreams or reality was irrelevant to the outcome of your dream training."

She leaned in. "Because dream training rewires the brain."

"Precisely," he replied with a nod. "Now it's my turn to ask a question." He leaned in, his eyebrows raised. "Back in the sleep laboratory with Davis—you were incredible. It was as though you knew exactly what to do. Have you ever witnessed an exorcism?"

She leaned back; her brow furrowed as she gazed into the distance, thinking back on the stories her father told her about his encounters with demonic possessions. Because of his successful track record, he was frequently called upon to assist with exorcisms across the city. Her father told her he had led over forty exorcisms over the course of thirty years, and she never doubted it—he told her the story behind every single one.

"I've never witnessed an exorcism," she said. "Until now, of course."

"Interesting." He folded his arms across his chest.

There was silence.

Emma sensed he wasn't convinced. "I have witnessed a demonic possession, though."

"What's the difference?" he asked.

"Someone can be possessed without having the demon exorcised. In my case, I witnessed a woman that was demonically possessed, but I didn't see the exorcism my father performed."

"I see," he replied. "Would you care to tell me more?"

She inhaled deeply. "I was a child when it happened. My mother rushed me out of my father's church when it became clear that a woman visiting that night was demonically possessed. It wasn't until I was older that my father told me what unfolded inside." She recalled what her father told her happened in the church that night while she waited in the car with her mother. She remembered how terrified she felt as it was happening. Over the years, though, she hadn't given it much thought.

"Are you comfortable telling me about it?" he asked.

She nodded. Since experiencing what happened with Davis firsthand, the thought of what happened that night didn't scare her nearly as much as it used to. "It took four men to hold her down. My father saw fear in one of the men's eyes and told him to wait outside. The man pleaded with him. He wanted to stay and help, but my father said he wasn't ready to be there and called upon a co-pastor to take his place. He ordered everyone else to join hands and pray from outside. Once everyone was out of the church, my father asked for the demon's name. She lunged at him. The men struggled to hold her back. The demon cackled in delight. It said its name was Juan; it spoke in a deep and ominous voice, but not clearly."

"What do you mean?" Dr. Clark asked.

"My father told me the voice was muffled, garbled, choppy, even high-pitched. He said it was as though the voice was coming through a broken speaker being filtered through layers of interference. He ordered the demon to leave the woman and rubbed his hands with anointed oil. The demon began growling obscenities at my father. It was as though it knew what my father intended to do next."

"What did he intend to do?" Dr. Clark asked.

"He was going to form a cross on the woman's forehead using the anointed oil. Her head turned from right to left as she resisted. The demon screeched in agony as the oil contacted the woman's forehead. It snarled and growled. She showed her teeth, signaling she was ready to bite. They pulled the woman's legs from under her, and each held her down by a limb. Then he placed the Bible on her stomach."

"That's how you knew to place the Bible on Davis's stomach," Dr. Clark said.

She nodded. The woman screamed in agony when the Bible touched her body, as if she had just been branded. She pleaded with my father to remove it. As she pleaded, my father told me she spoke in the woman's voice, not the demon's voice, and that she had a look of sincerity in her eyes. The men asked my father if they should release her. My father said the demon was trying to fool them. He knelt and placed his hand on the visitor's forehead and commanded the demon out. The woman's back arched and her body jerked, then she convulsed and foamed at the mouth. After some time, the woman lay motionless on the floor, sleeping peacefully, like Davis. The demon was gone."

"I see," Dr. Clark replied.

"And now you see why I never mentioned it before. I can't imagine you would have believed any part of it had you not experienced it yourself."

He nodded slowly. "You're probably right."

"My father told me it takes two things to take down a demon—authority and power. He compared it to law enforcement—you need a badge and a gun to take down the bad guy."

"Your father had the badge, the authority."

She nodded. "And, thanks to you, we had the gun. I couldn't have done it without you."

His lips curled up in a smile. "You know, I would never say something like this had I not experienced what I did with you in the sleep laboratory, but maybe there was a reason the memory extinction procedure didn't work," he said. "Maybe it was a part of the plan all along."

She stared at him with a raised eyebrow and a wrinkled forehead. "What do you mean?"

"Well, had the procedure worked, the memories of the stories your father told you, your memory of the demonic possession you witnessed, may have been eliminated."

She raised her brows, her mouth agape. "I hadn't considered that."

"I have another question for you." He crossed his arms. "Knowing now that the demons may have caused Davis to act out, would you have done anything differently?"

"No." She responded firmly and quickly, as though her response required little to no thought.

"Why not?"

"Davis was a narcissist before I met him, before he became possessed. He was already bad."

She paused.

"Perhaps that's why the demons chose him to begin with."

He raised his brow. "Well, his Narcissist Personality Disorder would have certainly been present well before you met," he replied. "It's believed it results from a combination of genetic and environmental factors, as well as parenting styles."

"He was abusive long before we ran into Rico at the Rumba Room, which is when I suspect he became host to most of the demons. The demons only amplified who he already was."

He scoffed.

"What?" Her brows narrowed. "Do you disagree?"

He shook his head slowly. "No, I don't. In all likelihood, what you did was a public service."

She turned to the sound of a single high-pitched squeal. A folding table was in the corner of the office. On it were seven cages, each containing a single rat. Their eyes emitted a luminous scarlet gleam, much redder and brighter than she remembered.

"What are they doing in here?" she asked.

"They've continued to show erratic behavior. I moved them here for round-the-clock observation." He directed his gaze to the rats. "They haven't slept since Davis left."

Their fur appeared dull and patchy. Ulcers covered their tails; inflamed open sores covered every centimeter of their exposed skin. Noticeable pockets of puss had formed just beneath their skin. Their ribs, spines, and hip bones were visible, their skin loose and saggy. "They don't look so good," she said. "Is it even humane to keep them alive at this point?"

"They've lost weight because of the extra energy they're expending while awake," he explained. "I've increased their food intake to compensate, but they continue to lose weight."

There was a knock on the door.

"Come in!" Dr. Clark shouted.

A woman and a young girl stepped into the office.

"Oh, hello, sweetheart, you're early," Dr. Clark said.

He turned to Emma. "Emma, this is my wife, Joan, and this is my daughter, Gabby." Gabby stood by her mother's side, smiling from ear to ear. She wore her hair down and curled. Under her pink coat, she wore a white dress decorated with pink roses.

"Today is Gabby's birthday, so I'm leaving the office to join them for lunch," he said.

Emma recognized the subtle red tones peeking through the little girl's dark brown hair. *Just like her father,* she thought; she smiled inwardly. "I love your hair," she said.

"Thank you! My mommy curled it for my birthday," she replied, visibly excited that Emma took notice.

"I love your dress, too. How old are you today?" Emma asked.

She squealed with excitement. "I'm nine." The chaotic cacophony of piercing shrieks that filled the air masked her squeal. She turned toward the unsettling noise. "Why are they doing that?" Gabby asked.

Emma stared at the rats as they slammed their bodies against the walls of their cages, as if trying to escape. She flashed back to the night at her father's church with the visitor. Her father's words boomed in her mind with a sense of divine revelation. *Remove the children!*

Her eyes widened. "We have to go. We all have to go. NOW!"

47

ER WORDS HUNG IN the air, leaving him utterly perplexed. Everything was fine just moments ago, but the look on her face told him something had changed. Drastically. He leaned in, scanning her body language for any clue that could help him make sense of the situation. "Emma, what's wrong?" he asked, still seated behind his desk.

Emma turned to Gabby. "Do you like taking the stairs?" she asked, crouching to make eye contact.

"Yes."

She extended her hand toward hers. "Do you want to take the stairs with me?"

She looked into her eyes and slowly raised her hand to Emma's. "OK," she replied with a smile.

"Let's go!" Emma exclaimed. Holding her hand, they raced out of the office.

Dr. Clark jumped to his feet. "What? Why?"

Joan rushed out after them.

Dr. Clark followed, nearly knocking his chair over in his rush to stand.

"Emma! Slow down!" Dr. Clark exclaimed. "What's going on?"

She hurried down the hallway toward the stairwell.

He moved fast to make up ground and was now just behind them.

She looked at Gabby, still holding her hand. "You're a big girl, right?" she asked with a smile.

"Yes," she replied.

"Can you run down the stairs?"

"Yes!" she exclaimed.

"Emma! Wait!" Dr. Clark shouted as they sprinted down the stairs.

Emma glanced back. "I'll explain once we're outside," she said, still charging forward.

"Stop!" Joan shouted from behind. "Stop right now, or I'm calling the police!"

She glanced back again. "Tell your wife I'm not crazy!"

"She's not crazy!" he shouted, still looking forward. "Emma, what are you doing? I trust you, but my wife doesn't know you. I've never seen her so angry." He pushed the exit door open.

"Does your wife know about Davis?" she asked.

"No. It's not ethical or even legal for a psychiatrist to reveal information about their patients to anyone. Not even their spouse. Why?"

"What the hell are you doing with my child!" Joan shouted as she emerged from the building, pushing the door open with the force of a charging ox.

Emma released Gabby's hand and stepped toward Joan. "Mrs. Clark, I'm so sorry; please let me explain."

Dr. Clark folded his arms across his chest, his nervous energy manifesting through his pacing.

"Sorry? The hell you are!" In a fit of anger, she raised her hands and forcefully pushed her away, propelling Emma backward with surprising strength.

As the argument escalated, tension filled the air. He stepped toward her. "Hey, honey, calm down. No touching," he said.

"Calm down? This fucking lunatic just tried to kidnap our child!"

She shook her head. "I know it must have appeared that way, but I assure you, I was trying to keep her safe."

Joan glared at her with eyes that pierced through her like daggers. "And how exactly were you trying to do that?"

There was silence.

Emma turned to Dr. Clark.

He looked at her with a look of puzzlement, shrugging his shoulders. "How were you trying to do that?" he asked.

She crossed her arms tightly over her chest. "Remember, during the exorcism, I told you that the demons needed something to enter once they were expelled from Davis?"

Joan lunged toward Gabby, pulling her in her direction, and placed her hands over her ears. She turned to her husband. "Exorcism? What the hell is she talking about?"

"I can't talk about it. It's doctor/patient confidentiality."

"But *I* can talk about it, right?" Emma asked.

He moved his face in a circular motion. "Uh, OK. By all means…" he replied sheepishly.

"Remember, I told you to plead the blood of Jesus so that you would be safe from the demons?"

"Yes," he replied, exhaling audibly. "How is this pertinent?" he asked.

"Demons seek the spiritually weak and vulnerable. The young are the most vulnerable. We never talked about your personal life." She turned to Joan. "Of course we didn't; why would we?" She turned back to Dr. Clark. "I didn't know if you were spiritually strong. That's why I had us both plead the blood of Jesus. To protect you, us both, just in case."

He threw his arms in the air. "What does this have to do with you storming off with Gabby?"

Joan's eyes widened. "Are you cheating on me?" she shouted, still covering Gabby's ears.

They turned to Joan. "OF COURSE NOT!" they shouted in unison.

Emma turned to him, her eyes locked with his, her gaze intense and unwavering. "Dr. Clark, Gabby is young and vulnerable! She's the same age as I was when the visitor came to my father's church."

"You *are* a lunatic," Joan said, her eyes focused on Emma with intense fury.

"Do you think it's a coincidence that the rats started going mad soon after Gabby walked in?" Emma asked.

Dr. Clark exhaled audibly. "I don't know." He reached for Gabby. "Sweetheart, how do you feel?"

"Good," she replied. "I had fun going down the stairs," she said, smiling.

"See. She's fine," he said.

There was silence.

Emma's cheeks flushed with embarrassment. "Good, I'm glad I could help," she replied, swinging her arms as if trying to distract from her discomfort.

"Glad you could help?!" Joan shouted, reaching for Gabby's hand. "You're a lunatic!" she shouted as she stormed down the steps of the building, each step carrying the weight of her anger.

Emma looked at him apologetically. "I'm sorry. I really was trying to help."

"I know you were. Look, if it makes you feel any better, I'll put the rats down when I return from lunch. They're in terrible shape, anyway."

"Yes, thank you, Dr. Clark."

He nodded. "No problem. I need to catch up with my family now. I have never seen my wife react like that before," he said jogging down the steps toward the parking garage.

"Dr. Clark, wait!"

He stopped and turned to face her. "Yes, Emma?" he asked. "What is it?"

She looked him in the eyes. "I'm sorry again about your wife…You know what they say."

"What's that?" he asked with a tilted head.

Her closed lips formed a secret smile. "Hell hath no fury…"

෫

KEEP READING
AN EXCERPT FROM

THE ETERNAL
SECRET

BY

MARY ROMASANTA

PROLOGUE

THE HOLLOWNESS OF THE EMPTY dwelling greeted him as he stood at its threshold, hesitant to go further. He inhaled deeply and, with a heavy heart, stepped inside. A profound vacantness hung thick in the air, seeping into his bones, and filling him with sorrow.

He turned his gaze to the kitchen table—yellow yarn spilled across it; needles, poised mid-stitch, stood frozen in time. Once alive with laughter and joy, the rooms were now void of all energy.

He set his keys down and pulled out a chair—the sound of its legs grating against the floor, deafening over the stark silence. A thunderous cloud seemed to settle over him…His fist clenched, and his lips curled into a snarl. A deep-seated pain within him demanded release. He picked up the chair and hurled it against the wall, causing the room to shake from the force of his fury— like a volcano erupting with anger.

That's not enough, he thought.

He stepped up to the wall with a clenched fist and unleashed a barrage of devastating punches through it. He pulled at the shattered pieces of plaster on the wall, exposing an arsenal weapons that he had hoped would never see the light of day again. His gaze moved from the weapon, as he calculated which would accompany him on his mission. His eyes landed on the Heckler & Koch P7—a 9 x 19 mm Parabellum used exclusively by the Feldjäger,

Germany's military police. He pulled it from the wall and brought it close to his face.

An ode to my roots, he thought.

With fierce determination in his eyes, he stepped into the bedroom and swung open the door to his wardrobe. He reached to the very back, using his sense of touch for his eyes, and pulled out another old friend—a sleek black Italian leather jacket. He put on the jacket, placed the gun in the inside pocket, and stepped toward the door.

Clad in black and a visored helmet, he swung his leg over his motorcycle and gripped the handlebars. With a swift kick, the engine roared to life, sending a surge of adrenaline coursing through his veins. With the quick twist of the throttle, he set off on his mission. The weight of the motorcycle beneath him settled like a familiar embrace.

Man and machine became one as they sliced through the narrow streets of Rome like a knife, tearing through traffic with ferocious intensity. With fearless grace, he weaved in and out of the gridlock of taxi cabs, leaning into every curve. The engine's growl echoed through the streets, a symphony of honking horns barely audible against the thunderous roar of the sleek machine.

There it is, he thought, fixing his eyes on the destination ahead of him.

A sign on the concrete wall read Casa di Santa Tomas. He positioned his body low and sleek and sped up, sending the motor-cycle roaring through the grand convent's iron gates.

An unsuspecting matronly nun stood nearby, raking leaves in the courtyard. Her body jolted at the deafening thrashing of the gates.

He stopped just in front of her. "Where is she?" he said in a deep, chilling whisper.

"Who?" the nun replied.

"MOTHER SUPERIOR!" he shouted, his bellow like a beast unleashed.

Her eyes widened, her mouth agape.

She pointed to the chapel up the hill.

He surged forward, the exhaust pipes unleashing a thunderous roar. The motorcycle's tires gripped each step, propelling it through the chapel's entrance. As he forced his way in, the church doors exploded in a dissonance of splintering wood and shattered stained glass.

A nun wearing a distinct crimson sash around her waist turned to the commotion. She bore her eyes into him like a dagger. "What do you think you're doing?" she said through a clenched jaw.

Without hesitating, Armonon reached deep into his jacket and withdrew his weapon, the metallic glint of steel reflecting in the darkness of his eyes. He extended his arm with deadly purpose; the barrel pointed ominously at her head. He tilted his head to the side and gazed at her. Behind the cold steel of his eyes lay a haunting emptiness, a reminder of the lives he had lost and the darkness that consumed him. Without Alice and his son, vengeance is all he had.

She raised her hands. "Now, now—" she said.

He pulled the trigger.

The bullet soared through the air like a vengeful spirit unleashed, racing toward its mark.

He returned the gun to his jacket pocket, confident that the bullet would reach its target, and watched as it penetrated her wrinkled forehead with lethal accuracy.

There was silence.

She stood frozen, her mouth agape.

A muted smile tugged at the corners of his lips as he admired the bright red blood splattered on the white wall behind her like a piece of modern art. *Magnificent*, he thought.

Milton Keynes UK
Ingram Content Group UK Ltd.
UKHW042006200224
438163UK00003B/10/J